Heart of Bone

Maggie James

To Mary

Thank you for all your help and support!

Best wishes,
Maggie James

Orelia Publishing

Published by Orelia Publishing 2022. All rights reserved. This book or any portion thereof may not be reproduced or used in any manner whatsoever without the express written permission of the publisher, except for the use of brief quotations in a book review. Please do not share or redistribute this novel. Thank you.

This novel is entirely a work of fiction. The names, characters and incidents portrayed in it are the work of the author's imagination. Any resemblance to actual persons, living or dead, or events is entirely coincidental.

Copyright ©Maggie James 2022.

The right of Maggie James to be identified as the author of this work has been asserted by her in accordance with the Copyright, Designs and Patents Act 1988.

This novel is dedicated to my wonderful accountability buddy, Jon Palmstrom, who always cheers me on when the going gets tough. Thank you for all your help and support!

CHAPTER 1

Greer Maddox remained in her car once she'd switched off the engine. Her gaze went to the third floor of Tom's block of flats, to a window on the right, her view partly obscured by the rain that pounded her windscreen. A gap in the curtains showed the lights were on. Her son was home.

Still Greer didn't move. Would Tom be annoyed with her for coming? If she left now, she'd be in bed before midnight, and he'd never know she'd been here. She'd not sleep if she did, though, what with worry weighing like a rock on her heart. Something was wrong with Tom, a darkness stretching beyond the depression that had marred his teenage years. The pain in his voice the last time she'd phoned—oh, how it had wounded her. As though, for Tom, living hurt too much these days.

A fortnight ago, he'd been so happy. All down to a former boyfriend, from the little he'd said. Tom never told her a great deal about the guys he dated. She didn't know the man's name, or how they'd met, but her son's glow of happiness had warmed her heart. On that occasion, his joy had overridden his customary reserve around her. 'Yeah, I'm seeing someone,' he'd admitted, after subtle probing on

Greer's part. 'We dated a couple of years ago, then split up. Now we're back together. He's all I've ever wanted.' Then, as if he'd revealed too much, too soon, he'd clammed up. Greer, reluctant to antagonise her son, hadn't pressed him.

Now, on this cold December night, she wished she had. Why hadn't she been a better mother?

Greer scratched at the burn scars on her arms. Stress always made them itch. She got out of the car and hurried through the driving rain to the entrance. A few minutes to reassure herself Tom was all right, then she'd head home. So what if he was angry about her turning up unannounced? He'd not responded to any of her messages, leaving her with little choice. As a mother, it was her duty to check he was okay. Besides, they needed to plan their Christmas together. It was only a week away.

She punched in the access code, sadness tugging at her. How reluctant he'd been to give it to her. Greer hurried up the stairs, her pulse racing, until she reached Tom's door. She paused for a moment to get her breath back. It was foolish to exert herself like this, what with her heart condition. Her doctor had warned her, more than once. Not that her health mattered right then. Tom's welfare was Greer's primary concern.

She pressed his buzzer, worry grating her nerves. No sounds came from inside Tom's flat; Greer glanced at her watch. Ten pm, too early for her son to be in bed. Besides, the light in his bedroom, his car in its space—both clearly indicated Tom was home. Why wasn't he opening the door? Her finger prodded his buzzer again, harder this time, as though to summon Tom by sheer willpower.

Still no response. Greer pulled open the cupboard to her left, which housed the gas and electric meters that served her son's flat. He'd never allowed her a key, probably afraid she'd invade his life more often if he did. Hurt squeezed Greer's heart at the thought. She reached up to access the top of the electric meter, her fingers scrambling through the dust. Ah, there it was. Greer closed the cupboard and inserted the key in its lock.

'Tom?' Her voice echoed through the small flat as she stepped inside. 'It's only me, sweetheart. You've not answered my messages, and I've been so worried—' Greer's heart leapt as she stared at Tom's open bedroom door. In the gap, she spotted a foot hanging over the edge of his duvet, along with a hairy leg. Oh, God, what if it didn't belong to Tom? What if she'd walked in on her son in bed with his boyfriend? He'd never forgive her. She shouldn't have intruded.

Why had neither of them reacted to her arrival, though? Maybe they were asleep—but Tom had always woken up at the slightest sound. An icy fist clutched Greer's heart. She edged towards the door. Her hand shaking, she pushed it fully open.

Tom was alone, lying on his back, his naked body sprawled across the bed, his cheek turned against a pillow. The rank stench of vomit filled the room. An inarticulate cry ripped from Greer's throat as she ran to Tom's side.

'Tom! Darling, can you hear me?'

No response. He didn't even stir. Greer grabbed his wrist to check for a pulse. Why couldn't she find one? Panic drained the saliva from her mouth as her fingers pressed harder. Wait, she'd found a beat. Weak, but definitely there. He was alive, thank God.

Greer turned her son's face away from the pillow, which was thick with vomit. His skin was a terrible greyish-white, his forehead clammy with sweat. Her gaze fell on Tom's bedside cabinet, bare apart from a folded piece of paper, a drained bottle of whisky and several empty blister packs. She dropped Tom's wrist as though his skin had burned her, and ran back to the hallway, where she'd left her handbag. Her fingers raked through it, desperate to find her phone.

'Ambulance. As soon as possible.' Her mouth was so dry it would hardly work. Somehow she managed to give Tom's address and her belief he'd overdosed. How else to explain the empty blister packs and the bottle of Scotch?

Once the call ended, Greer raced into the bathroom to wet a towel with warm water. Back in the bedroom, she flung the puke-covered pillow into a corner and knelt by the bed. She wiped the vomit from around Tom's mouth while her other hand stroked his hair the way she'd done when he was a baby. How had she not foreseen this? Not been there for Tom when he needed her? She should have ignored his 'keep away' attitude, insisted he seek psychiatric help.

Tears streamed down Greer's face. She'd failed him. Just like she'd done with Rose.

Where the hell was the ambulance? She knelt beside Tom's inert body and clasped his hands. Why were they so cold? What torment had forced her precious boy to believe the only solution was a bellyful of whisky and pills?

Her gaze fell on the folded paper on Tom's bedside cabinet. Greer got to her feet and moved as if in a daze towards it. Slowly, carefully, she unfolded the note.

Words danced, then blurred, before her eyes. How could she hope to read them through her tears?

A wail of sirens sounded from the street outside and flashing lights slashed through the gap in the blinds. Thank God; the paramedics were here at last. Greer stuffed Tom's suicide note into her jacket pocket, next to his spare key, and hurried to let them in.

CHAPTER 2

Greer stared at the profusion of tubes entering and draining from Tom's inert body as he lay in an intensive care bed at the Bristol Royal Infirmary. Around her, machines hummed and buzzed, along with the slow hiss from the ventilator that was breathing for her son. The sour whiff of vomit still clung to him. She didn't need to be a doctor to know the prognosis wasn't good.

She suppressed a sob. It was wrong to think that way. Tom would survive, because how could she live without him? He was her whole life. Especially since—

She mustn't think about Rose. It wasn't the time or the place. Right then, her focus needed to be on Tom.

'Please let him live.' Greer's voice had shrunk to a mere whisper.

She picked up Tom's hand, the one nearest to her, her fingers stroking his skin. Why was it so cold, so dry? Should she call someone? Then Tom's arm twitched, although his eyes remained closed, and Greer's attention flew to his face. Was he regaining consciousness? She waited, her heart pounding loudly in her ears. The machines around Tom's bed continued to hum and hiss. Tom gave no sign that he was regaining consciousness, however.

Wake up, Tom. Wake up, damn you.

Things would be different once her son was out of the hospital. He'd need nursing; he couldn't look after himself in that poky flat. Never mind what he or his new boyfriend might think. She'd insist on him coming home with her, back to his old bedroom, still decorated with his teenage posters. Greer would nurse him back to health, and they'd regain the closeness they'd shared when Tom was a child.

'I love you.' Greer spoke the words out loud, a tremor in her voice. Tom's hand quivered, and she let out a gasp of shock. Her plea had worked. He was waking up.

In a second, she was on her feet, running towards a nurse. She clutched the woman's arm with frantic fingers. 'Please come. It's my son. He's regaining consciousness.'

The nurse walked over to Tom's bedside, where she checked his monitors. A frown creased her brow as she turned to Greer. 'He's still in a coma, I'm afraid. A doctor will be round soon to check on him.' With that, she moved away. With a supreme effort, Greer sat beside Tom again.

She needed to make more of an effort. Didn't people still hear their loved ones, even when in a coma? Maybe feel touch, too? Greer reached under the sheet covering Tom's body, taking care not to disturb any of the tubes keeping him alive. She grasped his hands and eased them away from the bed, clasping them tightly. Now all she needed was for him to open his eyes.

'You can beat this, Tom.' Her lips grazed his knuckles in a kiss. 'You have to. I can't survive Christmas all alone. Fight, darling. I know you'll pull through this.'

Except that, deep down, she didn't. Dread uncoiled like a snake in Greer's belly. What if Tom died?

'Live, sweetheart.' She must, at all costs, keep the terror from her voice. 'You're all I have.'

A nurse, her face filled with concern, approached Tom's bed.

'Is there anything I can get you? Tea, coffee?' Her tone was sympathetic.

Greer shook her head. All she wanted was her son, conscious and on the road to recovery. She couldn't lose Tom. Not after what happened with Rose.

CHAPTER 3

On the morning after Tom's hospital admission, Greer called in sick to work, then phoned Charlie Prescott.

He'd driven to the hospital immediately, as she'd known he would.

Charlie burst through the door, his hair wild, face pale. Greer almost didn't recognise him. He looked a good ten years older than she remembered. He'd bulked up, but not with muscle; the surplus weight clung to his cheeks, strained his belly against his belt. Charlie's eyes were bloodshot and tired, and his skin had that ruddy hue associated with heavy drinkers. He'd not eased up on the booze, then.

She'd last seen him eighteen months ago, before he flew to Australia to go backpacking. Not long after—

Greer clamped down firmly on *that* thought. Charlie stared, his expression haunted, at the inert figure in the bed. Then he enveloped Greer in a fierce hug. She clung to him, desperate for the comfort he offered, his aftershave strong in her nostrils. Charlie understood what Tom meant to Greer. He'd always loved her son like a brother. They'd been best friends since primary school.

Now Tom lay pale and immobile, unaware of anything around him. Around his bed, the machines continued to pulse and hum. Greer squeezed his hands in hers, but Tom didn't respond.

'I don't understand.' Charlie's voice, hoarse and ragged, roused Greer from her thoughts. 'Why would he try to kill himself?'

She stepped away, fumbled in her pocket for a tissue. Her hand closed over the suicide note she'd taken from Tom's bedroom. Greer dragged it out with shaking fingers. 'He left this.'

Charlie pulled up a chair beside Greer's and sat down. He guided her to do likewise. He scrubbed a hand over his jaw.

'What does it say, Mrs M?' His affectionate name for her. 'I need answers. So do you.'

Greer nodded. She handed him the note. 'You read it. I can't bear to.'

Charlie unfolded the slip of paper. His face grew paler, something she wouldn't have believed possible. Tears swimming in his eyes, he screwed up the note and flung it across the room. Then he buried his head in his hands and sobbed, his large frame shaking with anguish.

Greer stared at the scrunched-up wad of paper like it was a demon from hell. 'Charlie? Do you know who did this to Tom?'

He wiped his eyes. 'I can't—'

Greer summoned every ounce of courage she possessed to walk over and retrieve the scrap of paper. Her heart pounding, she resumed her seat next to Tom's bed. She unfolded the note and read words that burned her eyeballs.

I wanted so badly for us to be together again. The lies have been the final straw.

A tsunami of torment swept through Greer. Tom's new boyfriend—he'd driven her beloved boy to try to take his own life. A tortured howl escaped her lips.

Greer's hands clenched in her lap. Her nails dug deep into her palms. Had the guy been in front of Greer right then, she'd have throttled him and gladly served time for his murder.

But he wasn't. There was only Charlie, and Greer, and sadness.

She needed to probe deeper. 'Did you ever meet this man he's been dating?'

'No.'

'You must know something about him. The two of you have always been so close.'

Charlie didn't reply at first. When his eyes met Greer's, she saw he was crying. Through gulps, he said, 'Tom doesn't tell me much about his love life. It's as if he thinks that, because I date women, I'll judge him. Like he's worried I'll stop being his mate because he's gay.'

'But you knew he'd been seeing someone?'

Charlie scrubbed his hand over his face to wipe away the tears. 'I think they split up. Well, they must have done. That's what the note, and this—' He gestured towards Tom. 'Is all about, right?'

Greer's gaze roamed over Tom's beloved face. Had it not been for the rise and fall of his chest, she might have thought him dead, so ashen was his skin.

He needed to get well. Then, together, they'd deal with everything, and everyone, that had hurt him.

'He's been so down recently.' Why hadn't she been more supportive? 'Depression—it's a terrible thing, Charlie. I'd been hoping he was getting better, and now this.'

Charlie took the note from Greer. '"The lies have been the final straw." I wonder what he means.'

Fury shot through Greer. 'He's obviously fallen in love with some bastard not fit to shine his shoes. A man who lied to my Tom, then dumped him, like he's worthless.' Her nails gouged blood from her palms, the pain a welcome relief. 'Whoever he is, I hate him.'

'Yeah,' Charlie echoed. 'Me too.' For a moment, they sat in silence, apart from the thrum and hiss of the machines keeping Tom alive.

'He will get better, won't he?' The agony in Charlie's eyes stabbed through Greer's heart.

'He has to.' Anything else was unthinkable. 'He's all I have left.'

Over the next two days, Tom showed some signs of improvement; he no longer needed a ventilator to breathe, but remained comatose. Greer spent every moment possible at the hospital, having negotiated compassionate leave with her boss. Not that she cared about work. Her data entry job barely paid enough to cover her bills, and was the least of her worries. As for sleep and food, who needed them?

Tom's doctors could offer little in the way of a prognosis. 'Your son ingested a large quantity of painkillers,' one told Greer. 'We're doing everything we can, but some of his internal organs have suffered extensive damage. Let's hope for a miracle, but you need to prepare yourself for the fact he might not recover, Mrs Maddox.'

CHAPTER 4

Greer filled her kettle. A quick coffee, and then she'd visit Tom. Her darling boy hadn't responded yesterday when she'd sat at his bedside. Not even a twitch. His colour hadn't been good, either, the waxy pallor of his skin a painful reminder of that terrible night she'd found him. Had that really only been a few days ago?

She spooned coffee granules into a mug. Tom *had* to get better. Didn't he realise she needed him?

If only she'd discovered him sooner. Or, heaven forbid, later, however awful the thought. Anything other than Tom forever trapped between life and death in a persistent coma. The knowledge that her son might never recover consciousness tortured Greer relentlessly. She raked her nails over her arms. Her burn scars were prickling like a bitch.

The kettle had just boiled when her mobile sounded from her handbag. Hope swelled in Greer's heart as she took it out. It must be the hospital phoning. Had—oh, please God—Tom regained consciousness?

As expected, the caller ID showed as Bristol Royal Infirmary.

'Mrs Maddox?' The voice was that of Sanjay Chatterjee, Tom's principal doctor and a friendly, caring man. Her son was in expert hands with him.

'Has he woken up? Is he okay? Has he spoken at all?' Greer paused for breath. 'I'll come right away. Can I bring anything?'

What might be required? Plenty of underwear, of course. Toiletries, books, sketchpad. A couple of packets of those tortilla chips he liked...

Why the silence? How come he wasn't answering?

Dr Chatterjee cleared his throat, and seconds later tore Greer's hopes to shreds. 'Mrs Maddox, I'm very sorry to tell you that your son has died.'

How remiss of the man. He must have confused Tom with someone else. 'That can't be right. You must have made a mistake.'

'He passed away a short while ago. We did everything possible, but as I explained to you before, the damage to his internal organs was too great. I'm so sorry for your loss.'

The dryness in Greer's mouth prevented any response. She sank into a chair, tears blurring her vision. Tom was dead. Nothing mattered anymore.

Tom, oh Tom. Why had her darling boy hurt himself? What had been so terrible that he decided to take his own life?

'Mrs Maddox? Are you still there?'

'Yes. I'll come right away.'

―ele―

'Mrs Maddox?'

Greer stared at Sanjay Chatterjee. Where was she, and who was this man?

'Mrs Maddox, do you understand what I'm telling you?' The words had entered her ears, but made no sense. *Died earlier this morning... suffered a fatal seizure... so sorry for your loss...*

'No.' The solitary word held a wealth of denial.

'Tom had taken a massive overdose, as you know, resulting in a lot of internal damage. Unfortunately—'

'You're mistaken. My son can't be dead.'

'I realise it must be hard for you to take in.' He fell silent.

This couldn't be happening. No way would the world still turn without Tom, alive and on the road to recovery. 'I want to see him.'

Dr Chatterjee frowned. 'I'm afraid that's not possible. Tom's body is now in our hospital morgue, ready for transfer to whichever funeral directors you decide to use. You'll be able to see him once that's done.'

He stood up. 'I'll leave you to collect your thoughts for a while. Then somebody will be along to talk to you.'

Greer had no idea what he meant, and didn't ask. What did it matter, anyway? She crawled off her chair, curled into a ball on the floor, horror washing over her. Tom had died, and life was now meaningless.

A loud knock at the door roused her. It opened, and footsteps approached. Greer stayed in her foetal huddle, her eyes tightly shut. Whoever it was needed to go away and leave her the hell alone.

The sound of a throat being cleared reached her ears, followed by a female voice. 'Mrs Maddox? Here, let me help you.' A hand on her elbow pulled her towards a chair.

'Mrs Maddox, my name is Susan Bartlett, and...' The woman said something about important details that needed to be discussed. Greer heard herself reply, but the words sounded as though they came from somebody else. She was swimming through an ocean of hurt, Tom on the other side. 'Come and meet me,' he urged. 'I'll tell you everything.'

'Mrs Maddox, can you follow me, please?' Greer nodded, not caring where she might be going. Susan Bartlett led her down the corridor into another room. She flipped the sign on the door to read, 'Occupied'.

'Take a seat.' She gestured towards a chair before choosing an identical one on the other side of the coffee table. On it stood a vase of white lilies, a box of tissues, and a plastic rack stuffed with brochures. The room stank of cheap air freshener and disinfectant.

Susan began to talk, and despair crept into Greer's consciousness. There had been no mistake. Her son was dead, and nothing would ever be the same again. Her failure to tell him more often that she loved him pierced her heart. She'd let him down when he'd needed her the most.

More words penetrated Greer's grief. *Organ Donor Register... clearly indicated his wishes... advise you that...*

Tom had intended to donate his organs, it seemed. Greer had no objection. Her boy was dead, and nothing would change that. Besides, she barely understood what Susan was saying. Greer heard herself agreeing to sign any paperwork. The woman droned on, her hand gesturing towards the pamphlets. Despite the fog in Greer's head, she read the title of the top one: *Grief Counselling—Practical Help for the Bereaved.*

Her hands clenched into fists so tight her bones would surely break. Damn this woman and her stupid leaflets.

Susan ended by mentioning the release of Tom's body, ready for whichever funeral parlour Greer chose. Burial. Cremation. How on earth could she organise any of it?

The other woman stood up to go. 'I'll be back soon.'

The clock on the wall ticked down the minutes. Greer sat immobile, her eyes on the vase of lilies. From behind the door sounds reached her: voices, footsteps, the scrape of trolley wheels. As though Tom wasn't dead, like Greer's world hadn't shattered. A tornado of fury spiralled in Greer's gut, threatening to explode inside her. She dug her nails into her palms, aware she was holding herself together by the slimmest of margins.

The door opened. Susan Bartlett plumped herself down again. She placed papers in front of Greer, laid a pen on the table.

'If you feel up to it, Mrs Maddox, here are the organ donation consent forms I mentioned.' Susan rambled on about how wonderful it was that Tom, in death, could help others live.

'I don't understand.' So what if Greer had interrupted the woman? 'Dr Chatterjee told me that the pills badly damaged Tom's internal organs. How can you use them for transplants?'

'People who have died from overdoses have successfully donated organs before. Here, the major damage was to Tom's liver. We've deemed his heart suitable for reuse.'

Greer didn't care. All she wanted was for this woman to leave her alone with her grief. She scrawled her signature next to the pencilled crosses, fury hot in her belly. No mother should expect to bury a child who, at twenty-seven, was still new to adulthood.

Why was she so cursed? Hadn't losing Rose already torn her heart in two?

The hurricane of rage inside Greer reached full force. Her right hand grabbed the vase of lilies. She wrapped angry fingers around its neck. Yanked it off the table. Hurled it against the wall. Watched as shards of glass fell to the floor along with the flowers. Drips of water splattered the tiles.

Greer picked up her handbag, ignoring Susan's stunned expression. Her legs on autopilot, she ran out of the hospital and into the downpour outside.

CHAPTER 5

Back home, her clothes sodden with rainwater, Greer huddled in an armchair, oblivious to the shivers that ran through her body. Images of Tom trooped through her head: as a baby, a toddler, a teenager nervous about telling his mother he was gay. Where had their relationship gone so wrong? All she'd ever wanted was to love him, keep him safe. Over the years, he'd pulled away, until the gap between them was so wide Greer had no idea how to cross it. Now she never would.

Charlie. She needed to call Charlie. She dug her phone out of her handbag and retrieved his number.

He answered on the first ring. 'Mrs M? How's Tom?'

Oh, God. How could she tell him his best friend had died?

Charlie's voice sounded in her ear again. 'What's happened? Has Tom regained consciousness?'

Greer shook her head. How stupid of her; they weren't on a video call. 'Nothing like that. I'm so sorry, Charlie.' She fell silent, sadness threatening to choke her.

She couldn't bring herself to say the words. He'd just have to understand.

His anguished cry told her he did. 'No. He can't be dead. I'd hoped—'

Greer wiped her eyes. 'Me too, Charlie. Me too.'

'He meant the world to me. I wish—' Tears in Charlie's voice. 'That he hadn't died the way he did. If only I'd convinced him his life was worth living.'

'You'll come to the funeral, won't you? Once I've arranged everything?'

'Of course. Just let me know when and where.' They exchanged a few more back-and-forths before Greer ended the call, desperate to give vent to her grief.

Except that anger was the dominant emotion in Greer's head. Fury against the man who'd trashed Tom's heart, lied to him, then tossed him aside. Whoever he was, she hated him.

Greer stashed the thought in a distant corner of her mind. She couldn't think about any of that now. Later, she'd track the guy down. Tell him what a shit he was for treating Tom so badly.

Make him pay for killing her son.

CHAPTER 6

Beth Randall hesitated, her finger poised to ring Greer's doorbell. Should she talk to her neighbour or leave her in peace? Greer's haunted face had bothered her ever since she'd seen the other woman hurry inside earlier.

Maybe Greer was simply desperate to escape the rain.

Or had Tom died? Please God, let it not be that.

Greer had already told Beth, sobbing her eyes out in her kitchen, that an ambulance had rushed her son to hospital the other day. A suicide attempt, she'd said, and Beth's heart clenched with compassion. She'd lost her sister that way a long time ago, the pain still sharp today.

Since Beth had bought the house next door to Greer's, the two women had struck up a friendship, sharing regular coffees together. Beth, bruised by a messy divorce, was lonely. She sensed Greer was, too.

Beth made up her mind. Now wasn't the time to be coy. If Greer needed a friend, and the white, harried face Beth had seen indicated that she did, Beth would be that person.

Her finger pressed Greer's buzzer. No response. She couldn't hear any movement within. She rang the bell again, then once more.

Footsteps eventually sounded in the hallway. Greer opened the door.

God, she looked rough. Greer's clothes were wet, her hair too, and she was shivering. Her eyes were red-rimmed and filled with tears, and her face was pale and haggard.

Time for Beth to take charge, as she often did. She bundled Greer inside and slammed the door behind them. With one hand on Greer's arm, she steered her towards the staircase. 'First, you're having a hot shower and a change of clothes. Then a strong coffee and some food.' To her relief, Greer allowed Beth to guide her upstairs without protest.

Beth had never been in Greer's bedroom. It was like the rest of the house: neat, decorated in neutral tones, the furniture a little dated. A hint of floral perfume hovered in the air. Beth spotted a doorway to the left that probably led to an en-suite bathroom. A push of the door proved her right. Beth turned on the shower, grabbed a towel off the rail, and handed it to Greer.

'While you're getting warm, I'll dig out some clothes, then get the kettle on.' Without waiting for a reply, she opened Greer's chest of drawers, hunting for pyjamas. From the corner of one eye, she watched Greer move towards the bathroom.

Beth tossed the first pair she found on the bed. She hurried downstairs, flung open the cupboards and grabbed a can of tomato soup and a bread roll. She spooned coffee into a mug and filled the kettle. A few minutes later, she carried a loaded tray upstairs, the smell of hot soup teasing her nostrils.

Greer was in bed, her face a healthier colour, and she was no longer shivering. Beth plonked the tray beside her. 'Get stuck into that. Then we'll talk.'

Once Greer had eaten, Beth took the tray from her and placed it on the floor. 'Tell me what's wrong. Please.'

Greer fixed her gaze somewhere to Beth's left. Her expression was world-weary, defeated. 'Tom died this morning.' Sobs wracked her body.

Oh, the poor love. Beth hugged Greer. 'I'm so sorry. I know how much he meant to you.'

'He was my world.' Greer pulled away to grab a tissue.

'I can only imagine how you must feel.' Greer would need Beth's support for Tom's funeral and the inquest. Throughout the long, empty days that would follow, too. Beth would be there for her, no matter what.

Greer snorted. 'You have no idea. None.'

Right when Beth was debating how to respond, Greer spoke again. 'I should have known I wouldn't have Tom for long.'

'What do you mean?'

A hollow laugh. 'Everyone leaves me eventually. Either they walk out on me or they die.'

'You mean your ex-husband? Or are you referring to your parents? But, my love—'

'Jake, Mum and Dad, Tom. Not just them, though.'

Damn, Greer was closing herself off. Should she leave her to get some sleep? Then Beth's eyes fell on the photo on Greer's bedside cabinet.

Its frame was large, probably ten by fifteen inches. In it, Greer had one arm around the shoulder of a young woman, who wore jeans and a white t-shirt. They were outdoors, the sky a cloudless blue behind them. The woman wore her blonde hair in a sleek bob. A small mole graced the side of her right eye. Her arm encircled Greer's waist. Both of them were smiling.

A niece, perhaps? But hadn't Greer said she had no siblings?

Now wasn't the time to ask. 'Talk to me, Greer. Please.'

'Let me tell you a story.' How bitter her neighbour sounded. 'About a child, very much a daddy's girl. He never had time for her, though. Always too busy. When the girl was eight, he left his wife for another woman. The girl's mother made lots of promises about how her daddy would stay in touch, but she was wrong. The father's visits were sporadic; soon they ceased altogether. He died from heart disease when she was twelve.'

'Greer—'

'For years I pined after Dad, but Mum did her best to compensate for the fact she'd married a deadbeat. Then, not long after I turned fifteen, she passed away too.'

'Greer, please stop scratching your arms. You'll make them bleed.' Beth had noticed Greer's burns before, but hadn't liked to ask about them.

Greer's frantic clawing stopped. 'Sorry. Bad habit. They itch when I get upset.'

'What happened?'

'A house fire. Years ago.'

'Is that how you lost your mum?'

A tear slid down Greer's cheek as she resumed savaging her left arm. Beth grabbed her hand, startling her from her trance. Her neighbour stared at Beth, pain and horror in her eyes.

'I tried so hard to rescue her.' Greer's voice was a mere whisper. 'The flames… oh, God, Beth, the flames. My hands and arms got burned trying to put out the fire, but it spread too fast. She died, and I couldn't save her.'

Greer wiped her eyes. 'I went to live with my aunt afterwards. She was kind enough, but didn't have kids herself. She had no idea how to deal with an unhappy teenager. I stayed with her until my early twenties. Then I met Jake.'

'Your husband, right?'

'Yes. We married not long afterwards. I was already pregnant, and so in love with him.'

'But the marriage didn't last?'

Tears filled Greer's eyes. 'No. He deserted me.'

'Does he know his son is dead?'

'No. I haven't a clue where he is, or how to contact him. Tom missed having a father when he was growing up. He kept asking why his dad left and if he'd come back.'

Beth's heart ached for the other woman. She'd endured so much pain and loneliness.

Greer shook her head. 'I still can't believe Tom's gone. I'd hoped that one day he'd open his eyes, and I'd be there when he did, and his life, and mine, would slowly get better.'

'You've always given me the impression the two of you were close, before—'

Whoa, Beth. She needed to stop right there, choose her next words carefully.

'Before he drank a bottle of whisky and filled his stomach with painkillers? You're right, we were.' Greer's gaze slid away, and Beth sensed she might be lying. 'I supported him when he came out as gay, throughout university, after his depression set in.'

She hauled herself up in the bed, her mouth a red slash of anger. Her hands clenched the duvet cover. She bore no resemblance to the grief-stricken woman who'd opened the door to Beth earlier.

'I'll tell you this much.' Fury flashed in Greer's eyes. 'Some bastard drove my Tom to take his own life, and I'm going to find him.'

CHAPTER 7

The next day, Greer drove to Tom's flat, her first visit there since the dreadful evening she'd found him unconscious. She'd already contacted his landlord, saying she wanted to collect Tom's things. Once she'd parked, she exited the car and grabbed some packing boxes from the boot.

Greer tapped in the access code to the building and walked up the stairs, every step an effort. She took the spare key from her tote bag, inserted it in the lock, and stepped inside.

A stale, shut-in odour greeted her, the air hot and musty. Greer strode into the kitchen, grabbed bin bags, microfibre cloths and cleaning fluid, and set to work.

Two hours later, she wiped sweat from her brow. She'd filled several bags with rubbish and most of the boxes with Tom's personal stuff. Why was it so hard to breathe? Inhale, in, out, one, two. Had she taken her heart medication that morning? Possibly not; she did sometimes forget.

The only room left to clear was Tom's bedroom.

Images besieged Greer's head. All those empty pill packets. The drained whisky bottle. Tom's face, all sweaty and waxen. Her hand flew to her mouth to stifle a gasp, and she sank to the floor, sobbing.

Hours later, Greer couldn't cry anymore. She stumbled to her feet, grabbed some bin bags from the kitchen, and pushed open the door to Tom's bedroom.

A sour smell of vomit greeted her. Greer glanced at the puke-stained pillow she'd flung into a corner, the towel she'd used to wipe his face. The rumpled bed where he'd lain, dying from those goddamn pills. Greer averted her eyes and headed for Tom's wardrobe. She chucked his clothes into bags, not allowing herself to think. If she did, she'd go mad.

A grey sweatshirt lay crumpled on the floor. Greer picked it up, inhaling a whiff of Hugo Boss along with a scent that was uniquely Tom. She pressed the fabric against her nose. By the time she stuffed it in her tote bag, it was wet with tears.

Greer emptied Tom's chest of drawers next. Only one area remained. Reluctance in every step, she approached Tom's bed.

The empty pill packets almost destroyed Greer. The whisky bottle undid her completely. She grabbed it by the neck and swung it against the wall, shards of glass raining onto the carpet. Fury filled her heart.

'How dare you leave me?' So what if the neighbours heard her screaming? 'You were all I had.'

Darkness had fallen by the time Greer pulled herself, shivering, off the floor. At some point she'd drifted into an uneasy doze, curled into a ball amid the slivers of glass. She grabbed a dustpan and brush from the kitchen and a fresh bin bag. Into it went the bottle fragments, the empty pill packets, and the soiled towel and pillow.

Greer realised she'd not checked Tom's bedside cabinet. In the top drawer were a couple of dog-eared paperbacks, which she threw into the bin bag. She tugged open the bottom compartment. Only one thing was inside. Greer took it out.

A thick notebook, A4-sized, covered in grey cloth. Printed on it were the words, '*My Journey to Mental Health*' in gold letters. Greer's fingers traced over them. Tom hadn't told her he'd been keeping a diary.

Should she open the notebook or destroy it? Hard to decide. To read it would be an invasion of his privacy. The journal might reveal the identity of the bastard who'd wrecked her son's life, however. Decision made. With trembling hands, Greer opened it to a random page, dated two years ago.

Words leapt at her, burning her eyeballs. *Felt suffocated... So clingy... Smother mother...*

A gasp ripped from Greer's throat. Hurt gripped her heart. She would have slammed the journal shut had it not been for a sentence that caught her attention.

My gorgeous, handsome, sexy Blue.

She'd been right. Within these pages, she'd discover who Tom's boyfriend had been. Greer would pay him a visit, and he wouldn't like what she had to say. Not one bit.

She wanted to go further than talking. Punish him for what he'd done.

Greer walked into the hallway and crammed the journal into her tote bag beside the sweatshirt. When she felt calmer, she'd read more of it.

Christmas Day dawned wet and windy. Beth, bless her, had invited Greer to join her for a turkey lunch, but Greer had refused. Beth meant well, but her son and daughter would be there, along with their partners, and Greer couldn't stomach spending the festive season with strangers. Not when she'd hoped to spend Christmas with Tom.

Greer snuggled further into her duvet. No point in getting up. Better to mull over her plan to track down the man who, in her head, had killed Tom. She'd not yet found the courage to open Tom's journal again, too burned by *Felt suffocated... So clingy... Smother mother....*

A memory sneaked, uninvited and unwanted, into Greer's head. Tom, aged eighteen, before he left to study graphic design at Newcastle University, talking to a friend on his mobile. His words had seared themselves into her brain.

'Can't wait to get away, if I'm honest,' he'd said. A pause while he listened. Then: 'She's so controlling. Always wanting more than I can give.'

So that was why he'd chosen Newcastle, three hundred miles north, when he could have studied at one of the two Bristol universities. Was it so wrong to love her son so much? Make him the centre of her world? She didn't have anyone else.

When Tom returned to Bristol after finishing his degree, hope had soared in Greer.

'I miss Bristol,' he'd told her during a rare phone call. 'Newcastle's great, but I've done my time up north.' Foolish to expect he'd move back in with her, but at least they'd be in the same city. Perhaps now they'd grow closer.

Her hopes came to nothing. Tom moved in with an old school friend, then into his rented flat in Redfield once he found work. She'd seen him on the occasional Sunday, a quick duty visit that always left her unsatisfied. Often he'd make an excuse not to come. Greer, Tom's 'controlling' comment echoing in her head, never pressed him, but inwardly she seethed. Was it too much to ask that he visit once a week?

As for Rose, the police had failed to find her. Not even a trace. It was unlikely they ever would.

Life held nothing for her anymore. Everyone who mattered had deserted her. Nobody would miss her if she died. Maybe she should join Tom in the cemetery at Arnos Vale. The only question was how.

She could allow her heart to harden into bone. Aortic valve calcification, common in her family, had that effect. Left unchecked, calcium deposits would build up and harden her heart; the pills Greer took each day prevented them from doing so. Ridiculous. She was way too young at fifty to suffer heart disease, but life wasn't fair, was it? Greer knew that better than most people.

Yes, she should toss her pills in the bin. Allow the build-up of calcium to thicken her heart until it no longer functioned. Or perhaps take an overdose of sleeping tablets.

A pounding on the door, following by her doorbell buzzing, roused Greer from her angst. Beth, of course. Her neighbour meant well, but she'd never lost a child. A sister, yes, but it wasn't the same. Why wouldn't Beth leave her alone?

Greer needed Tom, not Beth. An idea came to her then.

'Greer! Are you there?' Beth's voice boomed through the letterbox. The buzzer sounded again. Seconds later, a third time.

When she'd heard nothing for a few minutes, Greer breathed a sigh of relief. She pulled open her bedside cabinet and took out Tom's journal, along with his sweatshirt. The scent of her son drifted into her nostrils, touched her heart. Time to read what her boy had written. The opening entry was from two years ago.

CHAPTER 8

April 14. This feels weird. Stupid. I don't know what to write.

April 21. My second try, because I'm scared of what my counsellor will say if I don't tell her next week that I've made a start on this journal. She certainly chewed my ear off earlier about me not having done my 'homework'. In a nice way, of course. Counsellors aren't supposed to shout at their clients, and she didn't, just rattled on about how important it is for me to 'engage with the process'.

Linda's around Mum's age, but otherwise, they're completely different. She's far less tightly wound than Mum and doesn't have her difficult bits. At least they don't look alike. I can't imagine saying half the stuff in my head if they did.

I still don't have a clue what to write.

Perhaps getting all the dark thoughts out of my brain and onto paper will help. I'd hate for anyone to read this journal, though, especially Mum. Linda and I talked a lot about her today. We both suspect that part of the reason for my depression is bound up with Mum. And the father I've never known.

God, this is hard.

April 28. A better session this time. I'm comfortable now around Linda, more able to tell her stuff. How for years I've felt suffocated by Mum's love. She's so clingy, like I'm four, and she has to protect me from the world. She means well, but I wish she'd back the hell off. The way she fixates on me isn't healthy. For so long, I hoped she'd find herself a man, but she's too bitter about Dad walking out the way he did.

I am, too. I don't have a single memory of him. Linda thinks that's a contributing factor in my depression.

She also asked if I'd ever considered finding my father. I said that a man who abandons his pregnant wife isn't worth the effort.

I lied. I've thought of it many times.

Maybe someday I'll track him down.

I think I will. Eventually.

May 5. We talked a lot about Mum today. How guilty I felt about shouting at her after she'd cooked Sunday lunch for me. It was cruel of me to tell her she's a smother mother, how I wished she'd back off, just for a while. Mum looked so hurt, and the worst thing was, I was glad. I hugged her and told her I was just tired and in a bad mood, but I was lying. What kind of crappy son does that make me?

Bottling it all up is driving me crazy, though. Mum has that effect on me. She means well, but I can't stand all the fussing.

I've been thinking a lot about Dad. What if I approached one of those agencies that find missing people? If I had his contact details, would I get in touch with him? Ask him why he deserted his pregnant wife and unborn child?

Yes, I would.

I might not like the answers he'd give, though.

May 12. Oh, my God. I can't believe it. I'm over the moon. Blue, I love you. You're all I've ever wanted.

May 19. Linda asked today what's changed for me. She's obviously sussed out, although I've not mentioned Blue, that I'm different. No longer depressed. It's more than that, though. I'm actually happy, and it's so weird, because I've not felt this way for years.

I lied to Linda. Told her I thought the new tablets from the doctor are making a difference. Blue's a wonderful secret I'm keeping to myself for now. I'm not telling Mum. She'd start planning a wedding, and I don't need that kind of pressure. And Blue would hate it.

My gorgeous, handsome, sexy Blue. It's been a week now, the happiest one of my life. He laughed when I told him I'd nicknamed him Blue in my head, but that's how I think of him. He only has to look at me with those beautiful eyes, and I'm putty in his hands.

I know we're not exclusive. He's made that very clear. That's the only bit I'm not happy about.

I want Blue all to myself.

May 26. I've still not told Linda, or Mum, about Blue. Linda says I'm not ready to stop counselling, even though I seem so much happier. She reminded me that the issues I have with Mum, and my deadbeat missing father, haven't gone away, and that we need to talk more about them.

I'm still thinking about finding Jake Maddox, but not for a while. Right now, I want to enjoy being with Blue. Linda and I chatted about Mum, and how difficult some parents find it to let their children fly free in the world, especially someone like Mum, who's made me the focus of her life. It helped, I guess. I was more patient last week at Sunday lunch, and she didn't fuss so much. I even said I loved her, and she looked so happy. Linda's helped me realise that Mum's lonely. I've not been the best of sons, but that'll change. I must try harder.

She'll be over the moon about Blue, if she ever finds out.

Blue says we shouldn't tell anyone we've been screwing. His words, not mine. They hurt, because in my head we're dating, and faithful. I won't let myself picture him in bed with someone else.

He's a bastard. Sometimes I hate him.

I don't. I love him. I've adored Blue ever since I first met him.

Of course, I can't tell him that.

I don't feel so happy anymore.

June 14. It's over. Blue ended things between us today.

All I want to do is curl into a ball and cry. Or die.

I can't fool Mum. She's worried I'm depressed again, but I'm not—I'm grieving for Blue. For what might have been.

With a howl of rage, Greer hurled Tom's journal across the room. It slammed against the wardrobe with a loud thud. If only she could do that to Blue's head. Two years ago, her son's boyfriend had thrown him away like he meant nothing. More recently, he'd obviously done it again. Fury squeezed Greer's heart. Someday she'd find the bastard and make him pay.

First, though, she had to bury her boy.

CHAPTER 9

Four days after New Year, Greer dragged herself out of bed to attend Tom's funeral. Once washed and dressed, she forced down a slice of toast and a cup of coffee.

Today she would bid goodbye to her son.

She could do this. She had to, for Tom's sake.

Greer had arranged his burial at Arnos Vale, the Victorian cemetery that had become a tourist attraction, nestled in the suburb of Brislington. Time to lay her precious boy to rest among the trees there.

The day had dawned wet and dull, a steady drizzle accompanying Greer once she'd parked her car and was walking towards the magnificent Anglican chapel.

'Mrs M! Hang on a minute!' Charlie's voice, rendered faint by the wind. Greer had phoned him on New Year's Eve. He'd enquired about the funeral, and she'd told him when and where it was being held. No way would he have missed it.

He didn't look well. His eyes were bloodshot, heavy bags underneath them, and his skin looked grey. He'd probably hit the booze hard since Tom's death. Painful memories flooded Greer. Charlie and Tom on bikes as teenagers, doing homework in Greer's kitchen, setting off together for Newcastle University. Charlie must be suffering almost as much as Greer.

She wrapped him in a fierce hug. 'How are you?'

Charlie shrugged. 'I can't believe he's gone. How are you holding up?'

'I'm hanging in there. Barely, but still. Listen, can we talk? Afterwards, at my place?'

He nodded. 'Sure.' They proceeded in silence into the chapel. Greer spotted Beth in one of the pews, giving her a small smile, grateful that she'd come. Her neighbour was the closest she had to a best friend.

The turnout was good; Tom, it appeared, had been popular at work, and had kept in touch with his friends from Bristol Grammar School. Greer listened to the celebrant with one ear, her mind focused on Tom's body in the oak casket in front of her. The words from his suicide note sounded in her brain. *I wanted so badly for us to be together again. The lies have been the final straw.* Tom must have been referring to the man who drove him to despair. Who else could he have meant?

Why hadn't she gone to his flat sooner? Got there before the whisky and pills wreaked their havoc on his internal organs? It should be Greer in the coffin, not her beloved boy.

'Mrs M?' Charlie had hold of her arm. The celebrant was regarding her with a worried look. Had she said that last bit out loud?

She nodded at the man and managed a weak smile for Charlie. 'I'm fine.' The tension in the air ebbed away. Once the celebrant resumed speaking. Greer lost herself in memories of Tom.

Afterwards, she clutched Charlie's arm while the two of them made their way outside. The drizzle had slowed to a feeble trickle. Greer watched Tom's coffin being lowered into the ground, the odour of wet earth strong in her nostrils. She couldn't even cry.

Her son was leaving her forever, taking her heart with him. How could she live without him?

Charlie's arm wound around her. 'I'm sorry, Mrs M,' he whispered as Greer threw a rose on top of Tom's coffin. Moments later, the dark oak casket disappeared under spadefuls of earth.

'Goodbye, my darling.' Greer scratched at her burn scars, barely aware that they were bleeding.

She'd chosen not to hold a wake. Getting through the funeral was hard enough without having to make small talk with Tom's friends. The rain had begun again, and a stiff wind drove icicles through Greer's coat.

'Want some company?' Beth said from behind her.

Greer shook her head. 'Sorry, I can't.' Her eyes scanned around for Charlie. Ah, there he was, standing a few feet to one side, his gaze on her. He'd obviously remembered her request that they talk.

Beth edged closer. 'Listen, don't be a stranger, okay?'

'Thank you. You've been a good friend.'

Once Beth had walked away, Charlie took her place at Greer's side. 'You okay, Mrs M?'

'I've told you before. Call me Greer.' He never would, of course. He'd once confessed that he regarded her as a surrogate mum. His own had been too mentally ill to parent him.

'Can't do that.' He smiled. 'Wouldn't feel right. You still want to talk?'

'Yes. See you back at my place?' Charlie nodded his assent.

CHAPTER 10

Half an hour later, Greer's buzzer sounded. Charlie gave her a quick hug once she'd opened the door. 'God, this brings back memories,' he said, as he walked into the kitchen. It would do, of course. He'd not been to the house for what, eighteen months? He'd last dropped by to return a book he'd borrowed, right before leaving for Australia.

She gestured towards the kettle. 'Coffee?'

'Got anything stronger?'

Greer plucked a bottle of Merlot from her wine rack. 'Will this do?' Charlie wouldn't say no, of course.

'So,' Charlie said, once Greer had poured them both a glass and they'd seated themselves at the kitchen table. 'What did you want to discuss?'

'Tom. What else?' Greer sucked in a breath. 'Charlie, I've been thinking. About this boyfriend of his, the one who got Tom so wound up he killed himself.'

He took a gulp of wine. 'What about him?'

'I need to find him. Look that son of a bitch in the eye and ask him what right did he have? To treat Tom so badly?'

Charlie drained his glass. Without asking Greer, he refilled it, his hand trembling, and took another large mouthful. His eyes were wet. Well, of course they were. Tom and Charlie had been like brothers.

'Sorry, Mrs M. I don't know anything.'

Greer wasn't so easily put off. 'Can you tell me where they met? How long they dated? What the guy does for a living?'

'I've no idea.' Greer had never seen him so vulnerable.

'"The lies have been the final straw,"' Charlie said. 'I wonder what he meant by that.'

Greer didn't respond. She found she couldn't.

'You probably nailed it with what you said before, Mrs M. Tom loved some guy, and believed, rightly or wrongly, that he'd been lied to. What with the depression, his thinking got all out of whack.' Charlie drained his glass. The bottle was now empty. Greer saw his gaze travel to her wine rack, which was amply stocked.

'To kill himself, though? I wish—' Charlie glanced away.

'You wish what?'

He blew out a breath. 'That I'd been a better friend. If I had, this might not have happened.'

'You can't blame yourself.' Greer's voice was firm. 'I failed him, too. He felt suffocated by me. He was all I had, though. Didn't he realise that?' Her fist slammed hard on the table.

'He loved you, Mrs M. Even if he found you... difficult.'

'I just wanted to mother him. Was that so wrong?'

'No. But you need to let go. Grieve for Tom, and remember the man he was, his laugh, his sense of humour. Don't torture yourself by trying to find the bastard who hurt him.'

How stupid of her, not to have told him about Tom's diary. 'You don't understand. Finding him might be easier than you think.'

Charlie's wineglass almost slipped from his grasp; he caught it just in time. 'What? How?'

'Tom kept a journal.'

He looked alarmed. 'Mrs M, that's private. Tom wouldn't want you reading his diary.'

'I've only managed a few pages so far. He mentions this guy called Blue.'

Charlie's lips tightened. 'You need to respect Tom's privacy. He didn't write that diary for you.'

He set down his wineglass. 'Let's make a deal. I'll talk to Tom's other friends, see what I can find out. No more torturing yourself reading the diary, and Tom gets his privacy. Okay?'

Greer opened another bottle of Merlot while she considered Charlie's suggestion. It had its merits. That damn journal had sliced her up with every word. 'Okay.'

She refilled their glasses, and they drank in silence for a while. Greer's vision grew fuzzy. Too much booze; she'd eaten nothing since breakfast, and it was still only early afternoon.

Charlie cleared his throat. 'The police never found her, then?'

The abrupt change in conversation threw Greer for a second. 'No. I don't think they're even looking anymore.'

'They questioned me. Made me feel guilty, kept insinuating I might have hurt her.'

Shock punched through Greer. It made no sense. 'Why?'

He bit his lip, looked away. 'We dated. Only a few times, but it was wonderful.'

Hurt stabbed Greer. She hadn't known that. 'Why didn't she tell me?' As if she needed an answer. Rose, like Tom, had found Greer suffocating.

'I've no idea. Then she disappeared, and the police spotted my number on her phone records. Read our messages, including the one in which she dumped me. Got suspicious when I couldn't provide an alibi. I was home alone that night. They had no concrete evidence with which to arrest me, though.'

'I know you, Charlie. You weren't to blame.' Greer took a swig of wine. 'I wish I'd realised you were dating, though. And she shouldn't have ditched you. You'd have been perfect together.'

'Yeah, well, she didn't agree.' Charlie finished his wine, pushed back his chair, then got to his feet, his movements unsteady. He reached for his car keys, but Greer grabbed them first. Thank goodness she wasn't so drunk she'd lost all common sense.

'You're staying here tonight.' Her voice was firm. 'I'll make up a bed on the sofa.' She suspected Charlie wouldn't want Tom's old room. Too many painful memories. Rose's bedroom wouldn't be suitable, either.

A thought struck her. 'Was that why you went away? To Australia, I mean. Being questioned by the police... that must have been hard.'

'It was. The final straw, you might say.'

CHAPTER 11

Beth glanced up as she dragged her bins to the pavement. Greer was in the driveway next door, putting her own rubbish out for collection. Still in her dressing gown and slippers, she looked pale, tired, and defeated. Beth's heart went out to her.

'Greer!' Her neighbour glanced over on hearing her shout, then averted her gaze. Beth wasn't so easily deterred. She hurried down her pathway and into Greer's, laying a hand on her arm.

'Do you have time for a cup of coffee?' Beth forced a smile, taking in Greer's unwashed hair, the dark shadows under her eyes. 'It would be great to catch up. And I could use the company.'

Was Greer about to refuse? Apparently not. Her neighbour pointed towards her clothing. 'You'll have to come to me. I'm not dressed for going anywhere.'

Perhaps Beth should leave her alone. What kind of Christmas and New Year Greer had endured on her own, mired in her grief? But no, a genuine friend wouldn't desert Greer when her neighbour most needed support. Beth's sister and her tragic death served as a constant warning on such occasions.

She smiled at Greer. 'That would be great.'

Beth followed Greer into her house and took a seat in the living room. Greer headed into the kitchen, from where the rattle of cups and the clink of spoons soon issued. Beth glanced around her. The room was a mess; dirty plates and mugs on the floor, dust everywhere. A stale smell hung in the air. Greer being in her pyjamas at one in the afternoon was a worry, too.

Beth's gaze fell on a silver photo frame, the same one she'd seen by Greer's bed the day Tom died, standing on the coffee table. Greer with the pretty blonde woman with a tiny mole beside her right eye. Beth picked up the photo and studied it.

Greer's face was lit up with joy; a huge smile curved her mouth, deepened the crow's feet around her eyes. She looked as though she'd just won the lottery and found the Holy Grail all at once. Never had Beth seen Greer so happy as in this photo.

The other woman was somewhere in her mid- to late-twenties. She looked confident, like she knew her path in life. Unlike Greer's, her smile seemed a little forced.

Greer had told Beth she had no family or friends. So why was she staring at this woman with such love?

At that moment, Greer walked in carrying two steaming mugs. She stopped when she saw the photo Beth was clutching. Beth watched Greer's hand tremble, shaking the coffee so badly some slopped onto the carpet. Her neighbour's expression held a mixture of shock and dismay.

'I'm sorry, Greer. I didn't mean to pry.'

'I should have taken it back upstairs. I wanted to clean the frame, though, and the polish was in the kitchen.' Greer took the photo from Beth and studied it, clearly wrapped in her own world.

Her expression was so bleak. Who on earth was this young woman?

Greer sat beside Beth and handed her a mug of coffee. Beth's nose wrinkled. Was that stale sweat she could smell?

Greer set her drink down on the table. 'You must be wondering who she is.'

'I don't want to pry.'

A sad smile. 'That's Rose.'

Had Greer ever mentioned a woman called Rose? Beth didn't think so. 'Is she a friend of yours?'

Greer's gaze dropped away. Her hands twisted nervously in her lap. 'Rose was my daughter.'

Her daughter? Oh, dear God. Beth needed to tread carefully.

'You said 'was', not 'is'. What happened to her?'

'She disappeared eighteen months ago. Not long after I got her back.'

CHAPTER 12 - Before

Greer stared at her watch, counting down the seconds. Her daughter was returning home, and she couldn't wait. She pulled back the curtain and glanced out at the street, impatient for that magic moment when Rose would arrive. Greer shoved her thumb into her mouth and chewed the skin around the nail, her teeth working furiously. Four minutes past two. Rose *was* coming, wasn't she?

She'd promised. She wouldn't let Greer down, right?

A blue Citroen turned the corner and headed towards Greer's house, parking across the driveway. The driver's door opened, and Rose stepped out.

The tightness in Greer's chest eased. Her baby girl was home at last.

Greer raced into the hallway to fling open the front door. She slipped on a pair of shoes and headed down the driveway, her smile so wide her face would surely crack.

'You made it,' she said, throwing her arms around Rose. Her darling girl's hair was silky against her cheek. The musk of Rose's perfume, the scent of her shampoo, brought tears to Greer's eyes. She was hugging her baby too tightly, but couldn't let go. It wasn't every day a mother got her daughter back.

Rose gently extracted herself, then took a suitcase from the boot of the Citroen. 'Thank you. For saying I can stay here.'

'You're welcome.' How formal she sounded. Why couldn't she relax around Rose? Act like the mother she yearned to be?

She needed to give it time. Not rush things.

It had been hard not to so far. Greer had tiptoed around the subject of Rose living with her, although desperate to suggest it from day one. Instead, she'd dropped hints, fuelled by what Rose had told her. How she'd moved in with her father after dumping her boyfriend, but hadn't been happy. 'Dad's such an arsehole,' she'd said, her fingers picking at the hem of her t-shirt. 'I can't wait to find somewhere else, if I'm honest.'

At last. Time for Greer to make her move.

Now, here they both were.

Rose smiled. 'I'm going to enjoy living with you. But I promise—I won't outstay my welcome. We hardly know each other, after all. Maybe this won't work out.'

Later, once they'd shared a takeaway curry, Greer showed her Tom's photo. She'd already arranged for Rose's brother to come for Sunday lunch the following day. How could she ever wait that long? It would be such a wonderful moment. Her children were about to meet at long last.

Tom would adore his sister. She'd love him like crazy, too. Greer was sure of it.

'He looks like a nice guy,' Rose said. 'Tell me about him.'

CHAPTER 13 - Now

Greer raised her eyes to look at Beth. 'I gave birth to Rose six months after I married Jake. When she was born, my world became whole. I hadn't realised what was missing until she arrived. Rose was my everything. I had my beautiful baby to care for. Until I didn't.'

Greer seemed so fragile, like she might shatter into a thousand shards if Beth said the wrong word. Best to let her continue. She laid a gentle hand on Greer's arm and squeezed. 'I'm listening.'

'He took her from me,' Greer said.

'Jake? When he left, you mean?'

'Yes. I didn't see her again for twenty-six long, lonely, miserable years.'

This woman had suffered even more than Beth had ever imagined. 'You never tried to get custody of her?' Oh, God, that sounded judgemental.

Greer shook her head. 'I was so tired and brain-fogged back then. I was probably suffering from postnatal depression. I'd lost whatever fight I once possessed. By the time I got better, Jake was long gone, and I had no idea where.'

'Why did your husband take Rose and not Tom?'

'He never knew about Tom.'

'What? How come?'

'Jake didn't realise I was pregnant when he left. Neither did I. All I did was sleep, because that way I avoided the fact he and Rose were gone. I eventually took a test and found I was four months pregnant.' Greer wiped away a tear. 'It seemed like the end of the world. But when I'd thought it through, I was over the moon. Rose was gone, and nothing could replace her, but this way I'd be a mother again. I craved all of it, good and bad. Nappies, cuddles, bathing a child. I wanted that so badly, and Tom gave it back to me.'

'Oh, Greer. That must have been difficult. Single parenthood, I mean.'

'Yes, especially with the lack of money. Most of my life I've scraped by on benefits and with part-time admin jobs. I inherited just enough when my aunt died to buy this house with a bit left over.'

'You've had a hard life, my love.'

'I never forgot my baby girl, though.' Greer smiled, although her eyes were sad. She still clutched the photo of her daughter in one hand.

'And you didn't hear from Rose for... how long?'

'Twenty-six years. She told me she'd endured a succession of stepmothers, each worse than the last. More or less brought herself up.'

'How did that come about? Your reunion, I mean?'

'She tracked me down and got in touch, saying she wanted to meet. It was the miracle I'd prayed for.' Greer managed a smile. 'She'd had enough of her deadbeat father. Turned out she also needed somewhere to stay. So she ended up living here, like she always should have done. I was so happy. At first, anyway.'

'What happened?'

Greer raised tear-drowned eyes. 'One day, she didn't come home. She went on a blind date, even though I'd warned her about the dangers. I lay in bed awake, listening for the sound of her key in the door, but it never came. The next morning, I reported her as missing.'

This woman had suffered such misery in her life. Tom's death, her daughter's disappearance—it was a miracle Greer was still even halfway sane.

'Rose became just another statistic. Hundreds of thousands of people go missing in the UK each year.'

'You can't give up hope. Maybe she had mental health problems, stuff going on in her life you didn't know about—'

'No. Not my Rose. We didn't have each other for long, but we became close. The way a mother and daughter should be.'

'What do you think happened to her?'

Greer's mouth set in a tight line. 'That blind date? The police never found the guy.'

'You believe he—' Another occasion to choose her words carefully. 'Abducted her?'

'Of course he did. Rose wasn't the only woman who disappeared that summer.'

Shock hit Beth. 'Really?'

Greer nodded. 'At least one other, Lily Hamilton, went missing. I remember because my maiden name was Hamilton. And Lily—that reminded me of Rose. I've always loved flower names for girls.'

'People go missing all the time. For all we know, this other woman could be alive and well.'

Greer snorted. 'Yeah, right.'

'You think someone killed Lily Hamilton?'

'Don't you? Two women disappearing after going on blind dates? Oh, nobody's ever found their bodies.' Greer shuddered. 'But they're out there somewhere. My Rose, and Lily Hamilton. I'll never see my girl again.' She burst into noisy sobs. Beth pulled her close, one hand stroking Greer's hair.

Greer was probably right. Countless people disappeared each year, and while many turned up, others didn't. It was entirely possible for Rose Maddox and Lily Hamilton to have fallen victim to a predatory killer. One who'd successfully concealed their bodies.

'I only had her for a few short months,' Greer sobbed. 'I loved her so much. Now Tom's gone too. Why am I so cursed?'

For that, Beth had no answer. 'Are the police still looking for her?'

Greer shook her head. 'Like I said, she's just a statistic to them. Do you have any idea how awful it was to report her missing?'

CHAPTER 14 - Before

Greer paced the floor of her living room, her breath coming in short staccato bursts. In one hand, she clutched her mobile. Her heart was a dead weight in her chest, and for good reason: it was ten in the morning, and Greer hadn't seen Rose since the previous afternoon.

She'd lost count of how many messages she'd left on her daughter's phone, all of which remained unanswered. Now, as a light September drizzle tapped against her window, the time had come to take action. The police needed to know Rose hadn't returned home. Greer's fingers jabbed at her mobile, tapping out the number for Bridewell station.

'I need to report someone as missing.' She gave the operator her daughter's name. 'I'm so worried I can't think straight. Find her. Please.'

Within the hour, two uniformed officers arrived at Greer's house. 'Mrs Maddox?' the female one said, introducing herself as PC Alison

Hardwick. 'This is my colleague, PC Devin Gardner. May we come in?' Greer waved them inside.

'She's never stayed out all night before.' The police officers had already run through a few preliminary questions, but it was time for Greer to fill in the blanks. 'She's not answering her phone, either. I warned her something like this might happen. Those dating websites—you get loads of weirdos on them.'

'You said she had a date last night with a man she met online?' Alison Hardwick asked.

'I don't know any details. She can be very cagey at times. Doesn't tell me where she's going or who she's meeting.'

Devin Gardner leaned forward. 'Have you considered, Mrs Maddox, that she might have spent the night with this man?'

Greer sat up straight, eyeballed him full on. 'No. She's never done that all the time she's lived here. I don't like what you're insinuating.'

He spread his hands wide in a gesture of apology. 'My bad. These things happen, however. Do you mind if we take a few more details?'

Various questions followed. A request for a recent photo, what her daughter was wearing the previous evening, any distinguishing features, etc. Greer mentioned the mole beside Rose's right eye.

'Was everything fine between the two of you?' Alison asked.

No. But Greer couldn't tell this woman the truth. 'Yes. We get on really well.'

'Can we look around? Check her bedroom?' Greer nodded. Getting to her feet, she moved towards the door. 'If you come with me, I'll show you upstairs.'

'Are any of her clothes missing? Her passport?' Alison Hardwick asked once they were inside Rose's room. A hint of her sweet girl's perfume still hung in the air.

'No. It's like I told you. All she took with her yesterday was her handbag. I've no idea whether her passport was in it. But why on earth would she need it?'

'I've got it here,' Devin announced, holding it in his hand.

After what seemed an age, the two officers announced they'd had done all they could. 'We'll keep you posted,' Devin Gardner said, as the two of them left. 'Somebody will be in touch soon.'

CHAPTER 15 - Now

The morning after Beth's visit, Greer got her doctor to sign her off sick for a month. She could hardly bring herself to eat, let alone go to work. Besides, her dull data entry job sucked; she wouldn't miss it. She'd not forgotten her vow to find the man who'd ruined Tom's life, but it all seemed so pointless. Without Tom and Rose, was there any reason to carry on living? Her thoughts circled around the bottle of sleeping tablets in her bathroom. A fitting way to be reunited with her son.

Could she do it? Yes. No. Perhaps.

Greer's mobile sounded from her bag, startling her. When she extracted it, the words 'South West Organ Donation Services team' were on the screen.

Greer froze, her phone clutched tightly in her hand. Vague memories crowded into her mind. Some woman mentioning Tom being on the Organ Donor Register. Greer, too grief-stricken to think straight, signing the paperwork. Being told about the South West Organ Donation Team. How, if any of her son's body parts were suitable for transplant, a member of the team would contact her. With shaky fingers, she swiped the 'accept call' icon.

A female voice, heavily accented, met Greer's sharp, 'Hello?'

'Is that Mrs Greer Maddox?'

'Yes.'

'My name is Zofia Kowalski from South West Organ Donation Services. I'm calling in connection with your son, Mr Tom Maddox. First, let me say I'm very sorry for your loss.'

How presumptuous. This woman knew nothing of her loss. 'What do you want?'

Zofia Kowalski waffled on. Words slapped Greer in the face, stole the breath from her lungs. *Suitable recipient... your son's heart... operation a success, although it's still early days...*

Time to interrupt. 'You're telling me my son's heart has been used in a transplant, am I right?'

'That is correct. As per his wishes, and the paperwork that you signed.' When Greer didn't respond, the woman continued, 'I must apologise for not having been in contact sooner. What with the Christmas and New Year break, we've been short-staffed. Otherwise I'd have called you before.'

Greer's hand grew slick with sweat around her mobile. She sucked in a breath. Here was fresh pain, when she'd thought she couldn't hurt anymore. But what had she expected? She'd known about Tom being on the donation register, but her brain hadn't processed what that might mean. His body, now deep in the ground at Arnos Vale, was lacking a vital part. Tom's heart now beat in someone else's chest, and a nugget of anger took root inside her. It seemed all wrong to picture him with such an essential organ missing.

Zofia was still talking, but she'd missed whatever the stupid woman had been saying. 'Who was it?' Greer's voice hitched in her throat.

'You mean who received your son's heart?'

'Yes.'

'I can't divulge any personal details, I'm afraid. Patient confidentiality, you understand. What I can tell you is that the recipient is male, aged thirty-two, and had been on the waiting list for approximately two years. As I mentioned earlier, he's doing well. His new heart is settling in nicely.'

How dare Zofia talk as if this man had ordered a replacement from Amazon? Tom's heart may be new to *him*, but the guy had no right to it. It belonged in her son's chest, pumping his blood, keeping him alive. Anger pulsed through her.

'I've been told there's a letter from the recipient's family addressed to you. Would you like me to post it on once it arrives? Or else I can read it aloud to you. Whichever you prefer.'

No, no, no. Okay, so surgeons had removed her son's heart and inserted it into another man's chest. That person now lived while Tom was dead. A letter from his family would make the horror all too real.

'Mrs Maddox?'

'No. To both.'

'I understand how difficult this must be. You might find, however, that the letter helps. For many families, it's a comfort that their loved ones' organs are enabling others to enjoy healthier, better lives.'

'Well, that's not how it is for me. You can burn the damn letter for all I care.'

'Are you sure? I can keep it on file once I get it, in case you change your mind.'

'I won't.' Greer's index finger jabbed at the 'end call' icon.

Greer couldn't get the conversation out of her head, however. Words circled through her brain: *transplant, heart, recipient*. Images and sounds joined them. The rhythmic contraction and relaxation of the muscle, the *lub-dub* noise it would make. A strange sense of calm settled over Greer. She'd been wrong. Tom wasn't totally gone.

What might he have to say, this man who'd usurped Tom's heart? Some trite words of gratitude, probably. But what if Tom was reaching out to her from inside this man's chest? Shouldn't she hear what he had to say?

A fanciful notion, of course. Still, she had nothing to lose, because she'd already lost everything. This letter—why not read it? It wasn't her son who'd written it, of course, but curiosity nagged at Greer, wouldn't let go.

She'd call Zofia Kowalski tomorrow to ask her to forward the letter.

The sleeping pills in her bathroom could wait.

CHAPTER 16

The following morning, Greer called Zofia Kowalski and left a message on her phone. With any luck, she wouldn't have to wait long for the letter.

Except that she did. Three days passed, and it hadn't arrived. Her patience exhausted, Greer composed a curt reminder to Zofia. Two days later, Zofia responded.

'I've not received it myself,' she told Greer. 'I'm waiting for the patient liaison nurse to forward it.'

'Then chase him or her up. Today, please.'

Almost two weeks had slipped by since Greer told Zofia she wanted to read the letter. Now, at last, here it was.

The envelope felt smooth beneath her fingers. Despite the plain white exterior, she knew what was inside. She rarely received anything by post, so what else could it be?

Greer walked into her kitchen and set the kettle on to boil. A strong cup of Earl Grey was what she needed.

Half an hour later, her tea sat in front of her, stone-cold and untouched. As did the letter, taunting her from beside her teacup. In the background, her kitchen clock ticked away the seconds.

She shouldn't be such a coward. Why didn't she just read the goddamn letter?

Greer reached out a hand and picked it up with trembling fingers. A deep breath in. Then she tore open the envelope.

She read the covering letter. That, at least, held nothing alarming. Short and to the point, signed by Zofia. It reiterated how the enclosed communication contained no identifiers as to the recipient of her son's heart, and that if she replied, she should do so via Zofia, who would forward on her response. Greer set it aside and pulled out a separate letter, concealed in its own envelope. She could, if she wanted, rip it to shreds, bury it deep within her waste bin. Would it do any good to read it?

Her movements slow, as though in a dream, she opened the flap and unfolded the single sheet of paper.

Hello. We're strangers to each other, but we're both mothers—

Greer dropped the letter as though it had burned her. What the hell? She'd expected the writer to be the man who'd received Tom's heart. Her son, reaching out to her via him.

We're both mothers, though, women who know what it's like to love a son unconditionally. The gift of a baby is priceless, and mine will always be my little boy. You can identify with that, I'm sure.

I don't know your child's name, but I thank him. When the only thing that could save his life is a transplant, your son's selflessness makes a world of difference.

Please don't misunderstand me. It grieves me that your boy's death made my son's life possible. I hope it comforts you that his heart beats on in someone else, and that he didn't die in vain.

My son is taking his time in recovering from such a major operation, which is why this letter comes from me, not him. He's still in hospital, but if all goes well, he'll be discharged at the end of January. Like me, he owes your son a debt of gratitude he can never repay. From one mother to another, I thank you.

Greer crumpled the letter in a few savage movements, then tossed it across the kitchen. How foolish of her. She should never have read it.

Yet something drew her back to it.

Greer walked over to retrieve the letter. Time to chuck it in the bin where it belonged. Her fingers, however, had other ideas. Greer sat at the table and smoothed out the paper. That was when she spotted them.

Two small stains in the bottom right-hand corner. Almost unnoticeable, a shade darker than the paper, which was uneven and roughened in that spot. Greer's fingers traced over the tears another mother had shed, and her own eyes grew wet. She'd wept when writing to Greer, this unknown woman bound to her through Tom's heart. The bittersweet blotches unlocked Greer's own grief, and she sobbed, the letter still clutched in her hand.

When she was all cried out, she stared at the clock. Eleven o'clock on this damp Bristol day. Memories washed over her. Baby Tom, sleepy after his bath, gurgling in his cot. Greer, luxuriating in the rhythm of his heartbeat, one ear pressed against her son's chest. Her husband might have deserted her, taking Rose with him, yet Tom was strong, healthy and alive. Her son's heart beating against her own comforted her every time she hugged him. Somehow that sweet sound got Greer through the long, lonely years of single parenthood. Perhaps, if she heard it again, she might make peace with Tom's death.

Was that possible, though? Zofia had emphasised the need for patient confidentiality; Greer had no idea where this woman or her son lived.

Her mobile buzzed with a text. Beth's name was on the screen. *Fancy a quick coffee?*

Greer hadn't told her neighbour about Zofia's call or that she'd requested the letter. Now might be the time. Hadn't she already paved the way by confiding in Beth about Rose's disappearance?

Yes. I'll get the kettle on. Less than a minute later, Beth's finger sounded on the doorbell.

'How have you been?' Beth said, once Greer handed her a mug of coffee.

Greer sucked in a breath. 'Up and down. I've received this letter, you see.'

'Who's it from?'

She told Beth about her phone calls with Zofia Kowalski. Her decision to ask Zofia to post the letter to her.

'Have you opened it?' Beth asked.

'Yes. It was from his mother, not him.'

'What did it say? If it's not too personal a question?'

'She thanked me. Her words comforted me, Beth. I don't feel so lost now.'

'I'm glad, my love. You were brave to read it.'

'I'd give the world to hear Tom's heart again. I don't suppose that's possible, though. Patient confidentiality, and all that.'

'It might be more feasible than you think. Did this guy's mother propose meeting up?'

Beth's words hit Greer like a thunderbolt. In some dim recess of her mind, a long-forgotten television programme ran, one in which two people met in a park on a hot summer's day. It had held little significance to Greer at the time; she'd watched with only casual curiosity. She replayed the moment in her head, the memory fuzzy. A mother, listening to her daughter's heart in another woman's chest. The tears, the ecstasy on her face. Her grateful thanks.

Greer wanted that for herself. She needed to listen to Tom's heart again. The pain of her longing was almost physical.

'Greer? Did you hear what I said?'

'She didn't mention it, no. But her son's still in hospital. Do you think it's too soon for me to suggest it?'

Beth blew out a breath. 'Yeah, I'd say so. Maybe leave it a while.' She continued talking, but Greer tuned her out. A phone call to Zofia, proposing that they all meet up, was the way forward. Beth was right; it was too premature, but surely she'd understand, this mother who'd taken the time to write to Greer?

If all goes well, he'll be discharged at the end of January. Greer glanced at her phone; today was the twenty-seventh. In a few short days Tom's heart would leave hospital, ready for a new life. One in which Greer could, if she chose, play a part.

After Beth had gone, Greer returned to the sofa. Yes, she'd do it. She'd call Zofia Kowalski and ask her to set up a meeting. Her darling boy was calling to her. Before long, she might hear her son's heart beat again; perhaps it would ease the ache in her own.

Her mobile rang, startling Greer. When she glanced at it, Charlie's name showed on the screen.

'Thought I'd better call. A message seemed too impersonal,' he said, once they'd exchanged pleasantries. 'I've been doing some digging. Into Tom's boyfriend.'

In her zeal to reconnect with Tom's heart, Greer had forgotten her quest to track down Blue. 'Did you get the bastard's name?'

'Sorry, no. One guy said Tom didn't give any details, just that the bloke had dumped him and moved out of Bristol. He didn't know where. Meaning he'll be almost impossible to find.' Charlie cleared his throat. 'Time to let this go, Mrs M. No more reading Tom's journal. You need to accept Tom didn't want us knowing about this man.'

He was right. The memory of Tom's vomit-stained pillow, the empty pill packets, was still raw, but it seemed Greer stood little chance of finding Blue. Besides, she now had more important matters on her mind.

CHAPTER 17

Once Greer ended the call with Charlie, she scrolled through her contacts, in which she'd already programmed Zofia's direct-dial number. She drew in a deep breath, praying the woman would be sympathetic.

Zofia answered on the second ring. After Greer had identified herself, she didn't waste time with niceties. 'I want to meet him.'

'The recipient of your son's heart?'

Greer bit back her frustration. Who else could she mean? 'Yes.'

'As I've explained, Mrs Maddox, patient confidentiality is of prime importance. I can't give out contact details, I'm afraid.'

Greer gritted her teeth. 'Yeah, so you've said. But you could arrange a meeting.'

'Donor families and recipients do sometimes meet up. It's rare, however.'

Stubbornness swelled inside Greer. 'I want to make it happen.'

'Remember, Mrs Maddox, the recipient might still be in hospital. He—'

'He's being discharged in a few days. That's what his mother said in the letter.'

She heard Zofia fail to suppress a sigh. 'It's possible he'll be in for longer. Complications can, and do, arise where such complex surgery's concerned. A hospital stay of three months isn't unknown in heart transplant cases; if a blood vessel ruptures, for example.'

Damn this woman and her caution. 'I can at least ask, though. Right?'

'Of course. But, like I said, such meetings, despite what you see on television, are unusual. Even if the recipient of Tom's heart leaves hospital this month, he'll need a long recovery time at home. He might not feel up to arranging a get-together.'

'If I want to respond to the letter, I've every right to do so. Correct?'

'Yes. But—' Zofia launched into a speech about how meeting the recipient might worsen rather than ease Greer's grief. 'Emotions are complicated things, Mrs Maddox. You could react differently to how you think you will.'

'Please don't patronise me. I know my own mind. I want to meet him.'

'I'd need to be present if a meeting takes place, along with the transplant coordinator for the other party.'

'Fine.' Greer didn't care either way.

'There's no guarantee he'll agree. Many recipients prefer anonymity. I would urge you not to get your hopes up.'

Greer rolled her eyes. More verbal combat was clearly needed. 'How do I proceed? Is the next step to reply to the letter, saying I'd like to meet?'

'In a nutshell, yes. But Mrs Maddox—' Greer endured more pleas to reconsider, all of which she rebuffed. Zofia eventually capitulated, clearly too browbeaten to continue.

After the call ended, Greer made herself a coffee. All she needed to do now was find the right words. She'd start with the basics. *Thank you for your letter...*

CHAPTER 18

Greer hurried home from the shops, a greetings card tucked into her handbag. Nobody wrote letters anymore, so she had no writing paper or envelopes. Hence the card. As she dashed back, keen to escape the rain that had dogged that particular January, she spotted Beth getting into her car.

Beth waved. 'How are you doing? Fancy a coffee later?'

A nice idea, but no. The card was calling to Greer. Besides, after she'd composed her reply, she'd probably want to be alone. A shake of her head, a regretful smile, a tap of her watch, and Greer was safely inside her house.

Seated on her sofa, her lap desk on her knees, Greer took out the card, which boasted a bunch of roses along with 'Thank You!' in gold letters, and pulled a pen from the pot on the shelf. She already knew what she was going to write.

Many thanks for your letter. It brought me comfort to know my son's heart beats on, even if in another body. That was stretching the truth, but Greer considered it wise to temper her words. *Can I ask a huge favour? I'd love to meet your son. Would you, and he, please consider the idea? It would mean the world to me to hear my boy's heart beating in his chest.*

By the time you receive this, your son will have only just left hospital. When he feels well enough, I hope he'll agree to meet up. I'm free any time that would suit him, and am happy to travel to wherever he lives.

Greer read through what she'd written. Beth was right; it was probably too early to propose the idea. She imagined that, on the rare occasions when a donor family and an organ recipient met, it happened after several letters and a slow build-up of trust between the two sides. She didn't have time for all that. The urge to hear Tom's heart swamped Greer again. Her longing had become an obsession that wouldn't let go.

She slid the card into its envelope and addressed the outside to Zofia Kowalski at the South West Organ Donation Services team. If she hurried, she'd just make the five o'clock post collection.

She'd done her best. Now all she could do was wait. Again.

CHAPTER 19

Wait, Greer did, albeit reluctantly. Throughout the next week, no letter arrived, and Zofia didn't call. Greer checked her hallway multiple times a day, her impatience soaring with every disappointment.

Why hadn't either of them written back? What if the reply had got lost in the post?

Perhaps mother and son needed a while to consider. What was there to think about, though? If they were so damn grateful, why wouldn't they want to meet up?

By the end of the week, Greer's patience was exhausted. She needed a response, for God's sake. She was on the point of calling Zofia or sending a second card when her phone rang one morning. Zofia's name was on the screen.

Greer snatched up her mobile, swiping the 'accept call' icon. 'Have you heard from them? Are they okay with meeting up?'

Her mouth was dry with fear. What if the answer was no?

When Zofia replied, her voice was hesitant. 'What I can tell you is that I've received a letter for you from the other party's mother, along with a phone call from the Organ Donations Services team local to the family. I'm afraid, Mrs Maddox, that I don't have good news. The recipient of your son's heart prefers not to meet with you.'

No. No, no, no. She'd write again, stress how this meant everything to her. If she could just make them understand…

'His mother feels the same way. She asks you to allow her son to live his life in gratitude, but also in anonymity. From what I'm told, they're very private people, Mrs Maddox.'

'Can I write again? Make them see how important this is?'

'I'm afraid not. In her letter, which I'll forward on, the mother requests no further contact. I'd be happy to meet up, talk everything through with you—'

'Don't bother. The letter contains nothing I want to read.' With that, Greer ended the call. So what if she'd sounded rude?

What an ungrateful pair. Her son had gifted his heart to this man, and neither he nor his mother cared enough to thank her in person. How insulting to Tom's memory.

The echo of her boy's baby heartbeat filled Greer's head, and she wiped a tear from her cheek. She had to hear that sound again. Nothing else mattered.

There had to be a way. She'd do whatever it took.

Beth's mobile buzzed with an incoming call, Greer's name on the screen. Well, that was unexpected, but welcome. 'Hey, Greer. You free for a coffee?'

Greer was sobbing so hard Beth couldn't make out what she was saying. 'Hold on. Slow down, please. What's happened? Why are you so upset?'

Her ears strained to make out Greer's words. Something about a letter. 'You're at home, right? I'm coming over now.'

Greer opened the door before Beth had time to ring the bell. She collapsed into Beth's arms, tortured sobs escaping her. Beth steered her into the living room, towards an armchair, and dragged another close by for herself. The room was still dirty and untidy, and the stale odour seemed worse.

Best to let the poor love cry it all out. Beth squeezed Greer's hand and waited.

At last Greer seemed done. She wiped her eyes and gave Beth a sad smile. 'All I wanted was to listen to Tom's heart. But the guy's mother says he doesn't want to meet up. How they're grateful, but they value their privacy. If they're so damn grateful, why refuse when it means the world to me?'

'Greer—'

'You agree they're being selfish, right? I'm going to write again, make them see sense.'

Beth understood why the donor family had refused to meet her. Greer was expecting too much, too soon. How pale she was, how wild her eyes. Okay, so Greer's grief was finding an outlet, which was good. But how could she convince her neighbour to mourn her son, but also let him go? Beth wasn't a mental health professional, but Greer's obsession with Tom's heart didn't bode well for her future state of mind.

Still, she had to try. 'Promise me you won't write back. Please, Greer.'

CHAPTER 20

That night, Greer tossed and turned for hours, unable to sleep. Okay, so she understood that she'd pushed too far, too soon. But surely it was best for all three of them to meet while everything was still recent—Tom's death, the transplant of his heart, the recipient's hospital discharge? A get-together would help the guy come to terms with having a new heart and ease Greer's grief. So why the refusal?

The more she thought about it, the angrier she got. Damn that stubborn pair of fools.

Zofia had shut down firmly the idea of future attempts on Greer's part to arrange a meeting, so that option was off-limits. How else might she persuade the mother or her son—preferably both—to meet her? The donor transplant team had emphasised that personal details were not to be included in any correspondence. There had to be a way, though.

The hours slid past, and still sleep eluded Greer. It was only when the dawn light filtered through her blinds that a solution came to her.

Once up and dressed, Greer switched on her laptop and opened up Facebook. In the search box, she typed some keywords and checked the results. The top one had the label 'Heart Transplant Support UK' and was a private group with over two thousand members. Greer clicked the link and read the information.

This is a support group for UK residents who have received heart transplants or are on the waiting list, as well as their families and friends. We ask that members of donor families refrain from joining because of the conflict of interest. There is also recipient confidentiality to consider. No medical journalists either. To join, click or tap the link below.

Conflict of interest be damned. Greer put in a membership request, only to be met with questions designed to weed out unsuitable applicants. She typed out blatantly dishonest responses, then clicked on 'join group'.

Greer lied her way through more screening questions for two other groups, then sat back to wait. She'd done all she could for now.

Her stomach emitted a loud growl. Damn, she'd skipped breakfast again. She needed the bathroom as well; intent on her search, she'd ignored her full bladder. Food, the toilet—they'd have to wait. Greer typed 'heart transplant donor recipient meeting' into YouTube and worked through the results.

Wow, this was intense. A father, his face wet with tears, hugging the woman in whose body his dead daughter lived on. A mother, her ear against a young man's chest, listening to his heartbeat. She'd lost her only son a year ago in a car crash. Greer wiped her eyes as the young man thanked the woman. How she ached to be that mother, to hear the soft beat of Tom's heart again.

By lunchtime, all three Facebook groups had approved Greer for membership. A deep breath in, then she trawled through the posts. Many were heart-breaking. Tears pricked Greer's eyes as she read.

I've been waiting for a new heart for three years. Mine is very weak now. I can't hold on much longer.

Three months post-surgery, and I'm still in hospital. One complication after another. Will this hell never end?

My son's been rushed to intensive care, suffering organ rejection. Pray for him, please.

What these poor people must endure. Constant worry, fear and pain, all to pursue the bittersweetness of living. One particular post sent Greer's heart on a roller-coaster of emotions.

I'm doing well after my transplant. But it pains me to know someone had to die so that I could live.

Greer clenched her fists. Did the recipient of Tom's heart care that her darling boy no longer lived? Or was his chief concern his own well-being?

So selfish. His mother, too. She hated both of them.

Time for a break. Greer made herself a quick sandwich and a mug of coffee, relieved her bladder, then returned to her laptop. Enough browsing. She needed to do some digging. Tom had died two months ago, so she searched for posts in that time frame.

She almost missed it. A brief message from a woman called Heart Mum Isla. *Delighted to report that my son has his new heart! Thanks to everyone for their help and support.*

Heart Mum Isla had joined the group four years ago and spoke movingly about her son being diagnosed with hypertrophic cardiomyopathy. He'd suffered a heart attack aged just twenty-eight while playing tennis. Exercise was a trigger, apparently.

Huh. Wasn't there an incident on the news a while ago: a Premier League footballer, collapsing and dying during a match? Maybe he'd suffered from hypertrophic cardiomyopathy.

Twenty-eight. So young. Greer had been forty-eight when her doctor diagnosed her aortic valve calcification, and she'd countered with how she wasn't old enough for a dodgy ticker. She'd been told AVC that young was rare, but not unknown, especially given her family history. Heart disease wasn't the preserve of the elderly, it seemed. Greer read how hypertrophic cardiomyopathy led to the heart walls thickening, obstructing the flow of blood, with symptoms often starting in the late teens or early twenties. Isla's son had been unlucky; the disease rarely led to sudden cardiac arrest.

'I just want my son back. The way he used to be.' One of Isla's earlier posts. Well, Greer could relate to that. What she wouldn't give for Tom to be alive, healthy and well.

Was she on the right track, though? Suppose an unknown third party had received her boy's heart, not Heart Mum Isla's son? She clicked on Isla's profile. Her avatar photo showed a woman of Greer's age, standing beside a man who appeared to be in his early thirties. With them was a young woman, possibly mid-twenties. All three looked stiff, their gazes fixed on the ground.

Greer stared at the man in the photo. Isla's son, she presumed. Handsome, if you didn't mind a nose a little too big, lips that were loose and fleshy. Dark hair cut short, a few tufts swept off his forehead by the wind. Impossible to determine his eye colour. His features were coarser than Tom's and he was stockier, but his face shape was similar, as was the hair colour. He towered over Isla, but with no point of reference, Greer couldn't accurately gauge his height. A fit-looking guy; hadn't Isla mentioned her son used to play tennis?

That broad chest of his. Incredible to imagine Tom's heart pumping blood through it.

Isla's posts weren't public, so the amount of information Greer gleaned was minimal. Time to send the woman a friend request.

CHAPTER 21

Greer fretted throughout the rest of the day, checking Facebook constantly. Shortly before ten pm, her patience received its reward. A notification that Heart Mum Isla had accepted Greer's friend request.

Okay, time to dig deeper. Find out if her son had Tom's heart.

Isla didn't use Facebook much, but some crossover existed between her personal profile and that of the support group. After a minute of scrolling, Greer found what she was looking for. A post dated just before Christmas, accompanied by a photo of Isla and the same man. Just one line, but it said everything: *Grateful beyond words that my son has been given the precious gift of life.*

Greer clicked on Isla's profile. Ah, there was the information she needed. Nathan Taylor was the name of Isla's son, and the time frame fitted. Greer now possessed the identities of both the recipient of Tom's heart and his mother, assuming they shared a surname.

The young woman was Isla's daughter, Jessica. Not that Greer cared; her focus was entirely on Jessica's brother. What sort of man was he, this Nathan Taylor in whose chest Tom still survived? Was he a worthy recipient of that precious gift?

Greer's fingers hovered over her laptop, scared of what she'd find once she clicked on Nathan's hyperlinked name. How stupid of her. She'd come this far, so why not persevere?

Hmm, that was disappointing. Nathan had locked down tight on his security settings; Greer couldn't view his posts or glean any further information about him. He didn't even have a photo of himself as his avatar, just the default Facebook option of a generic head. If she was to find out more about the recipient of Tom's heart, she'd need to dig deeper into Isla Taylor.

Isla's profile listed her as living in Birmingham. That was convenient—less than a hundred miles up the M5 from Bristol. Buried in one of Isla's posts was a reference to Nathan also living in Birmingham. Food for thought.

Greer walked into her kitchen to make herself a coffee. Time to ponder her next step.

Maybe she should unfriend Isla and forget she'd ever stalked her and her son online. Where did that leave *her*, though? In the same miserable place as before—lonely, grief-stricken, suicidal.

Greer stared at a bottle of Merlot, veiled by a thin veneer of dust, in her wine rack. How easy would it be to drain it dry whilst popping pill after pill until oblivion came calling?

The kettle steamed and boiled until the automatic switch popped off, rousing Greer from her thoughts. She spooned coffee into a mug, her mind running on Tom's heart. The steady *lub-dub* of its beat, the rich red blood flowing through its chambers, the scars where the surgeons had stitched it into Nathan Taylor's body.

Greer's knees buckled; she would have fallen if she hadn't gripped the kitchen table. What on earth had she been thinking? She'd been stupid to contemplate forgetting about Isla and Nathan.

Greer wanted her son back, more than anything in the world. She needed to listen to Tom's heart one last time, and then she could die. Not before.

Wait, though. What about her own heart? Might it soften, the calcified deposits gradually melting to leave a healthy organ, if she were to hear Tom's heartbeat again?

A ridiculous thought. Yet seductive, intriguing. Tom's heart might hold the power to heal her own. Only if she could listen to it whenever she wanted, though. A reason for Greer to carry on living.

That meant tracking down Nathan Taylor. But how?

Greer glanced at the kitchen clock. The time was half-past eleven, and exhaustion was claiming her. Tomorrow. She'd sort everything out then.

CHAPTER 22

After breakfast the next day, Greer set to work. First, she typed 'how to find someone's address' into Google. The results were surprisingly helpful; why hadn't she considered checking the electoral register before? And websites existed that could do the legwork for her. This might be easier than she'd previously thought.

Greer chose the top result, typed in 'Nathan Taylor', and selected Birmingham as the city. Within seconds, dozens of results populated her screen; she had no way of knowing which was her target. To view them in more detail, she'd need to create an account and purchase online credits. Greer huffed her annoyance, but did so, taking advantage of the option to filter by Nathan's age. Still no luck; eight results remained. Any of them could be Nathan. She needed a different approach.

Isla Taylor might provide the answer. She searched the electoral register for Isla Taylor, Birmingham. And hit gold. Just one result.

Thank God for the woman's unusual first name. Greer grabbed her phone and added Isla's address to her contacts. Before long, Nathan's mother would lead her to her son.

Should she tell Beth what she intended? Greer doubted her neighbour would be too supportive; Beth obviously believed her to be obsessed with Tom's heart. Well, screw her. She'd never known the pain of losing a child, and if they stood any chance of being friends, Beth needed to get on board with this. Greer couldn't let Nathan Taylor slip away, not when she was so close to finding him. So tempting to hammer up the M5 to Birmingham that very day.

Caution was needed. She mustn't go rushing in. Far better to act with a cool head.

Maybe the emphasis Isla Taylor had placed on motherhood in her letter was the key. What if Greer appealed to the woman, mother to mother? Forced her to see how important it was that she met Nathan? Once Isla understood the depth of Greer's love for Tom, how could she still refuse?

CHAPTER 23

Beth read through her draft message to Greer. *Would be great to catch up. There's a new tapas bar opened in Redfield. Want to try it?* It would be good to get Greer out of her house into a more social environment. She sucked in a breath and tapped the 'send' icon.

To her relief, Greer replied straightaway. *I'd like that. Am free tonight. Have some news to share.*

Interesting. Hopefully not about that damn letter Greer had received. Beth tapped out a response. *Happy to drive. I'll come round at 7.*

At ten to seven, impatient to tuck into tapas, Beth started up the path towards Greer's house. Her neighbour must have seen her do so, because before Beth had time to ring the bell, she opened the door.

'I'll just grab my bag,' Greer said. To Beth's relief, she looked freshly showered and her clothes ironed. The house, from the little Beth could see, appeared clean and tidy. A positive sign.

It didn't take long to drive to the suburb of Redfield, or to walk the short distance from where Beth parked to Patatas Bristolas, the tapas bar she'd mentioned. A waft of garlic and sizzling meat met her nostrils as she pulled open the door.

Now she and Greer were at their table, menus before them. 'How have you been, Greer?'

A smile lit up Greer's face. 'I've found the recipient of Tom's heart.'

No preamble, just straight to the point. Greer was clearly far more obsessed than Beth had realised. And how on earth had Greer tracked the guy down?

When Beth didn't respond, Greer glanced her way. 'You don't seem too pleased. Aren't you happy for me?'

'Greer—'

'This makes all the difference. I know where he lives—where his mother does, anyway—and it's only a matter of time before we meet. I can't wait to see him. His name's Nathan Taylor, and his mother's called Isla.'

'How did you find all this out? Doesn't patient confidentiality apply here?'

Beth listened as Greer detailed the internet searches that had led her to Isla Taylor. Her neighbour's focus was totally on her dead son. Even allowing for the fact she was grieving, her obsession wasn't healthy, in Beth's opinion.

She needed to tread carefully. Greer was fragile, in need of a friend. 'I've no wish to rain on your parade. But don't you think you've gone too far? This woman and her son have said that while they're grateful, they prefer not to meet you. Many people would consider that understandable, given the circumstances. You know that part of Tom is alive in this Nathan guy. Isn't that enough for you?'

An angry flush stole into Greer's cheeks. 'No. Not even close.'

How could she make Greer see sense? 'I want to help you, my love. But I'd be a lousy friend if I didn't point out that what you're doing—well, it's veering into stalker territory. I doubt these people would be happy if they knew the lengths you've gone to. No, hear me out.' She mustn't let Greer interrupt. This was too important. 'You need to respect this woman's decision, and leave her and her son alone.'

Greer shook her head. 'This is the right thing to do. You're correct in saying Nathan and his mother have had a tough time. You don't think I haven't, given that I've lost my only remaining child? I can help them, give the support they need.'

'Nathan Taylor's been through a hugely traumatic surgery. He's fresh out of hospital and needs time to recover. Can't you leave him be?

Greer's eyes flashed fire. 'That man is only alive because of my son. He owes me, and I'm going to collect.'

To hell with treading carefully. 'You need to stop this nonsense. Now.'

'I want to hear my child's heart. Is that too much to ask?' Greer's eyes were wild, her hands clenched. The buzz of conversation around them masked her irate tone, to Beth's relief.

'No. But where does it end? When you've listened to Nathan's—sorry, Tom's—heart, will that be enough for you?' Greer's expression betrayed the answer.

Beth had to keep trying. 'You say you have Isla Taylor's address? Are you planning to write to her again?'

'No. I'm going to visit her.' Beth's worst fear confirmed.

'Listen to me, my love. I'm trying to save you a bucket-load of heartache here. You can't barge into other people's lives and demand their time, their attention. It's not fair. What about respecting their right to privacy?'

'I'm grieving for my son. *They* need to respect *that*.' Greer almost spat the words at Beth.

It was clearly no use arguing. The evening had already turned sour. Best to steer the conversation elsewhere. Beth handed Greer a menu. 'Let's order a few dishes. Spicy potatoes, marinated olives, and squid rings for me. What about you?'

Greer's tightly pressed lips indicated she was still angry. Beth should probably back off; her neighbour's mind seemed firmly made up. This was unlikely to end well.

Perhaps it was for the best. Isla Taylor would doubtless issue a firm rebuttal about meeting her son. Greer would sulk, and that would be that. What else could she do?

CHAPTER 24

The day after her evening with Beth—God, the woman had been no help at *all*—Greer's determination to track down Nathan remained strong. So tempting to jump in her car, drive to Birmingham, and find a cheap hotel. Allow Isla Taylor to lead her to Nathan. Then she'd meet him casually, as though by accident.

But no, that wouldn't work. Nathan was recovering from major surgery; he might not be well enough to go out. Besides, he probably wasn't a fool. He'd never believe the sheer coincidence of the mother of a man who'd donated his heart to him appearing in his local coffee shop. Neither would Isla. Much as it pained Greer, she had to be more subtle.

Whatever approach she tried was unlikely to go down well with the Taylors. The rules about patient privacy were there for a reason.

Hang on a minute. Why not try honesty? A coincidental meeting wouldn't work, so she'd appeal to Isla Taylor directly. Persuade her that a meeting would benefit all of them, especially emotionally. Probably best not to admit she'd stalked Isla on social media. In that respect, Beth was right—Greer's actions reeked of desperation, which wouldn't endear her to Isla and Nathan.

Decision made.

The following morning, Greer rifled through her wardrobe. What should she wear? Her one indulgence was designer clothing bought from charity shops. Beautiful clothes, many still with tags on, at rock-bottom prices. No way could she afford their original cost, not given her meagre income.

Ah, yes. Her woollen Peter Chauncey dress, a bargain at just a tenner, would be perfect. A Tom Cowley jacket she'd snapped up for a fiver completed her outfit. She'd disguised her grey roots with a blonde home-dye kit the day before. Greer strapped on a fake Cartier watch, bought from a market stall. A squirt of perfume, and she was ready.

She surveyed herself in the mirror. Not bad for a fifty-something.

Greer grabbed her bag and keys and walked out of the house towards her car. The scrap of paper with Isla Taylor's address was safe inside her purse. She programmed the postcode into her phone's sat-nav and set off for Birmingham.

Two hours later, Greer parked up in front of a large semi-detached house. She stared at it, taking in where Isla Taylor lived. The house and its front garden were well maintained; no peeling paint, the lawn neatly cut. The driveway was empty.

Was Isla at work? Or perhaps she was out shopping and would be home soon. It was now half eleven. If Isla wasn't back by twelve, Greer would use the afternoon to explore Birmingham and return about six o'clock. No way would she drive back to Bristol without meeting the woman, and if that meant a hotel for a few nights, so be it. To hell with the cost.

Wait. What if Isla was living with Nathan while he recuperated? Greer might waste valuable time hanging around here. She got out of her car, strode up the driveway of the house next to Isla's, and banged on the door.

A man, somewhere in his sixties, opened it. 'If you're collecting for charity or selling religion, I'm not interested.'

Greer pasted a smile on her face. 'Neither, actually. I'm an old school friend of Isla's, here to surprise her. Do you have any idea when she'll be home?'

The man stared at her. 'If you're a friend, how come you don't know she's at work during the day?'

Her lie needed to sound plausible. 'We've not been in touch for ages. I'll come back later. About six o'clock?'

The man nodded, then went inside and closed the door. How rude. No matter, though. Greer had the information she required.

She spent the afternoon in various cafes until she could return. When she parked up again outside number six, Spence Terrace, a silver Mercedes was in the driveway. Isla Taylor was home.

Just as Greer was about to exit her car, the front door opened and a woman appeared in the doorway. In her hand, she held a full rubbish bag by the neck. Greer's gaze slid to the right, where two bins, one grey, one green, stood beside the garage. She studied Isla as the woman walked to the grey bin, flipped open the lid, and slung the bag inside. She was tall, carrying a few excess pounds around her middle, hair pale toffee in colour. If Greer had to guess, she would have said Isla Taylor was in her early sixties. Her clothes spoke of money, her skin and hair of expensive beauty treatments.

Isla went inside and closed the door. Sweat prickled Greer's neck, despite the cool evening air. Might Nathan be inside the house with Isla?

Her pulse beat faster. She mustn't waste another second.

Greer slammed her car door behind her as she stepped onto the pavement. She walked up to the front door and pressed the bell once, twice, hard. The sound screeched in her ears.

Isla became visible in the hallway, her shape contorted by the crinkled glass. She stared at Greer once she'd opened the door, a polite smile on her face. 'Hi. Can I help you?'

Inside the house, footsteps sounded from the landing. A door closed upstairs. Nathan, perhaps?

'Can I help you? Isla repeated, irritation in her voice.

'My name is Greer Maddox. Could I come inside and talk to you, please?'

Isla frowned. 'What do you want?'

Before Greer could reply, she said, 'If you're selling anything, I'm not interested.'

'You've got this all wrong.' Why was this woman making things so difficult? 'I'm here about your son, Nathan.'

Alarm etched itself on Isla's features. 'How do you know Nathan? Is he all right? Has he fallen sick?'

Greer shook her head. 'Nothing like that. Sorry to worry you unnecessarily. The fact is—' She swallowed, desperate to dislodge the ball of nerves wedged in her throat.

'My son's name was Tom Maddox.' The words tumbled out in a rush. 'He died just before Christmas. He's who donated the heart that was transplanted into Nathan.'

If she'd thought Isla looked alarmed before, it was nothing compared to now. The woman's mouth fell open; she took a step backwards, her face pale. Her hands shot out, as if ward Greer off. 'You shouldn't be here. How did you find me? I specifically told—'

Greer reached out an arm, preventing Isla from closing the door. 'I know you did. But I had to come. Please let me talk to you. Just ten minutes of your time. That's all I ask.'

CHAPTER 25

After a few seconds' hesitation, Isla moved aside, gesturing into the hallway. 'You'd better come in, then.' Greer didn't need a second invitation.

'What is it you want to say?' Isla asked. The two women were sitting opposite each other at Isla's kitchen table, on hard-backed chairs that hurt Greer's hips. She'd have preferred their discussion to take place in Isla's comfortable lounge, but suspected Isla had shepherded her into the kitchen precisely so she wouldn't linger. She hadn't asked whether Greer wanted a coffee.

She must rise above it, not allow Isla's bad manners to affect her. Tom's heart was all that mattered.

Overhead, a door opened. Footsteps sounded, crossing the landing again. Greer's heart clenched with hope—was Nathan upstairs? Or was it Isla's daughter, Jessica?

She'd start with a polite enquiry. 'How's Nathan doing?'

Isla shrugged. 'He's got more energy now, but he still tires easily. Any physical exertion is a challenge. And he's on a whole cocktail of medication, like you wouldn't believe.'

To hell with caution. 'Is that him upstairs?'

'Nathan's not here. Say whatever you've come to say. Then go.'

Best to ignore such rudeness. 'Do you see him often?'

A sigh. 'Yes, although it's hard, what with working part time. Jessica, my daughter—she helps too. We cook his meals, do his laundry, etc. You'd do the same if the situations were reversed.'

Well, they weren't. Her Tom was dead, and Isla's Nathan was alive. Greer bit back the retort that threatened to burst from her lips. She mustn't antagonise Isla.

'I'll ask again,' Isla said. 'What do you want?'

Greer cleared her throat. 'In your letter, you said neither you nor your son wished to meet, and I understand your reasons. But please listen to mine. A few weeks ago, I lost my son. My only remaining child. Can you imagine what that's like?'

'Of course I can.' Isla's tone was curt. 'One day I got a phone call to say Nathan was in intensive care following a heart attack. My fit, active son, still in his twenties. He later developed scar tissue from a bout of myocarditis.'

Inflammation of the heart, often caused by a virus. Greer had heard of it.

'His heart didn't function properly afterwards. The doctors told him he needed a transplant. Month after month, I waited to hear that he'd found a donor, watching his energy levels decline, seeing him grow paler, more lethargic. Okay, so I've been luckier than you. My boy is alive, thanks to yours. But yes, I can imagine what it's like to lose a child, because I almost did.'

'You haven't even asked how Tom died. Don't you want to know?'

'No. And it wouldn't be appropriate for me to enquire.'

'He committed suicide.' Isla's expression turned from annoyed to startled. 'When the doctor told me, I wanted to die, too. Without my son, I had nothing to live for. Since I got your letter, though, everything's changed. '

'In what way?'

'More than anything, I'd like to listen to his heart. To know that it beats on in someone else—it would help me come to terms with his loss.'

There. She'd said it.

Isla looked thoughtful. 'How did you find where I lived?'

'It wasn't difficult. Through the electoral register. You're the only Isla Taylor listed on it in Birmingham.'

Fury blazed in Isla's face. She shoved back from the table, so hard the edge slammed into Greer's arm. 'Do you realise you sound like some weird stalker?'

As if Greer cared. Isla should have been more careful about her online presence. 'I'm sorry if what I did upsets you. I had no choice, however.'

'Of course you did. You could have respected our privacy, like we requested.'

'Please. I'm begging you. Mother to mother.' Greer glanced at Isla; the woman's mouth was a tight line of anger, her expression grim. 'My donor co-ordinator told me Nathan waited two years for his transplant. What if he'd died during that time? Your son has a new life, thanks to my Tom. Yes, it must seem odd, me getting your address that way. But don't you understand why I did it? Can you honestly say you wouldn't have done the same?'

Isla's expression remained hard. 'Maybe. But most people would have respected the wishes set out in my last letter.'

She sat down again. 'You probably think me harsh, but I get it. Everyone deals with loss differently, and you're grieving for your son. You acted inappropriately, but you're here now. Why not knock on Nathan's door, though? Or were you unable to track him down like you did me?'

Greer shook her head. 'I couldn't find him. Besides, I wanted to sound you out first. About how he's recovering, whether his health would allow us to meet up.' She looked Isla square in the eye. 'I thought you could also put in a good word for me. Once you'd met me and realised I'm genuine.'

A frown crossed Isla's face. 'I'm not sure Nathan would listen.'

'Why not?'

'My son and I don't get on that well. We haven't since he hit his teenage years.'

Before Greer had time to comment, Isla continued, 'He didn't grow up in a happy household. His father and I—let's just say there were problems.'

'Nathan's illness hasn't brought you closer, then?'

Isla shook her head. 'If only.'

'Maybe meeting me will help.' Greer warmed to her theme. 'Whatever issues the two of you have won't be there between Nathan and me. All I ask is the chance to listen to his heart, to know that Tom lives on in Nathan. Will you ask him to reconsider, please?'

'Nathan won't listen to me.' Isla wiped away a tear. 'He takes after his father, who's dead now. Both of them stubborn as a mule.'

'Then I'll ask him myself. I won't rest until I find him.'

'Don't. Please. Like I said to our donor co-ordinator, it's too much, too soon. You should never have come here.'

This woman couldn't stop Greer from discovering Nathan's address. All Greer had to do was fool Isla into thinking she'd backed off and then follow her. Isla would, with luck, lead Greer straight to Nathan.

Panic sounded in Isla's voice. 'Remember, he's recovering from major surgery. I don't want him upset.'

'I won't upset him.' Greer was determined to meet Nathan Taylor, and if Isla wouldn't help, then screw her. 'You can't stop me talking to him.'

'Oh, yes, I can. I'll warn him you're looking for him. Take it from me; he doesn't want to talk to you.'

CHAPTER 26

'I'm sorry if this disappoints you,' Isla said. 'But I'm acting in the best interests of my son. And my decision is final.'

The ingratitude of the woman. Who the hell did she think she was? 'You can't speak for him. Allow him to choose for himself, can't you? Give me his phone number so we can talk.' Greer practically spat the words out.

Isla leaned closer. 'Any normal person would have got the message by now. I'll say it again. Nathan doesn't want to meet you. He's only been out of hospital a short while and is still recovering. Don't you understand?'

She stood up. 'It's time you left. Please respect my family's privacy and leave us alone. I know you're grieving, and that's probably clouding your judgement, but you can't burst in here and demand Nathan's contact details. That's totally inappropriate.'

Isla wasn't getting rid of her that easily. Greer tamped down her fury; she'd not gain anything by provoking the woman. She stood up as well. 'If that's what you've decided, there's nothing more to say. I'll be on my way.'

Isla followed Greer down the hallway. 'Please don't think me ungrateful. But you need to let this go.' The second Greer was through the door, Isla slammed it behind her.

Greer walked towards her car. As she unlocked it, she glanced at the house. A movement at one of the upper windows caught her eye. A young woman, her hair cut in a mousy bob, stared back at her, then disappeared. Isla's daughter Jessica, recognisable from the family photo Greer had seen.

Greer sat behind the wheel, her jaw set tight, her hands clenched in her lap. How dare Isla say that grief was clouding her judgement? The woman could patronise her all she liked, but Greer was going to meet Nathan, come what may. How she wished she'd booked a hotel room so she could follow Isla the next day to Nathan's house.

Maybe it wasn't so bad having to return to Bristol. She'd use the time to plan a strategy. One that would end with her listening to Tom's heartbeat.

The next morning, Greer rose early to drive back up the M5 to Birmingham. Her plan was to tail Isla after she left to visit Nathan.

Once she reached Spence Terrace, Greer parked twenty metres further down the street, in case Isla recognised her Fiat. She settled herself down to wait. In her tote bag, she had a thermos of coffee, a cheese sandwich and a packet of crisps. With any luck, this wouldn't take long.

It didn't. Greer had been waiting less than an hour when Isla's front door opened and she appeared, complete with coat and handbag. She got into her car and drove away while Greer fumbled with her key in the ignition. She had to hope Isla was going to visit Nathan and not to wherever she worked.

Greer stayed two cars behind Isla as the streets grew ever more upmarket. Before long, Isla signalled left into the car park of a block of flats. Greer's pulse pounded; this must be where Nathan lived. She stopped her Fiat on the double yellow lines opposite and switched off the engine.

The building had a central glass panel that rose for five floors to the roof, revealing the staircase inside. Greer held her breath as Isla walked up three flights of stairs. Then she turned right and disappeared from view.

With any luck, Greer had found where Nathan lived. Time to get off these pesky double yellows. She drove until she located a multi-storey car park, parked up, and found a little backstreet bistro for lunch. Her sandwich and crisps held no appeal, not when she now had a reason to celebrate.

Greer checked Google Maps while she toyed with her tuna salad. Nathan, it seemed, lived in the upmarket suburb of Edgbaston. She glanced out of the window. The passers-by were well-dressed, the shops opposite her quirky boutiques. Not that it mattered. The only thing that was important was Tom's heart.

Once she'd finished eating, Greer walked the short distance to Nathan's block of flats, noting the name of the building, Wansbeck Heights, and the road, Nightingale Avenue. Now all she needed was the number of his flat.

It was vital to wait until Isla left, of course. Time to explore those intriguing Edgbaston shops. She'd come back in a few hours.

Greer lost herself in the joys of window shopping. Ooh, a Peter Chauncey dress, similar to the one she'd worn yesterday. No tag, but probably priced two hundred pounds higher than what she'd paid. Today she had on a Pierre Dupont trench coat that had cost all of twenty pounds. Appearances mattered. If she was going to meet Nathan, she needed to look her best.

At four o'clock, Greer trudged back to Wansbeck Heights. She headed into the car park, searching for Isla's Mercedes, but it had gone. Thank God for that. It didn't take long before she spotted an elderly man punching a code into the keypad mounted by the door. As he shuffled through, Greer followed him.

The lobby proclaimed wealth and affluence. A thick burgundy-coloured carpet covered the floor and stairwell, and the fixtures were solid and well made. A hint of citrus freshener lingered in the air. Greer glanced around. On one wall was a bank of post boxes. Eight in total, all of them locked, but bearing name tags. Nathan lived in flat six.

Oh, the temptation to run upstairs and pound on his door. Almost overwhelming, but she'd do better to wait. Her next move needed to be calculated carefully, back in Bristol. Time to drive back home, then.

She was too close to Tom's heart to screw up now.

CHAPTER 27

Two days later, Greer booked into a cheap hotel in Birmingham, having driven there that afternoon. The place was shabby, dirty, and miles from Edgbaston, but all Greer could afford. It hadn't taken long to unpack; she'd only brought one large suitcase and her laptop.

Excitement swelled inside her. Tomorrow, she was going to meet Nathan, although he didn't know that yet. With any luck, she'd get to listen to Tom's heart.

Greer's brain buzzed with anticipation. Various scenarios played out in her head. Nathan, a smile on his face, telling her how grateful he was to Tom. His fingers opening his shirt. Her head pressed against his chest.

More meetings would follow. The two of them strolling through a park, arm in arm. Drinks at his flat, long lunches together. Nathan confiding how cold Isla was, how he related much better to Greer. *Almost like you're my mother, not her*, he'd say.

How she yearned for that intimacy. Now she just needed to make it happen.

Once she had showered the next day, Greer dressed with as much care as for a first date. She pulled on a blue woollen dress and braided her hair into a French pleat. On went black patent leather court shoes, teamed with a matching handbag. A light application of mascara and lipstick, a squirt of perfume, and she was done.

Greer surveyed herself in the mirror. Would Nathan like what he saw?

She put on a thick coat—the weather looked cold and windy—and set off from her hotel towards Nathan's place. To save petrol, she walked, but it took ages; her feet were sore by the time she arrived.

Greer glanced at her watch: eleven o'clock, not so early that Nathan would still be in bed. Unless he was sick, of course. A terrifying prospect. Nathan dying, Tom's heart lost forever—she mustn't think about it. Suppose such negativity ruined the meeting she had so longed for, like some weird jinx?

Time to get her head together. Positive vibes only.

Greer pulled her coat around her, shivering while she waited for someone to enter or exit Nathan's block of flats so she could gain access. Within a couple of minutes, a woman shoved open the door, and Greer nipped inside. Not long after, she arrived at Nathan's flat. This was it: show-time.

Greer pressed her finger on the buzzer, the sound echoing inside the flat. She pumped up and down on her toes, her bag clutched in her hands. Her breathing sped up when she detected footsteps walking towards the door. Then it opened. Nathan Taylor stood in the gap.

The saliva drained from Greer's mouth, leaving her incapable of speech. All she could do was stare at him.

His complexion was pale, his face haggard, and dark circles ringed his eyes. In the flesh, he looked less like Tom, although his height and hair colour weren't too different. But no, his features were definitely coarser, his expression more guarded. No real similarity existed between the two men.

A prick of disappointment stabbed Greer. She was being unreasonable. It was silly to expect Nathan to resemble Tom, even if he was male and only a few years older.

She must remember why she'd come. Tom's heart was all that mattered.

Thank goodness she'd worn her designer gear. She offered Nathan a beaming smile.

His gaze raked over Greer. 'Who are you? What do you want?'

Nathan's brusqueness stole Greer's breath away. So uncalled for. Why be so unfriendly? Did he, like Isla and her neighbour, assume she was selling something? She stepped forward, her eyes drawn to Nathan's shirt. Incredible to think that Tom's heart beat beneath it.

'My name is Greer Maddox. I'm—'

'Mum warned me about you.' Nathan's tone had dropped several degrees. 'Didn't you get the message? Yeah, we're both grateful, blah blah blah, but the fact is, you shouldn't be here.'

Greer moistened her dry lips. 'Is there any chance I can come in for a few minutes? Just to talk?'

'Now is a bad time. So, no, you can't. How did you find this address, anyway?'

If she admitted she'd followed Isla, Nathan's anger might escalate. 'It's easy to find somebody through an online search if you know where to look. Aren't you interested in hearing me out?'

'No. Just leave.'

How rude. Ungrateful, too; an insult to Tom. Greer thrust aside her anger with some difficulty.

Her gaze trailed over Nathan's shirt again. 'My son died, but he's the reason you're alive. All I ask is that you let me hear his heart beating. It's all I have left of him, you see.' She smiled, confident that the man before her wouldn't reject such a fervent plea.

A dull flush crept into Nathan's cheeks. His jaw clenched. 'My mother said she had been very explicit. Both in a letter, and when you tracked her down. She told you, in plain English, that neither of us wants any contact with you. Why the hell can't you respect our wishes?' With that, he stepped back and slammed the door in Greer's face.

Shocked, she burst into noisy tears. How could he be so cruel?

Greer pressed the buzzer. When Nathan didn't respond, she tried again. A third time. Footsteps sounded in the hallway. Seconds later, she found herself before an enraged Nathan Taylor.

'What the hell is wrong with you? Fuck off! Leave me alone!' The door banged shut.

Her breath coming in anguished gasps, Greer retreated until she was flat against the wall opposite, shock pounding through her. She'd realised this first meeting wouldn't be easy. But never had she expected such a rude reception.

She swallowed hard. What on earth did she do next?

CHAPTER 28

Greer stumbled down the stairs to the entrance lobby and into the cold and wind outside. Coffee was what she needed. That little cafe over the road would do.

After the door to Nathan's block of flats closed behind Greer, a black Kia Picanto pulled into the car park. A young woman stepped out and headed towards Greer. She looked familiar; where had she seen that mousy bob before? Ah, yes. Jessica Taylor.

The two of them established eye contact, and Greer saw recognition sweep over the other's face.

'I know you.' Her voice held surprise, and something Greer couldn't identify. 'You visited Mum the other day. I saw you from my bedroom window. She told me about you after you left. My name's Jessica. I'm Nathan's sister.'

Greer stepped forward, oblivious to the biting wind. The other woman's face was a younger version of Isla Taylor's. She had little doubt that they were mother and daughter.

'Can I buy you a coffee?' The offer came before Greer had time to consider what she was doing. Really, though, was it such a bad idea?

Jessica, unlike Isla and Nathan, seemed friendly, and Greer might gain useful information.

Jessica looked surprised, but nodded. 'Sure, but I can't stay long. I have to cook for Nathan and do his laundry.'

Over espressos, Greer probed her about her brother. 'Can I ask—is Nathan always so unpleasant? He was really rude just now.'

Jessica shrugged. 'Nathan can be awful, like you wouldn't believe. His behaviour's got worse since his cardiac problems started. I'm sorry he gave you a hard time.'

Greer moistened her dry lips. 'All I wanted was to listen to his heart. To know that part of Tom lives on.'

'I understand that. I have to tell you, though—it's unlikely. Not if he's already told you no.'

'Could you talk to him? Please?'

Jessica laughed, the sound bitter. 'Nathan wouldn't listen to anything I say.'

Echoes of Isla. Was Nathan really so stubborn? 'What if I wait a while? Give him some space?'

'It's possible. But don't count on it.'

Greer grabbed her phone. 'Can I give you my number in case he changes his mind?' She stopped. Hard to imagine the enraged man she'd met earlier softening his stance.

Jessica nodded. Well, that was a start. They swapped mobile numbers, then Jessica finished her coffee. 'I need to leave. It was nice to meet you, Greer.'

Greer ordered another espresso while she pondered her options. They seemed few if Nathan Taylor wasn't willing to talk to her.

Number one: admit defeat and return to Bristol. How humiliating. Not to mention cowardly. She'd done so well in locating Nathan—was she really going to give up so easily?

No, she damn well wouldn't.

Surely Nathan would see sense, given enough time? Her visit must have come as a shock; she should probably have written first.

Wait. Could that be option number two?

The idea seized hold of Greer and wouldn't let go. She drained her coffee and hurried into a nearby Tesco, where she bought a blank greeting card with a spray of white lilies on the front. Hunched over yet another espresso, Greer wrote her contact details inside the card. Along with a heartfelt message, begging him to reconsider. Nathan could read it, let her carefully worded plea sink in, and perhaps he'd change his mind.

Greer was prepared to overlook his rudeness. She wouldn't even expect an apology when they met a second time. Tom's heart was all that mattered.

She drained her cup, then hurried back to Nathan's flat. Once she'd gained access, she made her way to the third floor and slipped the card under his door.

This would work. It had to.

Greer trudged back to her hotel, her feet getting sorer with every step. If she hadn't heard from Nathan within a couple of days, she'd pay him another visit. Somehow, she'd make him listen.

CHAPTER 29

Greer passed a restless night, tortured by the memory of Nathan slamming the door on her. She finally dozed off around five o'clock and awoke at ten. God, she felt exhausted. If only she could sleep for a week, and regain consciousness to find Tom's suicide had been a hideous nightmare.

She stumbled out of bed, her fingers groping for her mobile. Nathan must have left her a message, surely?

He hadn't, damn him.

Beth's cautionary words sounded in Greer's head. *You can't barge into other people's lives and demand their time, their attention. It's not fair.*

Greer brushed them aside. What did Beth know about a mother's grief?

No, she'd stick to her plan, at least for now. Wait and see if the card she'd slipped under Nathan's door produced results. She'd rushed him, and he'd got annoyed, defensive. Understandable, given that he hadn't been well. Once Nathan had had time to reflect, he'd change his mind.

Greer spent the rest of the morning exploring Edgbaston. She could picture herself living here, no doubt about it, but the house prices were so far beyond her budget they were a joke.

A small local deli proved a good choice for lunch. Just after Greer finished her sandwich, her phone buzzed with a message. *Unknown number*. Her fingers shook as she tapped her mobile. Might the card she'd slipped under Nathan's door have had the desired effect?

It seemed it had.

Sorry for the way I behaved yesterday. Wasn't feeling great, and you took me by surprise. Could we meet again? So I can apologise in person? Nathan.

Greer stifled a gasp. Her mobile clattered onto the table. This was more than she could have hoped for, coming so soon. Yes, she'd allow him to apologise, if only he'd let her listen to Tom's heart.

She tapped out a reply. *Of course. When and where?*

Greer waited, every nerve on fire. A minute later, a reply came through. *My place? Are you free now?*

Yes. I can come right away. Your mother won't be there, will she?

No. Just me. I think that's best, don't you?

I'll be with you in a few minutes. Nathan's last message gave her the entrance code to his apartment block.

Greer's heart beat fast in her chest. Should she return to the hotel and change her clothes? But no, there wasn't time, and besides, she was wearing her Pierre Dupont coat. That would have to do. Tom's heart was calling to her, pulling her to him. Greer needed to leave right away.

She called the guy who'd served her over to her table. 'Can I have the bill? Quickly, please. I'm in a hurry.'

Minutes later, Greer was rushing upstairs to Nathan's flat. She jabbed her finger at the buzzer, her breathing harsh and shallow. Footsteps sounded in the hallway. Seconds later, Nathan pulled open the door.

What a contrast between yesterday and today. His face was a better colour, the dark circles less pronounced. He looked much healthier.

Nathan gave Greer a rueful smile. 'Hi. Listen, I'm really sorry about before. Like I said, I was feeling pretty rough. That's how it goes after major surgery. You get good days and bad days.'

'I realise my visit must have come as a shock.'

'Yes, but not an unwelcome one, once I'd got my head in gear.' He stepped backwards, waving Greer inside.

'Make yourself comfortable, please.' Greer stared around Nathan's living room once she'd settled herself on his sofa, which was upholstered in cream leather and looked expensive. The walls were white and decorated with abstract art; from where Greer was sitting, they looked like originals, not prints. Vases of flowers stood at various points throughout the room, which could easily have featured in *Homes and Gardens* magazine. The scent of polish hung in the air; Greer guessed Jessica must have been in to clean for Nathan.

Nathan himself was wearing black chinos and a blue shirt; the latter enhanced the soft azure of his eyes. Her gaze traced over the buttons, imagining them undone. Soon she might hear Tom's heart beating in Nathan's chest.

'What can I get you? Tea? Coffee?' Nathan's words dragged Greer from her reverie.

'Coffee, please. Milk, no sugar.'

Once Nathan was in the kitchen, Greer took a further look around. No personal touches, such as photos of Isla. It seemed Nathan's mother been right in saying they weren't close. Jessica didn't feature, either.

Nathan reappeared, bearing a tray loaded with mugs and two plates. He placed it on the coffee table. 'You like chocolate cake, I assume?'

Greer nodded, despite her surprise. Should he eat refined carbohydrates when recovering from heart surgery? She was no angel herself with her own heart condition, but oughtn't he to be more careful? She perched on the edge of the sofa and sipped her coffee while Nathan devoured his cake.

'Nice watch,' he said in between bites. The fake Cartier on Greer's wrist had clearly fooled him.

'So,' Nathan said, once his plate was empty. 'You wanted to meet, and now we have. To be honest, I wanted that too.'

Greer fought to keep bitterness from her words. 'Your mother would beg to differ.'

Nathan blew out a breath. 'That's what I let her think. She can be very possessive. Overprotective, too. Acts like I'm twelve instead of in my thirties. Things only got worse once my heart gave out.'

Tom's accusations of how Greer was a smother mother flooded into her head. Nathan's relationship with Isla clearly mirrored her own with Tom. Not the kind of similarity she'd hoped to find.

Nathan took a sip of coffee. 'I knew she wouldn't take well to the two of us meeting.'

'Why not?'

'Have you ever had major surgery?'

'No, I haven't.'

'Something like that—it tears you up inside. Being prepped for the operating theatre, knowing that your heart is going to be cut out of your body, that you'll depend on machines and the skill of the surgeons, and that you might not survive anyway. Not to mention recovering from the anaesthetic, pumped full of drugs, accepting you've still got a long road ahead. Plenty of potential complications, including the risk of rejection. It messes with your mind.' Nathan's voice was strained, his face pale. 'Then there's the fact you're alive thanks to someone else's death. So no, part of me didn't want to meet you.'

Nathan leaned forward and, to Greer's surprise, took her right hand between both of his. His skin was warm and dry, and a single thought pounded through her head. How Tom's heart was pumping the blood that ran beneath her palms. Greer suddenly found it hard to breathe.

'You want to know why? It's simple. No words could ever express my gratitude for your son's sacrifice.'

Pleasure stroked soft fingers over Greer's heart. Nathan Taylor was a wonderful man; how foolish of her to have thought otherwise. She'd been rude, too, by intruding on Nathan's privacy and not making allowances for his health problems. Thank God he'd seen past her bad manners and reached out to her.

She stared into Nathan's blue eyes, their colour a stark contrast to Tom's brown orbs. Not that it mattered. The room faded away until only she and Nathan remained, her hand clasped in his, the blood that flowed beneath her fingers propelled by Tom's heart. A heady moment, one Greer never wanted to end.

'Tell me about him,' Nathan said. 'I want to know everything.'

CHAPTER 30

Once Greer started, she couldn't stop. She told Nathan how kind Tom had been, how generous. That, like him and Isla, she hadn't been close to her son. How they drifted apart during his teenage years.

Tears pricked her eyes. 'I'd watch him laugh and joke with his friends and wonder why he wasn't that way with me.'

Nathan squeezed her hand. 'That must have been tough.'

'Yes. It was.' Isla, despite being a cold fish, must have suffered the same hurt. Greer almost felt sorry for her.

She described how Tom could pick up a pencil and, with a few strokes, capture whatever he saw. How Greer had always thought he'd pursue a fine art degree. Her relief when he chose graphic design. Far more career opportunities for her boy.

Nathan, bless him, listened to her ramblings without interrupting. Tom's gym obsession, how he ran every morning before work, the foods he liked, the movies, his taste in clothes. The words tumbled out in a torrent.

'You loved him very much,' Nathan said once Greer fell silent.

Greer nodded. 'He was all I had left.' Impossible to mention Rose. Not yet, anyway. 'I always hoped we'd grow closer, perhaps when he gave me grandchildren. Although I wasn't entirely clear how he'd do that.'

His forehead puckered in confusion. 'What do you mean?'

Oops. She'd neglected to tell Nathan an important detail. 'Tom was gay.'

Something akin to distaste flickered in Nathan's expression. Then it vanished, leaving only a warm smile. 'Well, these things are more possible nowadays, aren't they?' He squeezed Greer's hand again. 'You'd make a wonderful grandmother.'

She must have imagined his antipathy. 'Thank you.'

Greer picked up her handbag and pulled out her mobile. 'Would you like to see a picture of him?'

Nathan nodded. Greer thrust her phone before his eyes. 'That's Tom, taken on his last birthday.' Her gaze flitted between the photo and Nathan. His features might be coarser than Tom's, but their face shapes were the same. Nathan's eyes were blue, Tom's brown, but her son's smile lived on in Nathan's.

She stared at him with a hazy sense of recognition. Something about Nathan seemed familiar, as though she'd seen him before, but she couldn't place when or where. His superficial resemblance to Tom must have confused her.

Greer's fingers swiped over the screen, once, twice, a dozen times. Tom, in cap and gown at his graduation ceremony. Seated on the bonnet of his first car. Greer and Tom enjoying a rare restaurant meal. Her heart swelled with pride while she paraded her son's life before Nathan.

'More coffee?' Nathan said, once Greer had exhausted her photos.

'No. Tell me about you.'

He shrugged. 'Get prepared to hear lots of cardiac-related stuff.'

'That's fine. I want to know everything.'

'Mum said she'd already told you the bare bones of what happened with my heart. The battle to manage my condition has dominated the last few years. Not what you expect to be dealing with in your late twenties and thirties.'

It must have been hard on him. Even given her own heart problems, Greer couldn't imagine what he'd been through. 'You'll be okay, won't you? Now you've had the transplant?'

'There's no guarantee. It's still early days, and rejection is a real possibility.' Nathan got up and walked into the kitchen, returning with a small plastic box. In it Greer saw rows of tablets and capsules split over various compartments. 'I'm on an insane amount of medication, along with weekly check-ups and blood work.' He placed the box on the coffee table and sat down. 'This helps keep me on track.'

Greer stared at it. It was split into four rows of seven, with markers down the side: morning, lunchtime, afternoon, night. She used something similar herself.

'What I just did? Walking into my kitchen?' Nathan leaned forward in his seat. 'Before my surgery, I struggled to make it across the room. Even a few steps were enough to exhaust me. That's how bad I was.' A rueful smile. 'Your son's heart—it's made all the difference.'

Her big moment had arrived. She opened her mouth to speak, but no words emerged. What if Nathan said no?

'I want—' Greer sucked in a deep breath. 'Would you mind if—I realise it's very personal, and I hate to put you on the spot, but—'

Nathan smiled again. 'I know what you're going to ask. You told me yesterday, remember? How you want to listen to Tom's heart.' He unbuttoned his shirt, pulling the two sides apart. Greer stared at the angry slash that cut through his chest. She extended a trembling hand to touch it. 'May I?'

Nathan nodded. Greer knelt to one side of his armchair and leaned in while Nathan inclined his body towards her. He pulled his shirt further open. Her fingers trailed in wonder along the scar's length. Greer tucked her hair behind her right ear, then placed it against the healing wound. She held her breath, and everything else disappeared as she listened.

There it was; one, two, lub, dub, the regular back-and-forth of Tom's heart pushing blood around Nathan's body. Tears fell from Greer's eyes onto Nathan's shirt, but she didn't care. Only this moment existed between mother and son, reunited. Tom hadn't died; her boy lived on in Nathan Taylor and the world was wonderful again. Greer flung her arms around him, forcing him into an awkward hug.

'Thank you.' Her voice was a whisper through her tears. 'This means the world to me.'

'It's the least I could do.' A lack of warmth coloured Nathan's words; as she pulled back to stare at him, Greer detected distaste in his expression again.

He probably wasn't good at handling emotions. What they'd shared was rare and precious; Greer had been more prepared than Nathan. She settled her ear against his scar once more.

Long before she was ready, Nathan pushed her away. 'If you don't mind, I need to use the toilet.'

When he returned, Greer risked asking the second question burning through her brain. 'Can we meet again? Please?' She held her breath.

To her relief, Nathan smiled. 'Of course. I'll be in touch.'

'Promise?'

'Yes.' Another smile. 'I hadn't realised how much I needed this. I feel a connection with you, Greer. More than I imagined possible.'

CHAPTER 31

Back at her hotel, Greer sank onto the bed, the memory of Tom's heartbeat precious beyond words. And—even better—Nathan had agreed to meet up again.

The room grew dark as fantasies blossomed in her head. She and Nathan, enjoying meals out at Edgbaston's many restaurants. Greer, finally telling him about the wound Rose's disappearance had slashed through her heart, mirroring Nathan's own scar. How he'd take her hands in his, the way he'd done earlier, and tell her he felt her pain. Hadn't he said how connected the two of them were, and after only one proper meeting?

Yes, which meant Greer could lay her head against his chest whenever she wanted. Nathan wouldn't refuse, surely? She couldn't wait to listen to that strong, regular sound again. Allow it to stop her own heart from turning to bone.

The harsh trill of her mobile jolted Greer upright. Nathan's name was on the screen. How wonderful. She answered straightaway. 'Hey, there. How are you?'

'Stay away from my son.' Isla Taylor's tone was curt. Shock leached the saliva from Greer's mouth.

'He's told me the two of you have met up. Twice.'

'You've got this all wrong. Nathan got in touch with *me*. The second time, anyway.'

'Only after you forced yourself on him the day before, despite me telling you to leave him alone. What the hell is wrong with you?'

Nathan's voice boomed in the background. 'Mum! Stop this, will you?' He came on the line. 'Sorry about that. She grabbed my phone while I was in the kitchen. Can't mind her own bloody business.'

Greer would wager a boatload of money he'd just shot a hostile glare at Isla. A pleasing thought. 'Ignore her. She's just jealous.'

'I'll call you soon, okay? I have to go.'

A few minutes after he ended the call, Greer's mobile pinged. Nathan, of course. But no, Charlie Prescott's name appeared on the screen.

Well, that was convenient. She'd meant to contact him, but with the effort of tracking down Nathan, she'd not done so. Charlie might claim not to know anything about Tom's boyfriend, but surely Tom must have let something slip? Or maybe Charlie could point her towards someone who could help, even though he clearly considered Greer's quest to be misguided.

She opened the message. *Hey, Mrs M. Just checking in to see how you're doing.*

Greer smiled. He always was a thoughtful boy. She should have contacted him much sooner, the minute she'd learned about the heart transplant. Charlie had the right to know that Tom's heart was still beating, albeit in a different body.

She tapped out a text. *All good here. A lot has happened, though. Can we meet? In Birmingham now, but returning to Bristol tomorrow.* She'd drive down the next day to get fresh clothes, do some laundry, check everything was okay at the house.

Charlie's response came quickly. *Sure. Get in touch when you're back.*

CHAPTER 32

'You're looking well, Mrs M.' Charlie smiled at Greer as he stretched his long legs across the length of her sofa. Greer, now back in Bristol, had texted him earlier, asking if he was available that evening to come round for a drink.

'I am. It's great to see you, Charlie.'

He grinned. 'Couldn't resist your offer of free beer.' He'd already been boozing, of course. Greer had smelled alcohol on his breath when he'd hugged her earlier.

Greer's doorbell buzzed. She rolled her eyes at Charlie. 'Best to ignore that. Probably Jehovah's Witnesses.'

The buzzer sounded again. Greer's letterbox opened, and Beth's voice trilled into the house. 'Greer! Are you there?'

Greer got to her feet. 'That's Beth. My neighbour. Do you mind if I quickly see what she wants?'

Charlie took a gulp of beer. 'Be my guest.'

'Sorry to drop round unannounced,' Beth said, as she pushed past Greer into the hallway. 'I baked brownies, but I got the quantities all wrong. Ended up with far too many.' She thrust a large plastic container at Greer, before catching sight of Charlie. 'Oh, God, you have company. I shouldn't have burst in like this.'

How sweet of her neighbour. Beth hadn't miscalculated her baking; she just wanted to check Greer was okay. She took the plastic container from Beth. 'Thanks for the brownies. Come and meet Charlie.'

Beth looked doubtful. 'I'm not intruding, am I?'

'Don't be daft. Of course you're not.'

Charlie stood up as Greer steered Beth into the living room, a smile on his face. 'Hi.'

'Beth, this is Charlie, Tom's best friend. Charlie, meet Beth, my neighbour.' Not wanting to linger, Greer hurried into the kitchen, where she busied herself arranging brownies on a plate. She could hear Beth and Charlie chatting: Charlie was telling Beth about Tom. They seemed to be getting on well. Not surprising; Beth's warmth put people at ease. She returned, carrying the plate of food.

'I won't stay,' Beth told Greer. 'It doesn't seem right, not if you have a guest. Charlie, it's been great to meet you.'

'Likewise.'

Greer smiled at Beth. 'Come round for coffee sometime.'

'I will. We'll catch up soon, okay?'

After Beth had left, Greer resumed her seat opposite Charlie. She took a photo of Tom from the side table and traced her fingers over his face. 'Missing him doesn't get any easier, does it?'

Charlie shook his head. 'Nope.'

'I've been meaning to ask. Tom must have given some clue about who he was dating, surely? That bastard broke my son's heart, Charlie. I need to look him in the eye and tell him what I think of him.'

'I told you already, Mrs M. I knew he was seeing someone, but not who it was.' Charlie's lips were thin with annoyance. Her questions must hurt him, but how could she stop when so much was at stake?

Greer set down the photo. 'I'll ask his work colleagues. He might have talked to one of them.'

'I doubt it. Why would he tell them and not me?' Ah, so that was it. Charlie was upset that Tom hadn't confided in him about his new boyfriend. Why he hadn't, she had no idea. Charlie might be straight, but that didn't mean he was homophobic.

'Could you ask Gary or Justin if they know anything?' Tom's two other closest friends were regulars on the gay scene. She didn't have their mobile numbers, but Charlie might, even though he didn't frequent the same bars.

Charlie finished his beer and placed the can on the table. Without a pause, he popped the tab on a fresh one. 'Can't you let it drop, Mrs M?'

'No.' The word came out more sharply than Greer had intended. Although Charlie had a point; she wasn't making any headway, so it was probably time to change topics. 'Listen, there's something important I have to tell you. About Tom.'

Charlie took a swig of beer. 'I'm listening.'

His eyes widened when Greer told him about the phone call from Zofia. 'Tom's heart has been used in a transplant? That's amazing.'

'There's more. I've met the recipient.'

Shock flew into Charlie's face. 'Really? How'd that happen?'

'His mum wrote me a letter.'

She ran through her meeting with Nathan, omitting the details of how she found him. It seemed best that Charlie assumed Isla had been cooperative. Greer's obsessive trawling of Facebook and her argument with Nathan's mother didn't paint her in a favourable light.

'I listened to his heart, Charlie. I can't tell you how much that meant. If all goes according to plan, I can listen whenever I choose.'

Charlie gulped another mouthful of beer. His face was flushed, and a slight slur rendered his words fuzzy. 'That sounds incredible, Mrs M.'

'Why don't you visit Nathan sometime with me? I'm sure he'd love to meet you.'

Charlie stared at her. 'That would be great. To shake his hand and know that Tom's heart is keeping him alive.'

'I'll mention it to him, shall I? We'll get something arranged.'

He nodded. 'I'd like that. I won't listen to Tom's heartbeat, though. That seems a little weird.' A smile. 'Not for you, of course. You're his mum.'

Relief hit Greer. It might be selfish, but she wanted to be the only one allowed to hear Tom's heart.

CHAPTER 33

The following day, Greer rose early. She couldn't wait to drive back to Birmingham. Nathan might contact her today, ask her to visit, and she needed to be close by.

By eleven am, she arrived at the hotel she'd booked. Her room was small, but well-furnished and clean, and came with a microwave, kettle and hotplate. Greer unpacked her suitcases; she'd brought more stuff this time, including Tom's sweatshirt. All she needed to do now was to buy groceries.

Back in the tiny kitchen area, Greer made herself a sandwich and a mug of coffee, one eye on her mobile phone. Would Nathan contact her today? So much remained for them to discuss; she'd still only scratched the surface of the man who'd received Tom's heart. They had time, though.

But did they? Nathan's remark about the ongoing risk of organ rejection—that was downright scary. The slab of chocolate cake he'd devoured—hadn't any of the cardiac team advised him about healthy eating? Greer made a mental note to raise the issue with Nathan, because obviously Isla hadn't bothered. In the meantime, there was much she could do to help. For one, educate herself about the after-care requirements following a heart transplant. Maybe Nathan had been too woozy post-surgery to understand the advice he'd been given, and Greer refused to count on Isla. The less she, and Nathan, saw of that woman, the better.

Greer retrieved her laptop and opened up her browser, typing 'immunosuppressant drugs' into the search engine. The large number of serious side effects such medication entailed made for disturbing reading. Nathan, it seemed, wouldn't be home and dry health-wise even if his body didn't reject Tom's heart. From what she could glean, he'd be at risk from the common cold. His bones might grow brittle. His kidneys would be vulnerable to problems. Greer read several more articles, each more alarming than the last. Not good.

Just as she was about to make another coffee, a link at the bottom of the page caught her eye. 'Cellular Memory—True or False?' How intriguing. Greer clicked on it.

Fascinating. She'd never heard of such a thing, but many people, scientists included, believed in cellular memory or conceded that it might exist. The theory was that every cell in the body stored memories, not just the brain. As a result, some transplant patients took on traits of the donor. Strange things happened; the living adopted the characteristics of the dead: their food preferences, their music choices, etc. Meat-eaters became vegetarians. Folk fans switched to jazz. Only a few cases documented the phenomenon; most transplant patients either hadn't experienced the issue or chose not to speak about it. The latter, most likely. Maybe they feared ridicule. Or being declared mentally ill.

The possibilities were dizzying. Incredible. If cellular memory was real, Greer's relationship with Nathan might skyrocket to a whole different level. Time to investigate further.

She found various YouTube videos in which organ recipients spoke of their experiences. A woman told how, pre-transplant, she'd loathed curry. Now the staff at her local Indian takeaway knew her by name; lamb bhuna with a side of mushroom rice was her regular Friday night order. On further investigation, she discovered the donor of her heart had loved spicy food.

In another, a man described his inexplicable urge to play the piano, despite having no previous musical training. When his fingers hit the keyboard, his level of skill astounded everyone. The man who donated his heart to him had been a keen amateur pianist.

Most fascinating of all was the account of a young boy who suffered horrific nightmares following his surgery. He described the sounds of screeching tyres, of metal crashing into metal, of flames erupting in front of him. Further enquiries revealed that the donor of his heart died not long after a multi-car collision.

Greer needed to find out more, and quickly. She ordered a book on cellular memory, called 'Outside the Brain' by Dr Thomas Webb. Dr Webb was an American surgeon who'd performed countless heart transplants, and the book concentrated on his conversations with the recipients. The 'next-day delivery' option was a straightforward decision, because even that was too long to wait.

Greer stepped away from her laptop to fill the kettle, her mind reeling. Cellular memory might happen with Nathan, and wouldn't that be incredible? In fact, what if it already had? Take Nathan forking chocolate cake into his mouth the other day. Her Tom had adored the stuff, despite his addiction to the gym and healthy living.

Was it possible? Could a miracle be about to happen?

Greer grabbed Tom's sweatshirt, held it against her nose, and breathed him in.

She was going to get her darling boy back. For good this time.

That meant a temporary halt to finding the man who'd broken her beautiful son's heart. Greer hadn't forgotten her vow. First things first, though. She'd establish a firm relationship with Nathan, and then she'd seek her revenge.

As the saying went, it was a dish best eaten cold.

CHAPTER 34

Greer drummed her fingertips across the table as she waited for Nathan. He'd messaged her the previous evening to suggest they meet for lunch. The place he'd chosen was an upmarket bistro, all leather banquettes, subdued lighting and soft music. The prices on the menu had made Greer blink with shock. She glanced at her watch; Nathan was already ten minutes late.

Panic clutched at Greer. Had his new heart given out? Might he have collapsed on the floor, unable to reach for his phone? Should she rush round to check?

She couldn't lose someone else from her life. Hadn't she suffered enough?

The door to the bistro opened, and Nathan strode through, his gaze falling immediately on Greer. He walked over and seated himself opposite her. 'What do you think of this place? Pretty swanky, isn't it?'

No apology for being late, or even a greeting. She mustn't be petty. He was here, along with Tom's heart, and that was the most important thing. Greer forced a smile. 'It looks lovely. So does the food.'

'I've eaten here many times. You can't go wrong, no matter what you choose.' Nathan picked up the menu and perused it. While he did, Greer studied him. He appeared healthy enough; his skin was a good colour and the dark circles around his eyes had faded.

He really did look familiar. Had she seen him before? Or was her imagination playing tricks on her?

Greer caught a whiff of his cologne as he shifted in his seat. It didn't smell cheap. The iPhone he laid on the table looked brand-new. She reached out a hand to finger his shirt, ignoring the surprise on Nathan's face. Egyptian cotton, of the best quality, and so soft. Nathan was clearly a man who appreciated the finer things in life.

'Steak and chips for me,' Nathan said. 'What about you?'

Should he be eating all that saturated fat? Almost certainly not. Later, perhaps, once they knew each other better, she'd discuss his food choices with him. As things stood, it was still early days between them. Best not to rock the proverbial boat. 'I'll have the coq au vin.'

A server appeared at their table. 'Hello there. What would you like to eat today?'

Before Greer could say anything, Nathan had ordered for both of them. 'And a bottle of your best red. Have you got—' He mentioned a particular French label and vintage. Greer knew nothing about wine and cared even less. It sounded expensive, though.

The server moved away, and Nathan turned his attention to Greer again. 'Mum's not happy that I'm here today. I probably shouldn't have told her. You'd think I'd know better.'

Oh, the sweet prickle of schadenfreude. Isla's son was obviously under no illusions about her. 'Your transplant hasn't brought you closer, it seems.'

'She fusses over me too much. A right old smother mother, if you know what I mean.'

Back off, Mum, you're suffocating me. Tom's words, spoken a few weeks before he died, echoed in Greer's brain. She mustn't make the same mistakes with Nathan. Was it so wrong for a mother to want to protect her child, though? Why had Tom rejected her love?

She needed to stop this negativity. Right now. Here was Nathan, lunching with her in this upmarket bistro, marking the start of a whole new relationship. She mustn't ruin it. Too much was at stake.

Their food and wine came, and the two of them made small talk as they ate. Greer's chicken was perfect, the sauce rich and sublime. Nathan attacked his steak with gusto, clearly enjoying it.

The enticing possibility of cellular memory at work in Nathan danced before Greer's brain. The book she'd ordered had arrived that morning, and she'd already read a couple of chapters. 'I have a question for you. Have you heard of cellular memory?'

When Nathan shook his head, Greer elaborated. 'Don't you think it's fascinating?'

He laughed. 'I'm not sure.'

'It's not widely acknowledged in the medical community, but the anecdotal evidence is strong.'

'It sounds like your son was a great guy, so maybe I'd do well to take on some of his characteristics.' Nathan picked up the menu. 'I think I can squeeze in some pudding.'

Well, that was disappointing. Greer had been so excited by what she'd read, so eager to share it with him, and Nathan had brushed aside what she'd said.

Perhaps she was being unfair. Many people probably dismissed the idea of cellular memory; it was a pretty wild concept to accept that other body parts might contain character traits and preferences, not just the brain. She'd talk to Nathan about it again sometime to see if she could open his mind a little.

'Do you want a dessert?' Nathan asked.

Greer didn't think she could eat another thing. 'Nothing for me, thanks. I'm full.'

'Well, I'm not. I'll go for the sticky toffee cheesecake.'

Greer pursed her lips. More unhealthy food choices. Wait, though. Hadn't Tom always loved cheesecake?

Oh, God. Yes, he had. Coincidence, possibly, but what if cellular memory was at work?

Once Nathan's dessert arrived, she watched as he slid his fork through the gooey mess and lifted it to his mouth. 'Is that what you'd usually order?'

Nathan paused, his fork in mid-air. 'Why do you ask?'

'No reason. Just wondered.'

He shrugged. 'Normally I'd go for ice cream. Just had a fancy for cheesecake, though.'

Greer stayed silent. Her hope that her son was alive and living on in Nathan sparked higher. Her eyes roved over Nathan's Egyptian cotton shirt. The style was the sort Tom had favoured. Cellular memory again?

The server appeared again. 'Can I get you anything else?'

'Just the bill.' Nathan smiled at Greer. 'Would you excuse me? I need the toilet.'

A moment after he'd gone, the server placed a leather folder on the table. Greer flicked it open. The numbers on the slip of paper inside made her gasp. The restaurant hadn't stocked the wine Nathan had wanted, but the bottle of red they'd drunk had cost more than their combined food. A far cry from her occasional pizza delivery.

Greer pulled her purse from her handbag and selected a credit card. This was a special occasion, and she wanted to impress Nathan. Her finances could ill afford it, but so what? She slipped her card into the folder and handed it to the passing server. When Nathan returned from the toilet, it was already back in her purse. He smiled as he slid into the booth. 'Ready to go?'

'We'll definitely eat there again,' Nathan said once they were standing on the pavement outside. 'It's been great to see you, Greer. Next time, I'll take you to an Italian place near here. They serve the best osso buco in Birmingham.'

Greer stepped closer. 'I'd like that.' What she *really* wanted, more than anything, was to listen to Tom's heart. But a light drizzle was falling, and they were in public, people bustling all around them. She was about to suggest coffee back at Nathan's flat when he spoke. 'My car's parked over there. I'll be in touch, okay?'

He mustn't escape so easily. Greer placed her hand on his shirt, close to where Tom's precious heart lay. Her face flushed hot with longing. 'Can we go to your place? Please? I'd like to listen to... well, you know.'

Nathan took a step backwards. Greer glimpsed distaste on his face, but it had gone before she could be certain.

Probably the fact they were standing on the pavement in the rain.

Or maybe Greer was being too pushy.

'I really have to go,' Nathan said. 'It's been fantastic seeing you, Greer. I'll text you about meeting up again sometime, okay?'

That was more than okay. 'I'd like that.'

He smiled. 'I'm so grateful to your son. I feel this is the start of something wonderful for us both, don't you?'

Greer could only nod, incapable of speech. Yes. Yes, she did, and it was incredible.

CHAPTER 35

By the evening of the next day, Nathan hadn't contacted Greer, despite his promise.

His words floated back to her. *This is the start of something wonderful for us both*. So why hadn't he texted? Was she expecting too much, too soon?

Two more days passed, and Nathan still hadn't been in touch. Was he ill? Should she drive to his flat?

No. She mustn't smother him. No texts, no phone calls. Nathan would contact her before long, and everything would be fine. Wouldn't it?

As Greer struggled through another sleepless night, she wasn't so sure.

It was the following morning when Greer's phone finally buzzed with a message from Nathan. *Sorry I've not been in touch. There's a good reason for that. Can we meet? There's something I want to discuss.*

Tension rushed out of Greer like air from a burst balloon. How silly of her. He wasn't abandoning her as everyone else had done; he'd just been busy. Time to call him.

To her relief, Nathan answered straightaway. 'Greer! How wonderful to hear from you.'

'Likewise. Of course we can meet up. Maybe that Italian place you suggested?'

'Sure. Are you free at lunchtime?'

How was it possible to be this happy? Lunch with Nathan beckoned, all shiny and inviting. He hadn't lost interest in her. All was well in her world.

By the time the call ended, Greer had arranged to meet Nathan at L'Oro di Napoli in Edgbaston at one o'clock. It was now just after nine. Time to shower and get ready. Black trousers and a teal-coloured blouse, teamed with a matching jacket, would do nicely. She'd spend extra time on her hair and her make-up, too. They were going to an upmarket restaurant; Nathan would expect her to look her best.

Greer arrived at L'Oro di Napoli half an hour early. She drummed her fingers on the expensive linen tablecloth while she waited. How quickly her feelings for Nathan had grown. Her grief over Tom remained a leaden weight in her heart, but her deepening connection to Nathan had soothed the pain a little. She'd been right to contact him, no matter what Beth thought.

The minutes ticked by, and Nathan didn't arrive. Greer shifted uneasily in her seat, aware of the hustle and bustle around her. Lunchtime diners packed the restaurant, mostly male, all in sharp suits and with neat hair. She didn't fit in here, even with her cut-price designer gear. Too downmarket by far.

Nathan would come soon, right? Although being late seemed to be his style.

Five past one. Still no sign of him.

Ten past. Should she call him? But no, there he was, walking towards her.

Greer's shoulders slumped with relief. His thousand-megawatt smile erased all traces of her anxiety. How silly of her. Not everyone valued punctuality the way she did.

To her surprise, Nathan grabbed both her hands once he'd sat down, leaning across the table. 'It's so good to see you. I've been looking forward to our lunch together all morning.'

'You have?' Pleasure fluttered in Greer's belly.

'Of course. Let's eat, and then we'll talk. Like I told you, there's something I want to discuss.' He grinned. 'Don't look so worried. It's nothing bad, I promise.' He handed her a menu.

Greer ordered a simple antipasto salad and bread. Her lips curled in disapproval when Nathan chose a traditional Italian beef stew, but she curbed the urge to comment.

Nathan talked a lot about himself over their meal: his last appointment with his cardiologist, how he got good days and bad days, his latest blood tests. Not that Greer minded. It was good to know Tom's heart was being carefully monitored.

A server appeared at their table. 'Can I get either of you the dessert menu?'

'Not for me, thanks.'

'I'll have some of your excellent tiramisu,' Nathan said. Really, all that sugar couldn't be good for him. She was about to say something, but Nathan got in first.

'Remember how I mentioned I had something I wanted to discuss?'

Greer nodded.

'It's the reason I've not been in touch. I wanted to be sure before I told you.'

'Told me what?'

'Things have been weird the last few days. Everything I've been experiencing, though—it makes me think this cellular memory stuff is real.'

CHAPTER 36

Greer stared at Nathan, her mouth open with shock. Her life currently hovered over a precipice; with his next words, Nathan might haul her to safety or push her over the edge. 'What do you mean?'

He reached into the messenger bag he'd brought and extracted a rectangle of card. 'I've had no interest in drawing before. Yesterday morning, though, I got this weird urge to do some sketching. It nagged at me, won't let go. In the end, I rummaged through my desk drawer, found a pencil and rubber and some paper. Next thing I knew, it was lunchtime, and I'd covered a dozen sheets of A4 with doodles, sketches, you name it. That afternoon I bought myself a sketchpad and spent the rest of the day drawing.' He placed the card before Greer. 'It's not great, I know. But what do you think?'

Two figures, one male, the other female, were walking through a forest, a small dog following them. Sunlight sparkled in a puddle, and fallen leaves carpeted the ground. The hint of love between the couple hung like a promise in the air.

Greer stared at the sketch, speechless. Nathan was being too modest. For somebody who had never tried art before, it was extraordinary. In her opinion, anyway.

'You don't like it.' Nathan sounded hurt.

'You're wrong. This is brilliant. Amazingly talented.'

He looked pleased. 'That sketchpad I bought is nearly full now.'

'Tom loved to draw. As a kid, he was always messing around with crayons.'

'That's not the only weird thing that's happened. I've had some really intense dreams. In them, I'm running through a park or along a beach. Wind in my hair, adrenaline rushing through me. I feel incredibly alive. I've always disliked running. But now I'm itching to experience that buzz in real life.'

He gave a rueful grin. 'Not that I can right now, of course. Too soon after the transplant. But one day I will.'

Greer pushed back her chair. 'Would you excuse me? Back in a minute.' Before he could answer, she rushed towards the toilets.

Once in the ladies', she hurried into a cubicle, locked the door and leaned against it. Sobs welled up inside her from deep within. Greer's heart pounded so hard she feared it might burst.

Tom had been a keen runner. Hadn't some transplant patients she'd researched also experienced vivid dreams? Ones that mirrored the lives of their organ donors. Now Nathan was dreaming about running.

This was huge.

Monumental.

Proof that cellular memory existed.

She really ought to get back to Nathan. What if he had more instances he wanted to share?

Greer wiped the tears from her cheeks, then made her way back into the restaurant. As she slid into her seat, she noticed a leather folder near her setting. Nathan, it appeared, had requested the bill.

He pushed back his chair. 'I need the toilet, too. I was waiting until you returned.'

After he'd gone, Greer settled the bill, despite being aghast at the total. Her bank balance could ill afford another such hit, but she mustn't be petty. It was only money, and Nathan's revelation had given her such joy. He could pick up the tab the next time.

Greer studied Nathan as he returned to their table. The more she looked at him, the more she saw similarities between him and Tom—his smile, the look in his eyes, the cast of his mouth. After the horror of his death, and Rose's disappearance, she could be a mother again. Or as close as she'd ever get, anyway. Life often kicked you in the teeth, but sometimes handed you a bouquet.

Nathan stood up. 'I'll see you back to your hotel.'

They walked the mile or so to where Greer was staying, the air around them chilly. Nathan trudged along, occasionally needing to catch his breath, but insisted he was okay. He waved away Greer's offer of help. 'I'm much better than I was,' he said with a smile. 'The exercise is good for me.'

Greer pulled open the door and stepped into the entrance lobby, Nathan behind her. The receptionist eyed her warily, clearly about to enforce the 'no visitors' rule. Screw that. Greer yearned to hear Tom's heart *now*. She'd waited too long already.

She pulled Nathan out of sight beneath the stairwell and placed her hands on his shirt. This was a public place, but so what? Nobody could see them. Greer smiled at Nathan, sure he wouldn't refuse. 'Do you mind if I listen to Tom's heart again?'

Nathan nodded, but his expression seemed strained. 'Go ahead.'

Her fingers trembling, Greer unbuttoned Nathan's shirt, then laid her head against his smooth chest, her eyes closed. Ah, there it was: the strong, soothing rhythm of Tom's heart. Greer wound her arms around Nathan's torso, pressing closer to that wonderful sound. If only she could remain there forever.

Strong hands gripped her. Why was Nathan pushing her away?

'I have to go,' he said. 'We'll get together again soon, I promise.'

'Can't we grab a quick coffee somewhere?'

'Sorry, no. I'll be in touch, okay?' Nathan made for the door, a smile on his face, but it seemed forced. What had she done wrong? Been too needy, perhaps? This was all new to him; she mustn't rush it.

Greer hurried upstairs to her room and fixed herself a cappuccino. It was as she had hoped; her beloved Tom was returning to her. Through Nathan, he was drawing, expressing his love of running, indulging his sweet tooth. What other cellular memory incidents might Nathan experience over the coming days and weeks? There had to be a limit to the influence it might exert. Or did there? Hope burned hot in Greer's heart.

Thank God she hadn't tried to kill herself. The thought was abhorrent now. Finding Nathan had changed everything.

There seemed no point in searching for whoever had broken Tom's heart. Besides, what could she do apart from yelling at him? No, she'd do better to concentrate on her relationship with Nathan. The man whom she might—one day—love the way she'd done Tom.

That night, as Greer fell asleep hugging her son's sweatshirt, her mind was on Nathan, not Tom.

CHAPTER 37

By the time Greer finished breakfast the next morning, she'd formulated a plan. It would be foolish to burn her bridges so soon, but her long-term goal was to move to Birmingham to be close to Nathan. A fresh start was in order.

She set her plate and mug in the sink. As she did so, her mobile pinged with a message from an unknown number. When Greer opened it, she found Isla Taylor was the sender.

Nathan tells me he's seen you again. Stop hassling him. Stay away from my son.

The old witch must have got Greer's number from Nathan's phone. Any rudeness, and she'd find herself blocked from Greer's pretty damn quickly.

Her fingers flew over her screen. *Why should I? Nathan's a grown man. He can see whoever he wants. Back off and leave us alone.*

The 'us' felt so good. She and Nathan together, with Isla the outsider.

Don't lecture me about how to behave. Nathan's my son, not yours.

Yeah, right. Biologically, yes, but otherwise? Nope. Greer's bond with Nathan would, over time, strengthen and deepen. No wonder

Isla was jealous. Greer didn't bother replying. Instead, she switched on her laptop and navigated to the Airbnb website.

Her goal was to find a short-term let close to Nathan. Greer soon spotted a fully furnished one-bedroom flat a mere two streets away. The same price as her hotel, but much roomier. She'd need to raid her meagre funds, but she wouldn't be there long. Once she and Nathan grew closer, she'd look for a suitable property to buy. A studio apartment, perhaps, funded by the sale of her home in Bristol. In the meantime, she'd rent her house out.

Greer reserved and paid for a month at the flat, making a considerable dent in her savings. She stretched out on the bed, a smile of satisfaction on her face. Everything was coming together nicely.

Her data entry job must go, of course. She'd worry about money later. Greer tapped out a quick email to her boss. Sorted.

Beth would say she was being impulsive, not thinking straight, etc. Well, Greer wasn't answerable to Beth Randall. She had nothing to keep her in Bristol. Her future lay in Birmingham and a fresh start with Nathan.

Maybe with Jessica Taylor too.

Greer had only met the young woman briefly, but she'd liked her. If Nathan was becoming Tom, might Jessica step into Rose's shoes?

Jessica seemed shy, sweet, self-effacing. Eager to help Nathan, even though the two of them didn't get on. Isla clearly hadn't created a happy, cohesive family unit. Well, Greer would change all that. She'd be a surrogate mother to Jessica and Nathan, and to hell with Isla Taylor.

The following morning, Greer checked into the Airbnb apartment, then drove back to Bristol to collect more clothes and personal items. Once she'd packed two more suitcases, she called a local estate agent who also handled rentals. Time to implement the next phase of her plan.

CHAPTER 38

Beth steered her car into her driveway and turned off the engine. Her gaze strayed towards Greer's house. Who was the woman with the elegantly coiffured hair, smart suit and high heels, chatting with Greer on her doorstep?

The woman shook Greer's hand, then walked towards a white car parked outside Greer's house. The sign-writing on the side proclaimed, in bold black letters, 'Kingswood's Premier Estate Agents—Your Key To A New Home'.

Wait, was Greer thinking of moving? And where to?

Beth hung back until the woman had driven away, then hurried up the driveway to press Greer's buzzer. The moment the door opened, she pounced. 'You're selling your house? Why?'

Greer looked taken aback, and a little annoyed. 'Hello to you too, Beth.'

Beth forced a smile. 'I'm sorry. Please forgive my bad manners. As well as my insatiable nosiness.'

To her relief, Greer laughed. 'You want to come in?'

The smell of cleaning fluid and polish hit Beth the minute she stepped over the threshold. In the living room, everything was tidy, but with a noticeable absence of any personal touches. The photos of Tom, of Rose—all gone.

Greer sat on the sofa and waved Beth towards an armchair. 'I'm not selling,' she said. 'Not yet, anyway. But I *am* going to rent the house out. I've taken a short-term let in Birmingham. So I can be closer to Nathan.'

'But you haven't even met him.'

'You're wrong. He's a wonderful young man. So grateful to Tom.' Greer's hands fidgeted in her lap; she wasn't looking at Beth. 'He wants us to spend time together. Eventually, I'll sell this house and buy somewhere in Birmingham.'

What in the world was Greer thinking? A move to Birmingham was an insane idea, especially so soon.

Time to reason with her. 'Are you sure this is wise?'

Annoyance crossed Greer's expression. 'Don't tell me how to live my life, Beth.'

'I'm worried about you, that's all.'

'Well, don't be. I'm a grown woman. I can make my own decisions.' The sharpness in Greer's tone delivered a stern rebuke.

Beth nodded, albeit reluctantly. 'My son and my daughter-in-law live in Birmingham. I often stay with them. Could we keep in touch? I know you think I'm overstepping the mark, but I'd like us to stay friends. Please, Greer.'

Greer pursed her lips. 'As long as you don't meddle in my life. I know what I'm doing.'

Beth disagreed, but what choice did she have? 'I'll let you know when I'm next in Birmingham. Maybe we can meet for coffee.' Interfering she may be, but Beth intended to keep a close eye on Greer. Her obsession with Nathan Taylor was heading into dangerous waters.

CHAPTER 39

Greer glanced around Nathan's flat. Here she was, spending time with him again, and wasn't it wonderful? Nathan was in the kitchen, opening a bottle of wine. The chink of glasses on the marble worktop reached Greer's ears.

She walked over to the archway that led to Nathan's galley kitchen. 'Done any more drawings?'

He appeared in the gap, a glass in one hand. 'Loads. It's like the urge to draw has taken me over.'

'Can I see them?'

He shook his head. 'I threw them away. Wasn't sure they were any good.'

'You're too hard on yourself. That one you showed me was excellent.'

'Thank you. That means a lot.' He walked back into the kitchen. 'Lunch won't be long.'

'Spinach, mushroom and garlic tagliatelle,' Nathan announced as he set a steaming plate before Greer a few minutes later. 'It's strange, but I've been fancying lots of pasta recently.'

Another of Tom's favourite meals. How amazing was that? Cellular memory was real, all right. 'It smells delicious. Did it take long to make?'

Nathan laughed. 'I'm useless in a kitchen. This came from a local deli.'

They ate in a companionable silence. Dessert was cherry cheesecake; Tom would have approved. Nathan pulled pills and capsules from his plastic dispenser without looking at them. 'Bloody medication,' he said when he noticed Greer watching him. 'No idea what half of these do, or which one's which. They keep me alive, though. Without the immunosuppressants, my body would spiral into rejection mode pretty damn quick.'

Greer shuddered. No way could she allow *that* to happen, not when her Tom was bringing about such wonderful changes. Nathan must have noticed her sombre expression, because he laughed, reaching across the table to squeeze her arm. 'Don't look so worried. I never miss a dose, despite not knowing what I'm taking. Too much at stake. I'll make us some coffee.'

Once he'd gone, Greer crossed the room to the desk under the window that served as Nathan's home office. He'd mentioned he was easing back into his sales manager role via remote working, just a few hours a day, which didn't sit well with Greer. He should rest, not fret about keeping his boss happy.

She rummaged through Nathan's waste bin but only found rubbish. No drawings. A disappointment, but perhaps he had emptied the bin recently.

Nathan had just brought Greer her coffee when the doorbell buzzed. He pulled a face. 'Bet you that's Mum. I told her you were coming for lunch, but she obviously didn't listen. Actually, that's probably why she's here. Wants to run you out of town.' He smiled, but his expression lacked humour.

Nathan walked into the hallway. Greer heard him yank open the front door. Seconds later, Isla's voice sounded in the flat.

Greer prepared herself for battle. Isla wasn't and never would be any friend of hers.

Isla strode into the living room and stopped short when she saw Greer. 'What are *you* doing here?'

'Mum! Don't be so rude. You know exactly why Greer's here. Have you forgotten what her son did for me?' Nathan sat back at the table, not offering his mother a seat. She took one anyway.

'Hello, Isla.' Greer pasted a false smile on her face. 'It's so nice to see you again.'

Isla's expression could have cut glass. 'You're right,' she said to Nathan, before switching her attention to Greer. 'I apologise for my bad manners. But you need to understand that Nathan's transplant was a huge emotional upheaval. Once the hospital discharged him, we wanted to get on with our lives without reminders of the operation.'

'I don't feel that way anymore,' Nathan said. He walked round to stand behind Greer, placing his hands on her shoulders. Their warmth penetrated her thin blouse. Greer's eyes closed momentarily in bliss. When she opened them, the full glare of Isla's hostility hit her square on.

'I owe an enormous debt of gratitude to Greer and her son,' Nathan continued. 'She's welcome here anytime. We're forging a genuine connection.' He shot a sly, almost triumphant glance at his mother.

Really, it was hard not to gloat. For Nathan to take Greer's side against Isla boded well.

She smiled at Isla. 'We've seen each other several times. Lunches out, meals here. Didn't he tell you?'

Isla's mouth twisted in a sneer. 'Maybe he didn't think it was important.'

Damn this wretched woman and her spite. She'd come back later, once Isla had gone. Time for a lie. 'I need to leave. There's somewhere I have to be.'

'Really? What a shame.' Isla didn't bother to keep the smirk off her face. Greer longed to slap the bitch.

She stood up, addressing Nathan. 'I'll call you tonight. We'll get together again soon, okay?' From her peripheral vision, she spotted Isla's expression turn sour. Well, two could play at her game.

'That will be great. I'll see you out.' Nathan followed Greer into the hallway. Once he'd opened the door, Greer hugged him. Their relationship was going much better than she'd dared hope; a move to Birmingham was definitely on the cards. She allowed her head to rest against Nathan's shirt, and there it was: the sweet *lub-dub* of Tom's heart, beating strong and sure.

Isla appeared in the doorway. Her expression turned even more vinegary, if that was possible. 'Oh, you're still here? I'll put on some fresh coffee for us, Nathan.' With that, she disappeared into the kitchen.

Greer gently disengaged herself. Had it been up to her, she'd have stayed there all day.

Nathan glanced behind him. 'Call me tonight, okay?' His voice was louder than normal, clearly meant for Isla to hear.

Greer kissed his cheek. 'I will.'

After Nathan closed the door, she hurried down the stairs. She'd just stepped into the lobby when footsteps clattered down the steps. Greer stopped, turned around. Isla stood behind her.

Anger dominated the other woman's face. She grabbed Greer's arm, hard enough to bruise. 'Listen here. While I'll always be grateful for the donation of your son's heart, I don't like the way you're monopolising Nathan. Do I have to remind you he's still not well? You're not doing him any good, pestering him all the time.'

Greer shrugged, signalling to Isla: *See? I'm not so easily riled up by your pathetic comments.* She smiled. 'Jealous, are we? Has Nathan told you he feels closer to me than he does to you?'

Hurt replaced the anger in Isla's expression. 'I won't deny it's upsetting that he's seen so much of you. Like I said when we first met, we're not close. He's my child, though, and I'll always watch out for him. I've been there through the bad times with his father, the diagnosis of his heart problems, then the transplant. You weren't.'

Rage flared in Greer. With difficulty, she shook Isla off. 'My husband was a bastard, too. He denied me my daughter, left me to raise my son alone. And, lady, your boy is still alive. Mine isn't.'

'I love Nathan,' Isla said. 'But I don't particularly like him. He's quite the woman-hater. Actually, that's unfair. Nathan loathes most people, male or female. Stay away from him. I'm saying this for your own good.'

'Like I said, jealousy.' Greer definitely had the upper hand here.

'No. Nathan's not a good person. It's not his fault; his father was a misogynist and Nathan is following in his footsteps.'

Greer thrust her face close to Isla's. 'I don't believe you. Two words: cellular memory. If you've not heard of it, read up on the subject. Nathan's becoming more and more like Tom. I see echoes of my boy in him every time we meet. And you know what? It's like getting my son back. So don't you dare—' She jabbed an angry finger against Isla's chest. 'Don't you dare tell me to stay away from Nathan. That's not going to happen.'

CHAPTER 40

Greer spent the evening after her lunch with Nathan in a stew of righteous indignation. That bitch Isla turning up—she'd face the rough side of Greer's tongue if she pulled that stunt again. Greer had enjoyed more quality time with Nathan, though, so that was a plus. And he'd sent her that lovely message earlier. *So good to see you. Really sorry about Mum's behaviour. How about getting together sometime this week?*

Greer had texted back immediately. *Of course. When's convenient?*

———

Two days later, Greer squirted perfume on her wrists, humming to herself. She was due at Nathan's in ten minutes; keen to look her best, she'd treated herself to a designer dress from an upmarket charity shop. A bargain at only a tenner, and the dodgy stain on the hem was barely noticeable. She put her coat on, then grabbed her coat and bag. What food might Nathan have ordered from the deli this time? Another of Tom's favourites?

It turned out it was. Once they'd sat down to eat, a bowl of thick fish stew swirled steam into her face; Greer closed her eyes, savouring the delicious aroma. Nathan had clearly put in a lot of effort. Her place setting was immaculate: a cotton napkin held in a solid silver ring, the cutlery chunky and expensive looking. He'd already pointed out how much he'd spent on the wine he'd poured into her glass.

How perfect it all was. 'This smells incredible.'

'Bouillabaisse,' Nathan replied. 'First time I've tried it. These days, though, I'm craving seafood all the time.'

So reminiscent of Tom. Greer smiled. 'Let's not leave it to go cold.' She dug a spoon into her food and raised it to her mouth, savouring the rich flavours. It didn't take long to finish the bowl.

Nathan, however, left half of his. At one point, she could have sworn he pulled a face. 'Is it too fishy for you?'

He shook his head. 'Just not hungry, that's all.'

A shaft of alarm shot through Greer. 'You're not feeling ill, are you?'

Nathan offered her a weary smile. 'I'm fine. Really. It's still early days, but my cardiologist says he's pleased with the way things are going.'

'You look exhausted, though. Are you sure you're okay?'

Nathan rubbed the bridge of his nose. 'I'm under pressure to get back to work full time, even though it's too soon. Oh, my boss doesn't want me in the office, just doing bits and pieces from home. It's vital I keep him sweet. My hours got reduced once I got diagnosed. I was lucky to keep my job.'

'Surely he can't fire you for being off sick?'

'Of course he can. He'll just dress it up so an employment tribunal can't touch him.'

'That's so unfair.'

'It's hard, because I'd rather be sketching. Let me show you.' Nathan crossed to his desk and pulled open the top drawer. He returned with a piece of paper in his hand and placed it before Greer. On it was a drawing of a rose, lying across a stylised heart, its petals weeping blood. Greer's eyes traced over the delicate lines, the intricate shading. It was perfect, beautiful. She could imagine Tom, in his home studio, sketching this.

'You can keep that,' Nathan said. 'If you want.' Greer most definitely did.

'I'll fetch our desserts. Back in a minute.'

Once he'd gone, Greer stood up to stretch her legs, walking over to the window near Nathan's desk. As she did, she spotted another of his drawings in the drawer he'd left open. Why was it wrapped in cellophane, though? With a price sticker attached?

Greer picked it up. The drawing was identical in style to the others, but portrayed a winter landscape. This one, however, bore the initials SC.

Well, that was strange. Perhaps Nathan had copied SC's artwork to help with his technique. He'd drawn those pictures, therefore felt justified in adding his initials. Yes, that must be it.

'Tarte tatin,' Nathan announced, setting two plates on the table. 'French apple pie, in case you didn't know.'

Dessert was pastry-and-fruit heaven, with whipped cream on top. Coffee rounded off their meal nicely. Once she'd drained her cup, Greer smiled at Nathan. 'Can I listen to Tom? Please?'

'Of course.' He unbuttoned his shirt, and Greer walked around the table to lay her head against his chest. Her arms wound around Nathan to pull him closer. Why was he so rigid, so obviously uncomfortable?

No matter; once he grew accustomed to this, he'd loosen up. It was only a matter of time.

The sound of her son's heart was a drug to her, one to which she was rapidly becoming addicted. Lub, dub, one, two. Such a thrill.

'Oh, Tom. I love you so much. You know that, don't you?'

Dear God. Had she said that aloud?

If Nathan had been stiff before, he now froze solid. Greer disengaged herself, not daring to look at him. 'I'm sorry. Slip of the tongue.'

Nathan cleared his throat. 'It's okay. Really. I don't mind.'

She risked a glance at him. 'You don't?' She couldn't quite read his expression.

'It's fine. Honestly.' He still seemed uncomfortable, however.

Nathan would get used to her loving him. Because she did, without a doubt. The realisation swept over Greer, pulling the breath from her lungs. A few short weeks ago, she'd been suicidal. Now hope gripped her heart. And it was thanks to this man.

Greer sat back at the table. 'Shall I pour us more wine?' Anything to cover the awkwardness. He nodded.

Nathan's fingers trailed over the sketch. 'I'd rather be drawing. But if I don't work, I won't get paid. I've already missed out on this year's performance bonus. I'll tell you, I'm pretty strapped financially. The mortgage on this place doesn't come cheap.'

While Greer was pondering how to reply, Nathan continued, 'Being so sick for ages didn't help. That damn waiting list—I thought I'd die before I ever got a transplant. I splashed out on lots of stuff, thinking I might as well enjoy myself before I croaked. Ended up with massive debts.'

How he must have suffered. Greer wasn't much of a spender, given her limited finances, but she understood Nathan's situation. Hovering on the brink of death probably did that to a person.

'I've asked Mum for help. Should have saved myself the trouble.'

Greer's dislike of Isla Taylor rose higher. 'She refused?'

Nathan snorted. 'Yeah. Straight away, didn't even draw breath. She's more interested in hoarding her money than helping her only son.' He grimaced. 'Guess I'll have to muddle through somehow.'

Greer didn't respond, merely took another sip of wine. Isla was more cold and unloving than she'd realised. What kind of mother turned her back on her son that way?

Maybe this was a good thing. Isla might not be there for her boy when he needed her, but Greer was.

CHAPTER 41

The following Sunday, Greer was cooking a roast chicken for Nathan in her flat. As she checked the vegetables and prepared the gravy, she juggled figures in her head. First, she'd sell her Bristol house and buy somewhere much smaller in Birmingham. With property prices the way they were, she'd have a fair bit of equity left, enough to pay off Nathan's debts. Any good mother would do the same for her son.

It would also piss Isla off. Well, the woman only had herself to blame. She'd had the chance to help Nathan, but chose not to.

The buzzer sounded. Greer threw her oven gloves on the table and rushed to open the door. Her world stopped dead, ceased to spin. Tom stood before her.

Nathan had cut his hair in a style that resembled the one her son had favoured. His striped shirt was almost identical to Tom's in Greer's favourite photo of him. He even smelled like Tom; was that a whiff of Hugo Boss she detected? Only the coarseness of his features, and his eyes being blue, not brown, belied the fact that Nathan wasn't Tom. Stupefied, she stared at him.

'Aren't you going to ask me in?' Nathan said.

Greer felt her face flush hot, as though he'd seen into her mind. She stepped back. 'Of course.'

'This is fantastic,' Nathan said as they ate. 'We should do this every weekend. Mum can't cook the way you do.'

Quite the compliment, and one in the eye for Isla. 'Thank you.'

This was what she'd wanted with Tom—the Sunday dinners together, the closeness. 'How would you feel about me moving to Birmingham?' The words tumbled out before she could rein them in.

Nathan's eyebrows shot skyward. 'Are you serious?'

Too much, too soon. Why did she never learn?

Nathan reached over to squeeze her hand. 'I'd love that.'

'You would? Really?'

'Of course. You're becoming more of a mother to me than my own's ever been.' He smiled. 'We've only known each other a while, but I already feel closer to you than to her.'

Greer threw down her knife and fork and rushed round the table to hug Nathan. 'Thank you. You don't know what this means to me. I've wanted so long to be a proper mother to you, Tom, but you kept pushing me away.' Her arms squeezed harder. Lost in her son, her hand edged towards his shirt buttons. She yearned to trace her fingers over that scar, listen to Tom's heart.

Reality jolted through Greer like an express train. Her words rushed back to haunt her. *I've wanted so long to be a proper mother to you, Tom...*

Except that this wasn't Tom. What must Nathan think of her? Her cheeks hot with shame, she returned to her seat. With a great effort, she glanced at Nathan. 'I'm sorry.'

He didn't look angry, thank goodness. Instead, a small smile played around his lips. 'It's okay,' he said. 'I don't mind.'

'You don't? It's just that—'

Nathan leaned across the table. She could smell the wine on his breath, the subtle scent of his aftershave. 'I understand,' he said. 'It's only been a short while since you lost your son, and you're still grieving after the shock of Tom's death. And now we've found each other, and it's amazing, and I hope we have many more times together like this. If you call me Tom occasionally, what does it matter?'

Oh, how wonderful. This was what Greer had wanted, but even better. Nathan had become Tom, but a more loving version. Considerate, too. It had killed Greer to know that her son had embodied those qualities, just not where she was concerned.

'I'll try not to. But I can't guarantee it won't slip out occasionally. You resemble him, especially now you've cut your hair, and what with the cellular memory stuff—' She stifled a sob. Through her tears, she managed a smile. 'You're becoming more like Tom than Tom ever was. I know that makes no sense, but it's how it is.'

'Does it help? With the grief, I mean?'

'Yes. It's as if he never left me.'

Nathan stood up, breaking the spell. 'I'll take these plates into the kitchen.'

'I've put two portions of raspberry trifle on the side. Can you bring those in, please?'

Once he'd gone, Greer took a few slow, deep breaths. That had been intense.

Nathan appeared with a plate in each hand. He sat at the table and set about demolishing his dessert.

Greer toyed with her fork. 'I have something to tell you.'

Nathan put down his fork and stared at Greer. 'Go on.'

'I wasn't being quite honest earlier. I've already decided to sell up and move to Birmingham. That way, we can spend more time together.' The last sentence whooshed from Greer in a rush of nerves. How would he react?

'That's a fantastic idea. I'm really pleased.'

So was Greer. And the best was yet to come. 'That'll release a fair amount of equity. If you'll let me, I'll pay off your debts, so you don't have that worry. The stress can't be good for you.'

Shock etched itself into Nathan's expression. 'That's incredibly generous. I can't allow you to do that, though. You hardly know me, and—'

'I know you well enough.' His resistance only made Greer more determined. 'You've already said I'm more of a mum than your own mother. Well, that cuts both ways. You're more loving than Tom ever was, and I don't give a damn how long we've known each other.'

Nathan sucked in a breath. 'We're talking a lot of money.'

'The amount's not important.'

'No, really. I added everything up this morning, and my debts are worse than I'd realised.' He named a figure, and shock ratcheted through Greer.

What did it matter, though, if Nathan's stress levels reduced? How wonderful that she could put the equity in her house to good use.

'I'm sorry.' Nathan said. 'You obviously didn't expect it to be that much.'

'It's not an issue. Consider it sorted.'

'I can't thank you enough. You're an incredible woman, Greer.' He cleared his throat. 'I don't suppose you could spare me a couple of thousand now? It would keep my creditors at bay for a while. I'll pay you back as soon as possible.'

Greer swallowed her dismay. She could ill afford to dip into her savings, but any loan would only be temporary, right? He'd promised to reimburse the money, after all.

'Of course. If you give me your bank details, I'll transfer the money today.'

Later, once Nathan left, Greer poured herself a glass of wine and got comfortable on the sofa. She switched on her laptop. Time to help Nathan with his financial problems.

Life was looking better at last. She'd never forget the horror of Rose's disappearance or Tom's death, but a wonderful future with Nathan beckoned instead. She'd not asked to listen to Tom's heart again, because what was the point? Nathan was becoming Tom to her, and yes, it helped soothe the grief. More than she could put into words.

That night, for the first time in ages, she didn't sleep with Tom's sweatshirt clasped in her arms.

CHAPTER 42

The following weekend, Greer was at Nathan's place, waiting for Charlie to arrive. A couple of days ago, he'd sent her a message, asking when would be a good time to meet Nathan. Good job he had; she'd been so bound up with the whole cellular memory thing that she'd forgotten she'd suggested the three of them meet up. Now they were all about to have dinner at Nathan's Birmingham flat. To her relief, Nathan had readily agreed when she'd mooted the idea.

'I want you to meet Charlie. He was Tom's best friend, and misses my boy almost as much as I do. If I'm going to move to Birmingham, and Charlie stays in touch, as I hope he will, you'll meet him eventually, anyway.'

Nathan had squeezed her hand. 'Let's set something up. Why don't you cook for us here?'

Ah, there was the buzzer. Greer pulled open the door to welcome Charlie. He looked like he'd lost weight. His football shirt hung loosely on his frame, and his face was gaunt. She walked towards the living room, Charlie trailing in her footsteps.

Nathan got up from the sofa when he spotted Charlie. 'Good to meet you. You're a friend of Tom's from Bristol, right?'

Charlie nodded as he shook Nathan's hand. 'His best mate, actually.'

'Sit yourselves down.' Greer ushered both men towards the table. 'I've cooked salmon with roasted vegetables and new potatoes. Nathan, can you pour the wine?' She handed him the bottle of supermarket-brand Cabernet Sauvignon Charlie had brought. Did she imagine it, or did Nathan's lip curl?

The conversation over dinner didn't go as well as Greer had hoped. Charlie seemed on edge, more concerned about how full his wineglass was. Should she talk to him about his drinking? Best not to. Hadn't Tom and Rose resented what they deemed her interference?

'I was telling Greer earlier how I bought a new brand of aftershave, then found out it was Tom's favourite,' Nathan was saying, as he pushed away his dessert plate.

Greer stacked it on top of hers, ready to clear away. 'Coffee, anyone?'

Charlie shook his head. His gaze seemed fixed on Nathan's desk across the room. Greer couldn't work out what might be so fascinating about the files on it or the digital photo display, currently displaying Nathan with his arm around someone, a wide smile on his face. Before Greer could shift her focus to the other person, the display had moved on.

While she was in the kitchen, a low rumble of voices, often heated, caught her ear, before the sounds stopped. She returned with coffee for Nathan and herself, only to encounter silence. Neither man was looking at the other. Charlie caught Greer's eyes, then glanced away.

Well, she'd better get the conversation flowing again. What had they been discussing before she left? Ah, yes, Nathan's new aftershave, which had been Tom's favourite.

'Cellular memory's fascinating, don't you agree, Charlie?' They'd discussed the topic when she'd phoned him earlier that week. Charlie had claimed he'd never heard of it. He hadn't sounded convinced by the idea.

'Very much so.' Charlie's response seemed forced, as did his smile.

'I think it's mind-boggling,' Nathan said. 'There's definitely something in it, as I'm finding out.'

Charlie stood up. 'I'm tired. Could do with an early night.'

Nathan also got to his feet. 'Yeah, me too.'

Greer clutched his arm in terror. 'Are you feeling all right? You haven't missed any of your tablets, have you?'

Nathan smiled. 'I never do. Relax, Greer. Everything is fine.' He turned to Charlie. 'It was nice to meet you.'

'Likewise.' The smile on Charlie's face didn't reach his eyes. Greer couldn't fathom the reason for his abrupt change of mood.

'I'll walk you downstairs.' Greer intended to have words with him about his attitude.

Once they were in the foyer, Greer rounded on Charlie. 'What the hell are you playing at? I arranged a meal here tonight because that was what you wanted. Instead, you barely spoke to Nathan. When you did, you bordered on rude.'

'Of course you'd take Nathan's side.' Charlie rubbed his eyes, reminding Greer of Tom as a toddler. Tired and cranky. He was definitely behaving with the maturity of a tetchy child.

'There *are* no sides. Why couldn't you have been more polite?'

'I'm sorry. I didn't mean to be rude. I'm tired, that's all.'

'You'll have to accept him in my life. You realise that, right? Tom is my son.' Damn, she'd messed up again. In front of Charlie, too.

'His name is Nathan, not Tom.' Charlie's tone was cold. 'And he's not your son. No matter how much you might want him to be. This fixation of yours on his heart is getting weird.'

Greer pursed her lips. 'So what if I called him Tom? A slip of the tongue, that's all.'

'You're too emotionally invested in him. Yes, it's wonderful that part of Tom lives on in Nathan. But, Mrs M, you're becoming obsessed with this man. And that's not healthy.'

'You're wrong.' The denial fell automatically from Greer's lips. 'Why don't you like him?'

'Because he's so phony. That fake laugh, the false confidence he projects—nothing about him seems on the level. And what about all that crap about cellular memory? Don't you realise he was saying exactly what you wanted to hear? I can't fathom what his game is. But he's got one, I'm sure. The bastard's stringing you along.'

His words stung. 'He doesn't have a game. Is it really so far-fetched that we've forged a connection? Brought together by Tom's heart?'

'Or perhaps he's just an arsehole.'

'That's offensive. You need to sober up.' Charlie, thank God, hadn't driven to Nathan's flat. He'd told Greer he'd walked from his hotel.

'But, Mrs M—'

'Leave, Charlie. Now. Don't make me ask you again.'

'Wait. There's something else, and it's really strange. The real reason I've got a bad feeling about this guy. Didn't you notice—'

She'd had way too much of Charlie's attitude for one evening. It was probably the drink talking, but his dislike of the man for whom she was developing powerful feelings grated. She hurried back upstairs, blocking the sound of Charlie's voice as he shouted after her.

CHAPTER 43

It was the Tuesday evening after Charlie's disastrous visit, and Greer was meeting Nathan for another meal. A pub this time, the Goose and Gosling, a ten-minute walk from Greer's rented flat. The March wind was chilly as she strolled along the pavement, her hands thrust into her coat pockets. She had so much to tell Nathan. The call from her estate agent in Bristol. The studio apartment in Birmingham that was up for sale, situated not far from Edgbaston.

Nathan, as usual, was late. The huge old-fashioned clock above the bar showed the time as ten past eight when he strode in. Greer had found them a quiet booth at the back of the pub. She watched him walk towards her. He looked so much like Tom these days.

'Cod and chips for me,' Nathan said, as he closed the menu. 'Strange, isn't it? I used to hate fish.'

Greer smiled. 'Cellular memory at its finest, hey?' She had one concern, though. 'Do you mind? Is it weird for you?'

Nathan shrugged. 'Not much I can do about it, is there? Besides, it's all good. I need to move away from red meat towards healthier food. And the drawing—it's like a whole new world has opened up. So no, it's fine by me.'

Joy squeezed Greer's heart. Strange how quickly life could flip around. Tom's death was still a raw wound, but the man before her might, with luck, heal her.

They placed their orders. Once the food arrived, Greer stayed silent about her plans, figuring they'd discuss them over coffee. Once they finished eating, she pushed back her chair. 'Would you excuse me? I need the loo.'

As she washed her hands, Greer's mind buzzed with everything she needed to tell Nathan. She pulled open the door to the toilets and walked over to their booth, her shoes noiseless on the thick carpet. Nathan had his mobile to his ear, his back to her.

A metre or so away from him, she froze. Around her, the pub stilled and grew silent, or so it seemed. All that remained were Greer, and Nathan, and the foul things he was saying.

'I hate queers.' Contempt filled Nathan's voice. Then: 'Every last limp-wristed one.' He laughed, the sound harsh and nasty.

Greer's mouth went dry with shock. She staggered back to the toilets and splashed water on her face, her breath coming in quick gasps.

She'd dissect what this meant later. Right now, her primary concern was to appear as though nothing was wrong. A few deep breaths, and she was ready, despite her inner turmoil.

Greer tugged open the door and walked back to their booth. Nathan's mobile, dark and silent, was now on the table. She stared at him. Why had she ever thought he looked like Tom? That wide nose, the fleshy lips, blue eyes instead of brown—the resemblance, if it existed, was slight. Instead, opposite her sat a snake, coiled and ready to strike.

She couldn't deal with this now. She'd process everything when she got home.

Greer snagged the attention of a passing server. 'Can we get the bill?'

'Are you all right?' Nathan said. 'You look really pale.'

'I've developed a bad migraine.' The lie slipped easily off Greer's tongue. 'It came on suddenly. Would you excuse me, please?'

'Of course. I'm sorry you're not well.' Greer was aware of him studying her. Try as she might, she failed to manage a smile. Desperate to get away, she grabbed her bag and jacket, conscious of the server approaching with a leather folder in his hand. Nathan, the goddamn bastard, could pay the bill for once.

'Will you text me either later or tomorrow? Let me know you're okay?' God, he was a wonderful actor. He seemed genuinely concerned.

Greer nodded. She forced herself to sound normal when she replied. 'I'm sorry to have to dash off like this. I'll be in touch.' With that, she scurried towards the door, not looking back. Damn Nathan Taylor.

CHAPTER 44

Back at her flat, Greer opened a bottle of wine, anger pounding through her skull. How dare he? Those hateful words—*I hate queers*—chased themselves round her brain, wouldn't let go. Impossible to overlook the vile slur on Tom. A gay man's heart beat in Nathan Taylor's chest. What an ungrateful bastard he was. A monster, no less.

Later, in bed, Greer tossed and turned, unable to sleep. *I hate queers. Every last limp-wristed one*. Nathan's words circled through her head, each syllable taunting her.

She ought to stride round to Nathan's flat and have it out with him. How dare he be so cruel, so awful? She'd been right to dub him a snake. Nathan had ripped the mask from his face, exposing the ugliness beneath.

How gullible she'd been. Nathan had shown his true colours the first time they met. She recalled Isla saying, 'I love Nathan. But I don't particularly like him. He's not a good person.' Something else about how Nathan was misogynistic. Misanthropic, even.

Homophobic too. Nathan knew about Tom being gay. Yet he still disrespected the man who gave him his new heart. The man was a vile hypocrite.

I hate queers. Try as she might, Greer failed to purge the terrible words from her brain. Such venom in Nathan's tone, too. The man she'd eaten fish and chips with earlier wasn't a worthy recipient of Tom's heart. Impossible to confront Nathan about what he'd said. He'd only spin her a load of crap, right?

Greer huddled into a foetal ball, the duvet over her head. How stupid to dream of a future with Nathan as her son. Like everyone else, he'd let her down, betrayed her. She should have expected it. Stupid, stupid.

What about cellular memory, though? Nathan's newfound artistic abilities, his growing preference for healthy foods, all proved it existed. But how could a man in whom Tom's heart beat be so homophobic?

Nobody knew much about cellular memory, though. Perhaps Tom's cells might exert influence over things like food choices, but hit a brick wall when confronted with entrenched attitudes. Maybe those took longer to respond, or didn't change at all.

An additional worry plagued her. What if cellular memory worked both ways? Suppose Nathan's nastiness corrupted the good in Tom's heart? If that happened, she'd lose the little that remained of her son forever. The idea was unbearable.

Could she overlook this? Put it down to crass male bravado? People often said things didn't mean in order to fit in. But how could she grow closer to Nathan, knowing that he'd have scorned Tom for his sexuality?

If only she had someone to talk to. Beth was out of the question. She'd say Greer should have heeded her advice to leave Nathan alone. The woman was probably right. Given their recent falling-out, Charlie wasn't a possibility either.

She needed to give it time, see how things went. One thing was for sure. She wouldn't be paying off any more of Nathan Taylor's debts, not a single penny.

A bolt of pain shot through Greer's chest, driving the breath from her lungs and causing sweat to bead on her forehead. Damn. Had she taken her medication that day? She'd been flaky on that front recently. All the excitement of being with Nathan had scuppered her usual routine. Once again, she yearned for someone to confide in.

Greer dragged in a few deep breaths and took a gulp of water from the glass by her bed. After a while, the tightness in her rib cage eased. Her breathing returned to normal.

Then it hit her. She *did* know somebody to talk to.

CHAPTER 45

The next morning, Greer picked up her mobile. Should she text Jessica or not? Nathan's sister was in her late twenties; why would she want to spend time with a woman old enough to be her mother? She was probably just being polite when she'd taken Greer's mobile number.

Greer eventually tapped out a message. *Hi, how are you? Can we meet for coffee? There's something I need to ask you.*

Less than five minutes later, a response pinged through. *Very busy this week, but I'm going to Nathan's after I finish my shift today. Why don't you walk there with me?*

Why not, indeed? They swapped texts, with Greer agreeing to meet Jessica at three that afternoon.

The sun's heat warmed Greer as she waited outside Willowbank Care Home. She was early—it was only ten to three—but she mustn't make Jessica late for Nathan, not if she was going there to help her brother. What a wonderful sister she was, despite Nathan's ugly attitude.

The door opened, and Jessica appeared, a smile lighting up her face when she spotted Greer. 'You came.'

'Of course.' Had she really worried that Greer wouldn't turn up?

Jessica waved a hand to her left. 'It's this way. About ten minutes in that direction. My car's in for its MOT, otherwise I'd drive.'

What a shame. Greer had hoped to spend longer with Jessica.

'I'm sorry I don't have more time. What with working, and cooking and cleaning for Nathan, I've barely got a minute to spare. As soon as I do, we'll grab that coffee together.'

A weight lifted from Greer's heart. 'I'd like that.'

They chatted as they walked. She learned Jessica had been a nurse at Southmead Hospital in Bristol. In fact, the whole family had lived in Greer's home city until recently. 'Mum relocated to Birmingham four years ago once she'd divorced Dad. She was born in Edgbaston, you see. After Nathan's transplant, she asked me to come and live with her. He transferred here before his operation. She finds it difficult to care for him, what with her job, and as a nurse, I'm better placed to help if he gets any problems.'

'You don't mind?'

A shrug. 'Not really. I was burned out in Bristol. Felt like a change.'

Greer sneaked a glance at her companion. Jessica's jaw was tight, her mouth thin-lipped. She couldn't blame Jessica for being resentful; she doubted Nathan was a model patient. And what was that nonsense about Isla struggling to cope? Isla's job was part-time, whereas Jessica's wasn't. How selfish of the woman. No wonder her poor daughter looked exhausted.

Jessica started talking about one of the elderly residents at the care home, and Greer only half listened, her mind elsewhere. How lovely to be walking alongside this sweet girl. Jessica became Rose in Greer's head, the two of them about to call in on Tom.

'Here we are.' Jessica's voice snapped Greer from her thoughts. They'd arrived at Nathan's block of flats. 'Was there something you wanted to ask me?'

Greer cleared her throat. 'Um. Look, this is awkward. Could you tell me a bit about Nathan? What sort of person he is?'

Jessica laughed, the sound harsh and humourless. 'He's upset you, hasn't he? He pisses everyone off eventually. I told you when we first met that he's not a nice guy.'

Greer wasn't sure how to respond. A light drizzle was falling, the wind whipping rain into her face. She took shelter under the building's entrance.

Jessica followed suit. 'Spill the beans. What's he done now?'

'He said horrible things. While he was on the phone. He didn't think I heard, but I did.'

'What did he say?'

'About hating queers, as he called them.' Greer's face flushed hot with anger. 'My Tom was gay.'

'I'm so sorry he was rude. Please don't take it to heart. Nathan slags everyone off.'

Greer wiped away a tear. 'It really upset me.'

'Nathan's ugly inside. He always has been. You shouldn't trust him.'

Greer stared at her. 'What do you mean?'

Jessica glanced away. 'Nothing. I'm just tired and mouthing off. I'd better go up. He doesn't like me to be late.'

'That's pretty hypocritical of him. He's never on time himself.'

Jessica shrugged. 'I know, but what can you do?' She gave Greer a quick, almost furtive hug. 'It's good to see you again.' We'll definitely grab that cup of coffee sometime, yeah?' Without waiting for a reply, she tapped in the access code, tugged open the door and disappeared inside.

Reluctant to return home immediately, Greer made her way to the coffee shop over the road. Once seated with her latte, her thoughts turned to Jessica. The girl was so sweet, yet utterly downtrodden. All thanks to Nathan and Isla bloody Taylor.

Greer's jaw tightened with anger. Had Jessica been *her* child, she'd never have taken advantage of her the way Isla did. Mothers should cherish their daughters. The way she'd tried to do with Rose.

Greer allowed herself to slip into a delicious fantasy. She and Jessica, strolling through a park, the midday sun hot on their faces. Jessica, telling Greer about her dreams of travel, marriage, a family. Greer, listening, being the mother Jessica so clearly lacked. Later, the two of them would enjoy ice creams while feeding ducks on the lake. Somewhere along the way, Greer's battered heart would heal a little.

In her head, her fingers tucked a strand of hair behind Jessica's ear. 'You're so beautiful, Rose.' Rose smiled at her, all soft and warm.

Greer lost herself in another, much kinder, world. Two hours had slipped by the time she saw Jessica emerge from Nathan's building. The girl appeared to be wiping tears from her eyes. What the hell?

Greer shot to her feet and grabbed her coat and bag. She hurried across the road to grab Jessica's arm. Shock registered on Jessica's face.

Her cheeks were tear-stained and blotchy, her eyes red and watery. In Greer's mind, Rose stood before her, needing Greer in a way she never had in real life.

'What's the matter, sweetheart? Has Nathan upset you?'

Jessica swallowed hard. She nodded, fumbling in her bag for a tissue. Greer watched as Jessica dabbed her eyes. She'd be having strong words with Nathan, that was for sure. He should damn well treat his sister better.

'You can talk to me, you know.' They were attracting curious stares. 'Let me buy you that coffee. The place across the road is good, and—'

Panic flashed into Jessica's eyes. 'No. No, I can't. Look, don't mind me. It's just Nathan, being a pig as usual.' Before Greer could find her voice, Jessica spun on her heel and strode away, leaving Greer open-mouthed on the pavement. What had all that been about?

CHAPTER 46

The following day, Greer was heading out to buy groceries. A quick whizz round the supermarket, and then she'd call Jessica, make sure she was okay. Find out what had upset her. She'd just stepped into the lobby when Nathan opened the door to the building. Greer froze.

'Hey,' he said. 'You've not answered any of my messages.'

Greer's lip curled. 'I've been busy.'

'Are you still unwell?' He eyed the handbag slung over Greer's arm. 'I guess not, if you're going out.'

She tried to push past him, but he grabbed her arm. 'Something's wrong. Have I upset you?'

I hate queers. Every last limp-wristed one. 'Yes. You have.'

'Why? What have I said, or done?'

Greer jerked away from his grasp. 'Leave me alone.' They needed to talk, sure, but not when she was still so furious. She strode out of the door, aiming to cut through the nearby park to the supermarket, but she'd reckoned without Nathan. As she headed towards the swings, he caught up with her. 'Tell me, Greer. How can I put things right if I don't know what I've done wrong?'

Ahead of them stood an old bandstand, now converted into a shady spot to sit. Greer gestured at it. 'Over there. I'll give you five minutes, no more.'

The bandstand's only occupant was a teenage boy, his gaze on his phone. When Greer and Nathan entered, he pulled a face and left. Greer sat on a bench and Nathan joined her.

'I thought everything was great between us. Now it's not. What changed, Greer?'

'You did. As soon as I wasn't around, you showed yourself in your true colours. Your mother was right about you.'

A hint of anger crossed Nathan's face. 'Mum? What's she said to you?'

'She warned me about you. I should have listened to her.'

Nathan frowned. 'Mum's bitter because her marriage to Dad ended in divorce. She has a downer on men, even me.' He edged closer, his voice pure silk. 'We were getting on so well. Tell me what's upset you. Please.'

Greer's anger ebbed a little. Maybe she'd misjudged him. She owed him the chance to explain.

'It was what you said when we had fish and chips in that pub. I needed the toilet, and when I came back, you were on your phone. Saying how much you hate gay men.' Nathan's expression morphed into one of shock. 'Pretty nasty of you, given that you have a gay man's heart inside you.'

For a second, Nathan didn't respond. Then he took Greer's hand. 'I'm sorry you heard that. I didn't mean it, Greer. It was an awful thing to say.'

'Then why did you?'

Nathan pulled a face. 'I've known Eddie, the guy I was taking to, for years. We were at school together. He's always been Mr Macho, hates gays. Back when we were teenagers, we'd slag them off without a second thought. Pure bravado, but he's never grown out of it. I carry on the charade with Ed solely to keep up appearances. I don't hate gay men, Greer.' Nathan smiled, and Greer lost herself in the blue of his eyes. 'How could I, given that I have Tom's heart inside me?'

Greer bit her lip. She didn't like Nathan's cowardice, but was reluctant to be too hard on him. He still faced a long road back to health. The guy couldn't afford to alienate a close friend, even an unpleasant one.

'You're okay with gay men? Really?'

'Yes. I'm sorry you overheard what you did. That's not who I am, believe me.'

'What you said was ugly. Cruel and spiteful.'

'I know. I'm ashamed of myself, honestly I am. I can't bear to think I've upset you this way, right when we were establishing such a strong connection.'

When she didn't respond, he pulled away, unbuttoned his shirt. 'Listen to Tom's heart, Greer. That will tell you much better than words how grateful I am. Don't let my stupidity come between us. Please?'

Greer glanced around. A group of children occupied the swings, their shouts lost in the wind. An elderly couple were walking their dachshund. Nobody was paying Nathan or her any attention.

The lure proved irresistible. Greer laid her ear against Nathan's scar, oblivious to everything around her. The steady beat of Tom's heart pulsed inside her head, reassuring her. Nathan had been stupid and thoughtless, but he deserved a second chance, right?

―

Later, back at her flat, Greer couldn't get Nathan's face out of her mind. The nagging conviction that he looked familiar wouldn't leave her alone. Had she seen Nathan before, and if so, where and when?

A reminder beeped from her mobile. Time for her heart pills. She padded into the kitchen for a glass of water with which to take her medication. Her fingers twisted off the cap of the bottle and shook out an oval white tablet. The penny dropped in Greer's head with a resounding clang. She knew exactly where she'd seen Nathan Taylor before.

Nathan, as he and Jessica had both told her, had lived in Bristol until a couple of years ago. His heart problems had begun in Greer's home city. He'd have attended the cardiac unit at Bristol's Royal Infirmary. The same unit Greer had attended for her own heart issues.

That was how she knew him. She could picture him clearly now. He'd been paler, thinner, obviously ill, but it was him all right.

Snippets of memories forced themselves into Greer's mind. Nathan, behaving rudely to the staff. Not dissimilar to his behaviour that first time they'd met at his flat.

What was it Isla had said? 'I love Nathan. But I don't always like him.'

So who was the real Nathan Taylor? The boorish individual who'd spouted awful things about gay men, or the charmer who claimed they were forging an amazing connection?

The latter. It had to be. Despite Nathan's bad behaviour, Tom's heart still beat in his chest. How could she ignore *that*? And what about the question of cellular memory? Nathan might be shallow and had behaved like a pig, but what if he changed? Suppose Tom's gentle nature predominated, wreaking a positive influence?

She was lonely. Nathan offered her something she didn't have in Bristol. Jessica was here, too. Didn't she owe it to herself to stick around? And forgive Nathan?

CHAPTER 47

The next day, Greer hurried down the street, grocery bags in hand, eager to escape the driving rain. She was almost back at her Airbnb flat, and desperate for a rest. As she rounded the corner, her phone trilled from the depths of her bag.

Greer darted into an empty doorway and pulled out her mobile. The caller's name on the screen was Nathan Taylor.

He'd pester her with a multitude of texts if she didn't answer. 'Hey. How are you?'

'Any chance you can come round?' His voice sounded flat. 'I've had an argument with Mum. You know what she's like. Honestly, Greer, you're more a mother to me than she is.'

She hesitated. A cup of tea, followed by a nap, held more appeal. Besides, Nathan wasn't her favourite person right then, even though she'd decided to overlook his nastiness.

'Greer?'

He'd explained his vile comments, hadn't he? Shouldn't Greer be more forgiving?

She rolled her eyes. 'I'll come over right away.'

'Good to see you,' Nathan said once he'd opened the door. 'I'll make us some coffee.'

Once they'd seated themselves in his living room, Greer studied him. How exhausted he looked. His skin was pale, and dark smudges underlined his eyes.

He'd better be looking after Tom's heart. 'Are you all right?'

Nathan waved a dismissive hand. 'A bit tired, I guess. Everything was okay at my last check-up, however.'

'You're still having them weekly? Every Monday?'

He nodded.

'And keeping up with your medication?' Greer glanced at the plastic pillbox on the coffee table. From what she could see of the days and time slots, he was.

'Of course.' Nathan's voice was huffy with irritation. 'Like I told you, it's dangerous to miss even a single dose. Anyway, let's not worry about that. I had a big row with Mum.'

'What about?'

'She's so unsupportive.' He rubbed his hand over his jaw. 'She knows it's important for me to avoid unnecessary stress. I still can't work much, so I don't have a lot of income right now. Mum, though—she's loaded after the divorce.'

Greer tensed. A request for more money seemed probable, and she didn't have much left to give.

'There's one credit card company that's really hounding me. I'd overlooked them when I totalled up my debts before. You've already been extraordinarily kind in loaning me a couple of grand, so I didn't want to bother you again. Like a fool, I asked Mum, and she refused.'

When Greer didn't respond, he continued, 'I'm being threatened with a potential court case and all the associated fees. So I was wondering. Is there any way you can advance me a short-term loan, just until I'm back on my feet at work?'

'How much are we talking about?'

'Five grand. I know that's a lot. But I'm so stressed, and all I can think about is money. How it'll be a while before I earn a decent income again. I wouldn't ask if there was another way. If I had a mother who actually cared. But I don't, you see.'

Greer's mouth was dry with panic. Five thousand pounds would wipe out her remaining savings, leaving her with nothing.

'I'll pay you back as soon as possible. With interest, too. Can you swing it for me, Greer? I'm worried my health will suffer with all the stress.'

'Well, I—'

'I'm not eating properly or sleeping much. I'm terrified I'll mess up my medication because I can't think straight.'

That clinched it. Tom's heart mustn't be endangered, despite her misgivings. 'Of course. I'll transfer the funds to you now.' *Take that, Isla Taylor.*

'Thank you. You don't realise what this means to me.'

Nathan stood up. 'I'll make some more coffee.'

Greer got up to pace the room, her thoughts a mess. She couldn't really spare the money. He'd pay her back, though. Of course he would, in time.

Her future was here in Birmingham, with Nathan. She had to trust him and the connection they were building, because if she didn't, what meaning did she have in her life?

Nathan walked in, bearing two steaming mugs, one of which he handed to Greer. 'Have you sent the money? Sorry to press you, but it's kind of urgent.'

Greer took her mobile from her bag. 'I'll do it now.'

She accessed her online banking app and transferred five thousand pounds into Nathan's account. Her savings balance now stood at £36.98. Money would be tight for a while. She'd simply have to cut her spending, get her house rented out, or apply for an overdraft. Tom's heart was all that mattered.

CHAPTER 48

Beth leaned back and closed her eyes. God, it had been a long day. Shopping, visiting an old school friend, volunteering at a food bank. A hot drink was what she needed. She hauled herself to her feet and walked into the kitchen.

A minute later, she returned with a mug of coffee, settled herself on the sofa and grabbed the TV remote. First, she'd watch the evening news, then a movie, all nice and chilled-out.

She'd reckoned without the usual global mayhem. Beth listened to reports of an earthquake in Japan, stabbings in London and tension in the Middle East. The main bulletin ended, followed by the local one. By now, she'd finished her coffee. Did she really want another?

A quick refill wouldn't hurt. As Beth stood to take her empty mug into the kitchen, a name from the television caught her attention. She froze in place, her gaze on the screen.

'Missing woman discovered dead in local woodland,' the caption read, as the opening music faded. The camera focused on the two newscasters.

'The body of Lily Hamilton, the Bristol woman who disappeared eighteen months ago, has been found in a wooded area on the outskirts of the city,' the male news anchor said. 'Local building contractors discovered her corpse while clearing the site for future development. We have this report from Penny Lucas.'

The image changed to show a young woman, blonde hair blowing in the wind, dressed in a beige trench coat. Blue-and-white crime scene tape fluttered in the background. 'As my colleague has said, Lily Hamilton's body was discovered this morning under a rocky outcrop when workers were clearing undergrowth in preparation for a new housing development. Police officers are treating her death as suspicious but have not released further details at this stage. Lily went missing after telling friends she was meeting a man she'd contacted through a dating website.'

Beth's buzzer sounded. A minute after opening the door, she slammed it shut on the hapless political canvasser who'd dared to disturb her evening. He wouldn't be calling on *her* again in a hurry. By the time she returned, the news had shifted to a local robbery.

Lily Hamilton. The name seemed familiar, but why? Wait a minute. Hadn't Greer mentioned a woman called Lily Hamilton who disappeared the same year Rose did?

She really should phone Greer. The discovery of Lily's body was important news in Bristol, but the Birmingham television stations wouldn't report an event that wasn't local to them.

Her friend needed to know, however. Hadn't Greer told Beth she believed Lily and Rose had fallen victim to the same predator?

Beth picked up her mobile.

Wait. How would she ever find the right words?

Greer rubbed moisturiser into her face. God, she was ready for her bed.

As she pulled back her duvet, her phone rang. Beth's name was on the screen.

Greer frowned. Wasn't it a bit late for a phone call?

'Beth. This is a lovely surprise.' They exchanged pleasantries—*How are you? Fine, thanks*—then Beth's tone turned serious. 'I know it's past eleven, and you're probably tired. The thing is, I've been agonising for hours over what to say.'

What a strange comment. 'What do you mean?'

'I don't want to upset you. But do you remember telling me about your daughter Rose going missing? You mentioned another woman as well. Was her name Lily Hamilton?'

Shock drained the saliva from Greer's mouth.

'Greer? Are you still there?' When she didn't respond, Beth continued, 'I doubt it made the news in your area. Lily Hamilton's body's been found, Greer. I realise this must come as quite a bombshell. But say something. Please.'

Greer moistened her dry lips. 'Who found her?' Stupid question. What did that matter?

'Construction workers, apparently. In woodland just outside the city. The site's under development for a future building project. I'm so sorry, my love. I know this must reopen old wounds.'

Tears filled Greer's eyes. 'They never healed.'

Once the call ended, Greer poured herself a glass of water from her bedside jug and drank it in one go. It didn't help; her mouth remained dry with shock.

Sleep was out of the question. She pulled on her dressing gown and retrieved her laptop. A Google search confirmed what Beth had said. As well as how Lily Hamilton disappeared after going to meet a man from a dating website.

Just like Greer had once told Beth Rose had done.

CHAPTER 49

Was it morning already? Greer was positive she'd only dozed off a short while ago. Time to drag herself from bed, however groggy she felt. It was hardly surprising she'd slept badly. How could she rest when Lily Hamilton, and the discovery of her body, had haunted her during the long hours of wakefulness?

What had Beth said? *I know this must reopen old wounds.* Her neighbour was right. The pain of Rose's loss was as sharp as ever.

Oh, to stay in bed forever, nursing her misery. She needed the loo, though. Greer's stomach was rumbling, too, and she had nothing in for breakfast. Time to get up.

She showered, dressed, and made her way downstairs, all the while feeling sick. The stairs needed more effort than usual, and her legs were heavy, like concrete encased her feet.

Greer dragged open the front door to the block of apartments and turned right towards the nearest supermarket. The day seemed unusually warm, given that the sky was dull and overcast. She wiped sweat from her brow. Why did her chest feel like it might explode?

The tightness under her ribs worsened as she browsed the wine aisle. An iron hand squeezed her lungs in a deadly grip, the nausea worse now. Then a lightning bolt of pain struck. Greer slumped to the ground, dimly aware of voices around her. *Oh my God... are you all right, lady? Someone call an ambulance...*

Greer regained consciousness to a world of white. Where on earth was she? She glanced around; monitors, beeping sounds, tubes. The blue scrubs of a nurse. Ah, yes. She was in hospital, of course. Tom was too, wasn't he? He was much sicker than her, though. She must tell him how much she loved him. Before it was too late.

Wait. It already was.

She remembered now. Her darling boy had died. Shame she hadn't. Why bother living when Tom was gone?

The nurse was speaking, but her words made no sense to Greer. All she knew was that Tom was dead and something bad had happened to her. She slid into unconsciousness once more.

An indeterminate amount of time later, Greer opened her eyes again. Her brain seemed clearer, sharper. No confusion about where she was, or why she was here. She'd suffered a heart attack. No need for a doctor to tell her *that*.

'Ah, you're back with us, I see.' The voice was male, laden with cheer, and Greer hated its owner before she even looked at him.

'Go away.' So what if she sounded rude?

The doctor didn't seem to take offence. No doubt he'd been on the receiving end of far worse. Greer turned her head, intent on ignoring him, but his words filtered through. *Coronary artery calcification. At risk of a second heart attack. Review of your medication. Diet and lifestyle modifications.*

'Your GP has discussed all this already with you, of course.'

Greer's mouth twisted into a sneer. 'Yeah, sure. We've had many conversations on the subject. My heart's turning to bone, right?'

The doctor nodded. 'That's one way of putting it.'

Greer spent the next few days in Birmingham City Hospital's cardiac unit. She'd sent messages to Nathan, Beth, Charlie, and, as an afterthought, Jessica. Beth and Charlie had expressed their concern—*Sorry to hear that, Greer! Can I do anything to help?* and, *Look after yourself, Mrs M! Hope to see you soon*—and she'd chatted via video with both.

'The news about Lily came as an awful shock,' Charlie told her.

'I can't talk about that. It's too upsetting.' He never mentioned his argument with Greer. Fine by her. A heart attack made one take stock of life; she had no wish to fall out with Charlie.

As for Beth, she'd been keen to visit, but Greer had assured her it was unnecessary.

'I'm fine. As heart attacks go, it was minor. More of a warning, really.'

'If only I'd not phoned you about that woman's body being found.' Anguish in Beth's voice. 'I feel so guilty.'

'It wasn't your fault.' Their conversation had strayed into dangerous territory. She forced herself not to think about Lily Hamilton, or Rose, or even Tom. Her heart, already fragile, might shatter if she did.

Nathan hadn't been in. The hospital allowed patients one visitor per day, for an hour only, subject to prior arrangement. The real reason Greer had discouraged Beth from visiting; that precious time-slot bore Nathan's name. A heart attack definitely made petty resentments disappear; she'd forgiven him for his vile words. Tom's heart beating inside Nathan—*that* was what mattered.

He'd declined, much to Greer's disappointment. 'I daren't risk it,' he'd told her during a video chat, his voice filled with regret. 'Hospitals are full of sick people, and I can't jeopardise what's left of my immune system that way. You understand, right?'

Greer, hurt but determined to hide it, had agreed. Inside, though, his rejection stung. This was a cardiac ward, not a covid one; was the risk really so great? She supposed he was right to be cautious, though.

How selfish of her. She couldn't lose Nathan, not now. With Tom and Rose both gone, and with her planned move to Birmingham, he was all she had left.

Wrong. How could she have forgotten Jessica?

The girl had pleasantly surprised her. Her reply to Greer's message about being in hospital was warm. Concerned. Kind. Further ones flew back and forth, and they also chatted via video. Greer told Jessica about Tom, and Jessica vented her frustrations over her job and her brother. 'Can we meet up once you're discharged?' she'd said the last time they spoke.

Greer's heart swelled. 'I'd like that.'

'Let me collect you. I'll drive you to wherever you're staying, make sure you're okay. I'm a nurse, don't forget.'

How caring of Jessica. 'That would be lovely. Thank you.'

CHAPTER 50

Jessica had been as good as her word. A few minutes after Greer texted her with her discharge details, she'd replied. *I'll be there.*

Greer hadn't notified Nathan, Beth, or Charlie. What was the point? She'd catch up with the latter two back in Bristol, and as for Nathan, she planned on visiting him soon. Listening to Tom's heart would help heal her own.

Jessica was waiting for Greer in the hospital's discharge lounge that morning. The two women hugged. 'Come on,' Jessica said. 'Let's get you home. Hey, why are you crying?'

Why, indeed. Because such kindness felt unfamiliar. It was wonderful, but strange.

Impossible to explain that without sounding weird. 'I'm okay. Just glad to be out of here.'

Jessica drove Greer to her Airbnb flat and stayed until late evening. She hoovered, dusted, and cooked them both spaghetti bolognese, refusing to let Greer lift a finger. 'You need to rest,' she said. 'I can sort everything out.'

A bit of pampering felt good. Greer could get used to having Jessica in her life. It was as if Rose had returned, but in a more loving version.

Jessica was putting on her coat to leave. 'Sorry to rush off. I need to get back to Mum.'

'Thank you so much. You didn't have to go to all this trouble.'

A shrug. 'I'm a nurse, remember? And it's just a few hours of my time. No big deal.'

'Oh, I think it is. If you're half as caring with Nathan, he's lucky to have you as his sister.'

A cloud passed over Jessica's face. 'Yeah. About him. Could we chat sometime? Please?'

'Whenever you want.' One day, she'd find out why Jessica and Nathan didn't get on. 'I'm hoping to see him tomorrow.'

Jessica's eyes widened. 'Can we talk first? It's important. You need to hear what I have to say.'

Greer slept in late the next morning. It was to be expected; according to the cardiac team at Birmingham City Hospital, tiredness was common after a heart attack. They'd also advised gentle exercise. A walk with Jessica in the nearby park, already arranged for two o'clock, fitted the bill perfectly.

She sang in the shower and while she dressed. In her own way, Jessica was becoming as important to her as Nathan; her affection for the girl might easily grow into love one day.

The afternoon, thank goodness, was dry, the sky pastel-blue with no sign of rain clouds. Greer shuffled her feet as she waited, risking a glance at her watch. 2.05 pm. Jessica wouldn't let her down. Right?

Ah, there she was. How silly she'd been to worry.

'Sorry I'm late.' Jessica hurried up to Greer. Her breath came in rapid puffs. 'Work was manic. Didn't think I'd ever get away.' She eyed Greer with a critical gaze. 'How are you? You sure you're up to walking?'

Greer laughed. 'Don't worry, I'm fine. I'll tell you if I need to stop.'

'We won't go too far. Just to those benches over there, and then we'll sit down.'

They set off, with the wind ruffling Greer's hair, the sky pastel-blue. The shouts of children rang loud in her ears as the two of them strolled through the park. Jessica was walking slower than usual, clearly for Greer's benefit. Such a caring girl.

What a great idea this had been, spending time together. Jessica was Nathan's sister; she deserved Greer's attention too. The girl lacked Nathan's confidence, being almost mousy in comparison. She needed encouragement, that was all. Greer doubted Isla bloody Taylor was much of a mother to Jessica.

Greer could fill that gap. If this sweet girl wanted her to.

They'd reached the benches Jessica had mentioned, next to a wooden shack that sold refreshments. 'Let's sit down,' Jessica said. 'I could do with a rest.'

Greer smiled at the obvious lie. How considerate, but she felt fine. A little breathless, but otherwise okay.

'I'll buy us both a coffee.' Without waiting for a reply, she headed towards the shack.

While Greer waited, she kept a watchful eye on Jessica. The girl's shoulders were hunched, her gaze downcast. She didn't look happy. Had Nathan upset her again?

Probably. He definitely wasn't Mr Nice Guy. The sooner Tom's heart worked its magic, the better.

Happy times would then follow. Nathan and Jessica, visiting Greer, the three of them laughing and chatting. Both saying how much more of a mother than Isla Greer was. Greer, hugging Jessica close. 'I'll always be your mum, Rose. Yours too, Tom.'

Oh, dear God. Had she really just thought that?

She needed to be more careful. One slip of the tongue, and she'd ruin everything.

'What can I get you, love?' The stallholder's voice snapped Greer back to reality.

'Two flat whites, please.' She couldn't remember how Jessica took her coffee, so it seemed a safe choice. She paid the man and headed back over to Jessica.

Greer sat beside her and handed her a coffee. 'How's work?'

A shrug. 'Same old, same old. Bedpans. Wiping backsides. Changing sheets.'

Greer squeezed her arm. 'It's only as long as Nathan needs help, right? Once he's well again, you can apply for a new job.'

Jessica shifted restlessly. 'You sound like Mum.' Her tone was bitter. 'The thing is, I work long hours and go home drained. I barely get time to look after myself, let alone someone else. And Nathan—well, you've seen how abrasive he can be. How ungrateful.'

Jessica looked stricken. 'Oh, God, I'm so sorry. I didn't mean that as a dig at you. You were so appreciative yesterday, whereas Nathan—he doesn't even say thank you. No wonder I get annoyed.'

'I think you're doing a wonderful job. And you have me now, remember? I'll help, especially with the cooking.'

'That's really kind. Thank you.' A pause. Followed by a deep breath. 'Um, this is really difficult for me. But can we talk? About Nathan?'

'I'm listening. What's wrong? Tell me, Jessica.'

'During our video chats, you told me a bunch of stuff. About Tom.' She sighed. 'I'm sorry. I don't want to dredge up terrible memories for you. I just thought I should tell you.'

'Tell me what?'

'You said Tom had been dating someone. You didn't know who, but you believe the guy drove Tom to take his own life, right?'

'Yes.' Where was Jessica going with this?

'And how you hated that guy. Wanted him to suffer.'

Greer nodded. One day, she'd find Tom's killer, with or without Charlie's help. Make him pay.

'Nathan won't have told you this, but he's bisexual,' Jessica continued. 'He doesn't treat the men he sleeps with any better than he does his girlfriends, believe me.'

'I don't understand. If he's bisexual, why would he slag off gay men?'

'It's all a front to maintain his image. His employers are pretty old-school and don't have a clue, neither do his mates. Even Mum doesn't know. I'm the only person who does.' She grimaced. 'I wish to God I didn't. Nathan's always bragging about the men he's shagged. He gets a kick out of embarrassing me.'

Anger flared in Greer. *I hate queers.* Nathan was a bigger hypocrite than she'd realised. 'How did you find out? Did he tell you?'

'No. I dropped by one day unannounced while he was with some guy. The two of them were naked in his living room.' Her cheeks flushed. 'He swore me to secrecy. '

Jessica cleared her throat. 'Here comes the hard part. I remembered Nathan banging on about some guy he hooked up with in Bristol a couple of years back, before his heart problems escalated. Nathan was a regular in the gay clubs there.'

Icy fear clutched Greer's heart. She didn't like where this was heading.

'Yet another one he ditched once he'd got what he wanted.' Contempt laced Jessica's tone. 'He said the guy was a graphic designer. And that his name was—' She bit her lip, her expression troubled. 'Tom.'

CHAPTER 51

The world stilled around Greer. She stared at Jessica, unable to respond.

'I agonised over whether to tell you. I realise how close you've got to my brother. But he's not a good person, Greer. Honestly, he isn't. And you're so sweet, and so kind, and I knew I had to say something, even though I didn't want to.' Jessica's words tumbled out in a mad rush.

'It can't have been my Tom. It's a common enough name. Besides, lots of guys are graphic designers.'

'Listen to me, please—'

'You're mistaken. The odds of Nathan getting the heart of an ex-lover must be a million to one.'

'I wanted to be sure before I said anything. So I told Nathan that a friend in Bristol needed a graphic designer. How I thought he'd once mentioned some guy called Tom.'

Greer licked her dry lips. 'What did he say?'

'The usual shit. But yeah, he confirmed he'd had a fling with a graphic designer called Tom. I asked if he still had his number, or remembered where he lived.' Jessica blew out a breath. 'Nathan laughed.

Said he never kept mobile numbers from random hook-ups. I pressed him about the address, and he said—' She glanced away. 'Redfield. Didn't you say your son lived in Redfield?'

Icy dread stilled Greer's tongue. She ran through the facts.

Okay, so Nathan was bisexual. He'd dated, then dumped, a graphic designer called Tom. By itself, that meant little. A weird coincidence, nothing more. If the guy also lived in Redfield, though? Coincidence might then turn into something more solid.

'I was worried he'd make the connection,' Jessica continued. 'But he didn't. Men, like women, are two a penny to Nathan. And he's totally self-absorbed. The possibility that he'd once dated the man who'd donated his new heart never occurred to him.'

Oh, God. This was all too much. Nathan had been Tom's secret boyfriend.

She now understood Tom's nicknaming him Blue. Nathan's most striking feature was his piercing cornflower eyes.

Something seemed off, though. 'Okay, so Tom dated Nathan in Bristol. But how did they hook up again a while ago, if Nathan was so sick? He told me he could hardly walk across his living room. Besides, he'd moved to Birmingham by then.'

'You can't trust a word Nathan says. Yes, he struggled with his breathing. His energy levels, too. But nowhere near as badly as he pretends. Tom got Nathan's contact details from a mutual friend. Told him he wanted another chance, but Nathan laughed in his face. Only after they'd had sex, of course. Said he didn't like reheated leftovers.' Her face flushed. 'I'm sorry. This must be hard to hear.'

Jessica had no idea. Her beloved Tom, spurned by a man not fit to grovel in the dirt before him.

A lone magpie hopped in front of Greer, eyed her with a beady stare, then flew off. One for sorrow, as the nursery rhyme went. She shivered, and not just from the breeze.

'I understand you care about Nathan,' Jessica said. 'And that you've given him money. He'll hassle you for more, but you have to say no, because he already has loads. If he told you otherwise, it's a pack of lies. Don't let him take advantage more than he's already done.'

Too right. Nathan wouldn't be getting another penny.

'That was the reason I was so upset that day I ran away from you. I'd just found out, and I had no idea how to tell you, or even whether I should. Oh, God, now I've made you cry.' She fished in her bag for a tissue and handed it to Greer. 'My brother is vile. You deserve better. So does Tom's memory.'

Jessica was correct. Nathan had brought about Tom's death.

For that, Greer intended to make him pay.

There was one problem, though. Her darling boy's heart still beat in Nathan Taylor's chest.

CHAPTER 52

Beth picked up her mobile. Time to contact Greer, who, as far as she knew, was still in Birmingham, recovering from her heart attack. With any luck, she'd be back in Bristol soon; they'd have a proper catch-up then.

Greer answered straightaway. 'I'm so glad you called.' She sounded like she'd been crying. 'Something awful's happened.'

The poor love. Right after her heart attack, too. 'What is it, Greer? Talk to me, please.'

More sobs, but Greer didn't reply. Beth tried again. 'How are you feeling? Are you out of hospital yet?'

A muffled 'yes'.

Better not to press Greer. Let her talk when she was ready.

Eventually Beth heard Greer blow her nose, clear her throat. 'It's about Nathan.'

Beth suppressed a sigh. Wasn't it always?

'I hate him. So much. I want to kill the bastard.'

Greer had clearly fallen out with Nathan. That was probably for the best. Her preoccupation with him would die a natural death, and she could grieve properly for her son. 'What's happened?'

Greer told her.

This wasn't good. Not at all. Her neighbour's obsession with Nathan Taylor was getting stronger, not weaker. Just in a different direction. Besides, what Greer was telling her all seemed very unlikely.

She exhaled a long breath. 'This is all so weird. It doesn't sound right to me, if I'm honest, Greer. An incredible coincidence, don't you think? That the man who received your son's heart is the same person who drove him to suicide.'

'That's what I thought at first. But then I realised bizarre coincidences happen all the time. Did you hear about the man who got killed by a taxi while riding a moped? One year later, to the very day, his brother was killed riding the same moped. By the same taxi, driven by the same driver.'

'I still reckon you and Jessica are making something out of nothing.'

A huff of annoyance from Greer. 'Jessica said Nathan dated, then dumped a graphic designer called Tom who lived in Redfield. And Tom's boyfriend had blue eyes. So does Nathan.'

'Lots of people do. Tom's a common name, and graphic designers are two a penny.'

'You're not listening. Nathan Taylor is an opportunistic bastard who preys on people, me included. He conned me out of thousands of pounds. I should have listened to his mother when she told me he was rotten.'

Why was Greer being so stubborn? 'You're jumping to conclusions. So is Jessica. What if Nathan told Jessica Redland, not Redfield? Easy to confuse the two.'

'No. Nathan's the bastard who killed my boy, and I'm going to make him pay. You see if I don't.'

Whoa. Crazy talk. Beth needed to rein Greer in, and quickly. 'I think you need professional help, my love. A trained counsellor, someone to talk to about Tom's death. That's what started your obsession with Nathan Taylor.'

'You don't understand. Nathan's warped, evil. He killed Tom. Not directly, but as good as.'

'Let's not fall out over this. Can we talk again when you're not so upset?'

Her neighbour's words roared through Beth's head. *I want to kill the bastard...*

Greer didn't mean it literally, of course, but all this stress was bad for her heart. The sooner she was back in Bristol, where Beth could keep an eye on her, the better.

Greer threw her mobile across the room. Damn Beth Randall and her scepticism. No matter what her neighbour thought, Nathan Taylor was a snake in human form who'd caused Tom's death. She'd been naïve and was now paying the price. Literally, what with all the money she'd given Nathan.

He'd suckered her from day one. Seen her designer clothes, the fake Cartier, and assumed, wrongly, that Greer was wealthy. With funds he could tap, if he kept her sweet. He'd obviously had a rethink after throwing her out of his flat that first time.

All that crap he'd spouted about cellular memory. The bastard was just recycling what she'd already revealed about Tom. Those drawings—he'd simply bought them, erased the artist's initials and substituted his own. Not once had he mentioned stuff she'd not told him, like Tom's love of D H Lawrence's novels. Fake, all of it.

And what about all the sugary flattery? *You're becoming more of a mother to me than my own's ever been.* How had she not seen through Nathan's blatant insincerity?

Because she'd been desperate to believe him. The rhythmic *lub-dub* of Tom's heart had lured Greer into Nathan's web, rendering her helpless. She should have listened when Isla warned her about Nathan. Unlike Greer, Isla saw her son as he really was. Not how a foolish, grieving woman like Greer had hoped he'd be.

She'd proved a sucker for Nathan's machinations. So had Tom. Not only had Nathan broken her son's heart, but he'd nearly destroyed Greer's, too. The deception was almost too much to bear. Greer curled into a ball and cried.

Images pulsed through her head. Tom, lying naked on his bed, self-poisoned by pills and whisky. Greer, listening to Nathan talk of his newfound love of fish dishes. Her joy at seeing those beautiful drawings. The demands for money, the honeyed assurances of a prompt payback. Round and round the mental pictures swirled. A hard shell was forming around Greer's heart, right when she'd hoped it was softening.

She sat up and wiped her eyes. Anger, sweet and slow-burning, was replacing self-recrimination. One word beat, louder and stronger, in her brain. *Payback. Payback. Payback.*

Hadn't she vowed to confront the man who killed Tom?

Yes, she had.

Wouldn't punishment be better than confrontation?

Another yes.

Means, motive, and opportunity, as the saying went.

Means. Easy enough to substitute Nathan's medication with homeopathic pills, or aspirin. He never looked at them anyway, just downed them with a swig of water.

Motive. That one was obvious.

Opportunity. Greer knew where Nathan kept the spare key to his flat. As well as the date of his next hospital check-up. A time when he definitely wouldn't be home.

Food for thought.

She liked the idea. A lot.

But what about Tom's heart? Could she lose her last link with her darling boy?

Dare she risk that precious organ being corrupted by Nathan, though? What if cellular memory worked in reverse, as she'd once feared?

CHAPTER 53

The next morning, Greer made herself breakfast, deliberately blocking any thoughts about revenge on Nathan. Better to allow the idea to percolate for a while.

As she bit into her toast, her phone vibrated with a text. Charlie's name was on the screen. *Can we talk? Please?*

There seemed no reason to refuse. Charlie had been rude to Nathan, and acting weird, when they'd last met, but now she understood why. What was it he'd said about Nathan? *He's so phony... That fake laugh...*

Charlie was obviously a far better judge of character than she was. Besides, he'd been Tom's best friend and almost a second son to her. She couldn't stay mad at him for long.

Greer tapped out a quick reply. *Of course.*

I'm in Birmingham to watch City play Sheffield United. I need to tell you something. Could I come to your place?

Interesting. Might Charlie also have found out about Nathan and Tom? Well, he'd get a surprise once he realised Greer already knew of Nathan's duplicity.

Tonight at eight? Charlie confirmed that was convenient, so Greer gave him her address. It would be good to see him again.

At eight pm precisely, Greer's doorbell buzzed. Charlie greeted her with a wide smile once she opened the door. She smiled when she spotted his Birmingham City football shirt. He'd always been a huge fan.

'Hey, Mrs M,' he said, once he'd hugged Greer. 'How are you doing? I've been so worried about you. What have your doctors told you?'

Greer waved a dismissive hand. 'Nutrition, exercise, the usual. Different pills.' She steered him inside her living room. 'Have a seat. Can I offer you a drink?' Knowing Charlie, he'd have taken a taxi in order to consume alcohol. Before long, they'd be having a serious chat about his drinking. Tonight wasn't the time, though.

She'd guessed correctly. 'My car's back at the hotel. So I'm good for a beer.'

London Pride for Charlie, and Merlot for Greer, then. Once they'd settled themselves with their drinks, Charlie cleared his throat. 'I'm sorry about what happened at Nathan's. I realise I appeared rude. There's something I need to tell you, though. About who he might have dated when he lived in Bristol.'

It was as she'd thought. The strange way Charlie had stared at Nathan's digital photo frame. He'd obviously seen a picture of Nathan with Tom. By the time Greer had spotted Charlie's shock, the display had moved on to Nathan with someone else. 'I already know.'

Surprise flashed on Charlie's face. 'You do?' Then he nodded. 'I'm guessing you've seen the photo too. The one on his digital display.'

Greer shook her head. 'His sister told me.'

'I presume the police discovered the connection, questioned him, and ruled him out. I can't help wondering, though. Whether he killed her.'

Greer stared at Charlie. What on earth was he talking about? 'Killed who?'

'Lily Hamilton, of course. Who else?'

Greer set her wineglass on the coffee table. 'I don't understand. What makes you think Nathan had anything to do with her death?'

'That's who I saw on his digital display. Lily Hamilton, Nathan with his arm slung around her.'

She'd not expected that. A simple explanation existed, though. 'Nathan's heart problems began in Bristol. Lily was a cardiac nurse, remember. Given his medical history, Nathan must have met her at the BRI.'

'I'm not disputing that. The way he spoke about her when you were making coffee pissed me off, though. Pure spite. It was pretty obvious she'd rejected him when he'd asked for a date.'

'That doesn't mean he's a killer.'

'Some guys react badly to being spurned. Anyway, Lily was too smart to fall prey to a stranger. She must have known whoever murdered her.'

'Not necessarily.'

Charlie looked unconvinced. 'Besides, this is personal. The cops questioned me about her disappearance, remember?'

'He probably has photos with all of his nurses. Leave Lily Hamilton's murder to the police, Charlie. I doubt Nathan was involved.'

'But—'

'We've obviously been talking at cross-purposes.' She relayed what Jessica had told her about Nathan having dated Tom. 'He's the one who hurt my boy, Charlie. I hate the bastard. He deserves to die.'

Charlie drained his beer, then popped the cap on a fresh bottle. 'It all sounds a bit implausible, Mrs M. There was probably more than one graphic designer called Tom in Redfield back then. Or perhaps Jessica misheard, and Nathan said Redland, not Redfield.'

'That's exactly what Beth said. You're wrong, both of you.'

'You need to be careful here, Mrs M. You're in danger of going off at half-cock at him on zero evidence.'

'Like you with that photo of Nathan and Lily?'

'Perhaps you're right. I just don't like the guy.'

Well, that made two of them. 'After Tom's death, I made my boy a promise. I swore I'd hunt down the man who'd hurt him, and I'd make him pay. And now I've found him. Nathan's guilty as hell. Soon he's going to be sorry. As soon as I decide how.'

'Please stop with the crazy talk. You don't look well.' Concern filled Charlie's face. 'Hardly surprising. You had a heart attack, remember?'

'Don't patronise me. I'm fine. I just wish you'd believe me about Nathan.'

'Let it go, Mrs M. Please.'

'I can't. I won't. He's lied, conned money from me, and now this. All the evidence fits. Tom's journal mentions he nicknamed his boyfriend Blue. You've seen Nathan's eyes, right? And you told me Tom dated a guy who moved away from Bristol.'

Shock flew into Charlie's face. 'Have you been snooping through Tom's diary again? Mrs M, we talked about that. It's a huge invasion of privacy.'

'Only the first few pages. I'm his mother. I needed to know.'

'I'm begging you. Don't read any more of it. Please. Tom wouldn't have wanted that.'

He was right, of course. 'I don't need to now, do I?

Charlie blew out a breath. 'I can't help feeling that Nathan might have been involved in Lily's murder, though. The police should at least interview him again.'

'Take your own advice, Charlie. Let it go.'

Charlie drained his beer. 'Not sure I can, Mrs M.'

CHAPTER 54

Nathan Taylor deserves to die. Five words on constant replay in Greer's head.

Impossible to face him, not yet. Nathan had messaged several times, asking about her health, should he come round, etc. What a bastard, trying to pretend he cared. He needed to stay the hell away from her. She'd not be responsible for her actions should he walk through her door.

It was vital he didn't realise she'd rumbled him. A brief message did the trick. *Been told to rest. Will be in touch soon.*

Greer had lied about needing to rest. Since her heart attack, she tired easily and needed more sleep, but overall she felt fine. More than capable of going out each day.

Her journeys always took her to Nathan's block of flats. Greer would sit in the coffee shop opposite, staring at the building, thinking. About his spare key, hidden in the utilities cupboard outside his flat. His pillbox of medication. How he never looked at his tablets before taking them.

What was it he'd said? *Without the immunosuppressants, my body would spiral into rejection mode pretty damn quick.*

A few times, Nathan left and didn't return for hours. It would be so easy to cross the road, take the key, and slip inside his flat. Switch out his pills, the way she'd previously imagined.

So very easy.

―—⁓⁓―—

Greer's anger had festered long enough; plotting Nathan's death had done nothing to calm it. She needed to confront the bastard with what he'd done.

Late one afternoon, she arrived unannounced at Nathan's flat. There were things she needed to say to Nathan bloody Taylor. At the very least, she'd force him to admit his hypocrisy. His vile behaviour. How cruel he'd been to Tom.

Irritation flashed across Nathan's features upon opening the door, before he pasted on a false smile. 'Greer! What brings you here? We hadn't arranged anything, right?'

'Correct.' She stepped past him and into the living room.

Nathan lounged against a bookcase, his expression wary. 'This isn't a good time, Greer. Mum said she might call in. To be honest, I'm feeling pretty rough. Can't breathe properly, got chills all over me, and I'm running a temperature.'

'Take a paracetamol. It's probably just a cold.' He definitely looked ill. Sweaty and unnaturally pale. As if Greer cared.

'You don't understand. This might be the start of organ rejection. I need to get to the hospital, but I'm not up to driving. I should call an ambulance.'

What if he was right? Suppose Nathan's body was spurning Tom's heart?

Nathan rubbed his hand over his forehead, which was slick with sweat. 'This can't be happening. I've been taking all my medication. My weekly checks have been fine.'

'Then you're probably okay. Stop fussing.'

'I'm really not well. Can you take me to the hospital, please? It's not far.'

Greer shrugged. 'You're overreacting. Try to keep things in perspective. Pop a paracetamol, and if you're not better in half an hour, I'll drive you to a hospital. How's that?'

Nathan blanched. 'I might be dying. Can't we go now?'

'There's something I need to ask first.'

'Some other time, for Christ's sake. I feel like shit.' Nathan stared at her. 'What the hell's wrong with you? You're not yourself today.'

'How perceptive.' Greer's tone was as sharp as her anger.

Nathan slumped in a chair. He looked worse now than when Greer arrived: sweatier, paler. She remained standing, her arms folded.

'Well, spit it out,' Nathan said. 'Can't you see I'm ill?'

'You could drop dead and I wouldn't bat an eye. Not after what you did to Tom.'

Shock flooded Nathan's face. 'What did you just say?'

'You heard me. You're a cold, misogynistic, homophobic monster, and I want revenge.'

Bewilderment showed in his expression. 'What are you talking about? This is no time for games. I need to call a fucking ambulance, except I can't find my phone. Where the hell is Mum? Why couldn't the useless bitch turn up like she promised?'

'I'm here about Tom. Did you, or did you not, have a sexual relationship with my son?'

Nathan stared at Greer, his mouth slack with shock. 'What the hell? I never even met him.'

The lying bastard. 'Wrong. You drove my boy to take his own life.'

'Where's all this crap coming from? Why would you say such a thing?'

No way would Greer land Jessica in trouble. Nathan had obviously forgotten his conversation with his sister. 'Tom. My son. He was a decent guy. You should have been grateful to get his heart. Instead, you slagged off gay men. Quite the hypocrite, aren't you?'

'I—'

'As well as a liar. You faked cellular memory to con money out of me. All that crap about how you'd started liking fish, how you developed an aptitude for drawing. You may have duped me for a while, but not any longer.'

A sneer. 'You stupid bitch. You lapped it up, didn't you? So fucking gullible.'

'You've no reason to pretend anymore. So go ahead, tell me about it. How you broke Tom's heart, then dumped him. You might as well have put those packets of pills in his hand yourself.'

Nathan struggled to get up from his seat. The effort proved too much, and he slumped down again. 'I'll say anything you like if you grab me some paracetamol, then drive me to a hospital. Bathroom cabinet, top shelf.'

Greer walked from the room towards Nathan's bathroom. When she returned with the paracetamol, a wheeze sounded from Nathan's chest. 'Check this out,' he said. He pulled up his trouser legs to reveal ankles that were swollen and red. 'I've developed a stomach ache, too. Fucking hell, this can't be happening. I need an ambulance. As soon as possible. Where the hell is my phone?'

Greer handed him the bottle. Nathan twisted off the cap and dry-swallowed some tablets.

'You don't think you just need extra rest?'

'No, of course I don't need some fucking rest! My body is going into organ rejection, you stupid cow. For God's sake, call me a bloody ambulance!' Nathan tried to stand up but collapsed back on the sofa. His skin was an ugly grey colour. The wheeze in his chest had increased in volume.

'You goddamn cow. I know you've got your phone on you. Call me an ambulance, for God's sake. Before it's too late.'

Greer opened her handbag, extracted her mobile. She waved it in front of his face, just out of reach. 'You drove my son to commit suicide. All you have to do is admit it. Then I'll call you an ambulance.'

Another wet wheeze. 'You're insane.'

'Say it. Say, "I killed Tom Maddox".'

Nathan's lips had turned blue. 'Yeah, you mad bitch. I shagged him, then I killed him. Happy now? Now call me a fucking ambulance.'

CHAPTER 55

The buzzer to Nathan's flat sounded. Fists pounded on the door. Followed by Isla's voice, shouting through the letterbox. 'Nathan! Greer! Open the door. Now.'

Greer cast a glance at Nathan. Was he still alive? His eyes fluttered, so yes. She grabbed her mobile, stabbing the 'nine' button three times while she opened the door to Isla. Nathan's mother pushed past her, spotted her son, and ran to his side.

Meanwhile, Greer, still in the hallway, spoke into the phone. 'He's collapsed. Hardly breathing. He had a heart transplant recently. I'm worried he's suffering organ rejection.' Greer gave Nathan's address before the operator ended the call. He'd assured her an ambulance would attend as soon as possible.

Greer ran into the living room. Isla's arms were around Nathan, tears soaking her cheeks. 'What the hell happened? That was 999 you were calling, I presume?'

'Oh, God. Is he still breathing?' Nathan's lips were now almost purple. 'Yes, of course I called an ambulance. As to what happened, I came round earlier to speak with Nathan. He told me he wasn't feeling well. Then he collapsed. Right before you arrived.'

Isla didn't appear to be taking any notice. 'He's still breathing.' Her tone sounded strangled. 'Still breathing. He's still breathing.' As though the words were a mantra that could save her son.

It was probably too late for that. The bastard needed to die. That way, Tom got the justice he deserved.

They waited in silence for what seemed like forever. 'Where is the ambulance? Why is it taking so long?' Isla's voice was a wail of anguish.

Sirens sounded in the distance. Hope edged into Isla's face. Minutes later, footsteps pounded up the stairwell. Fists banged on the door, rang the bell. Greer rushed to let them in, pointing to the living room. 'He's in there.'

'Move aside, please, ma'am, so we can help him,' the male paramedic said to Isla. His female colleague listened as Greer spun her version of events. Beside, Isla stood pale, silent, spent. Her gaze fixed on Nathan.

'We need to transport him to a hospital immediately.' The two paramedics transferred Nathan's inert body to a stretcher and carried him from the flat. Isla followed them, with Greer close behind.

'That's my son,' Isla said. 'I'll ride in the ambulance with him.'

'Me too.' It was vital Greer knew whether Nathan lived or died.

'Like hell you will. I'm his mother. You're nothing to him, do you understand?' Isla shoved Greer out of the way, then hurried down the stairs after the paramedics.

Greer dragged in a deep breath. Damn Isla bloody Taylor. If she hadn't arrived when she did, by now Nathan would be dead. If he survived, it would be Greer's word against his about their discussion before he'd collapsed. Nathan couldn't prove anything.

CHAPTER 56

Greer made her way back to her rented flat. Once home, she poured herself a glass of wine and sprawled on the sofa. It was too soon to phone the hospital, and the staff wouldn't discuss Nathan with her anyway, given that she wasn't a relative.

Impossible to ask Isla about her son. That left Jessica. Isla might be a lousy mother, but she'd still tell her daughter that Nathan was critically ill. Sorted, then. Greer would text Jessica tomorrow.

Not that Greer cared a jot about Nathan. What concerned her was Tom. If Nathan died, so would her beloved boy's heart. Her last connection to him.

Earlier, everything had seemed so simple. Justice for Tom had been all that mattered. Now the future of his heart meant everything.

Wait a minute. Might the hospital remove Tom's heart from Nathan and reuse it? Two transplants of the same organ—was that even possible? For part of Tom to still live on?

Her only hope. All Greer had to cling to.

Between bouts of wakefulness that night, Greer snatched a few brief dozes. Exhausted, she stumbled out of bed at six am, reaching straight for her mobile. A quick text to Jessica. *I was with Nathan yesterday when he became ill. Can you keep me informed, please? Thinking of you. X.*

The morning dragged by without so much as a beep from her phone. Midday came. Should she call Jessica? Leave it another hour?

Her mobile rang. Jessica's name appeared on the screen. Greer stabbed the 'accept call' icon.

'Nathan's dead.' Jessica sounded like she'd been crying. 'He died not long after he got to the hospital. The doctors did their best, but he was too far gone.'

'Oh, my God. I'm so sorry, sweetheart.' Greer exhaled a guilty breath. What had she said the day before to Nathan? Ah, yes, that was it. *Quite the hypocrite, aren't you?* The pot calling the kettle black, no less. Jessica had just lost her brother, though. What else could Greer have said?

'Organ rejection's always a risk,' Jessica continued. 'Despite the medication, the check-ups. Mum's out of her mind with grief, of course.'

Greer didn't doubt that. Jessica was her chief concern, however. 'Can I do anything to help? Will you be all right?'

A strangled sob. 'Thank you. I'll be fine, honestly. Mum's my priority. She needs all the love I can give her.'

Greer swallowed. She longed to ask about Tom's heart, but it wasn't the time. Later, when Jessica was less raw with grief. 'I'm here for you, sweetheart. Call me if you need me.'

Jessica didn't call or text over the next few days. Greer realised she shouldn't trouble the girl when she was grieving. Better to wait a while, then go to the care home where she worked. Assuming she wasn't on compassionate leave, that was. She'd hang around until Jessica finished her shift, and then they would talk.

How hard it was to wait, though.

Once she judged enough time had passed, Greer set off to drive to Willowbank Care Home. She parked up outside, prepared to stay for as long as was necessary. A nearby bus shelter provided the perfect spot to wait, despite the chilly breeze. Greer huddled into her coat, counting the minutes.

After half an hour, the front door opened, and Jessica emerged. As she drew nearer, Greer stood up and walked over to her. 'Hello, sweetheart. How are you holding up?'

Not good, it seemed. The girl looked tired, pale, and had shed weight she could ill afford to lose. Well, it couldn't be easy for her. She'd just lost her brother, and Isla was too wrapped up in her own pain to care for her daughter.

Jessica shrugged. 'I'm okay. Sorry I've not been in touch. It's been a difficult time.'

Greer nodded. 'You're right.'

Jessica smiled, but it didn't reach her eyes. 'It's good to see you again. I need to get back to Mum, though. She's in a bad way.'

'I understand. I just wondered if the hospital had transplanted Tom's heart into someone else. Nathan was on the donation register, and—'

Jessica's smile was sad. 'I might have guessed you'd ask that. The answer is no.'

Greer's throat constricted with disappointment. 'Why?' Her voice was a dry croak.

'Too damaged. His body rejected it, remember?'

So that was that. She'd never hear Tom's heart beat again. Grief almost drove Greer to her knees, but somehow she stayed upright.

'I'm sorry, but I really should go,' Jessica said. She touched Greer's arm, concern in her expression. 'You take care of yourself, okay?'

At her Airbnb flat, Greer packed quickly, then messaged the landlord to say she was leaving. Birmingham held nothing for her anymore.

That night, back in Bristol, she slept holding Tom's sweatshirt for the first time in ages. It no longer smelled of him. She'd lost every last trace of her son.

CHAPTER 57

Beth hacked away at the dead plants in her garden. What was going on with Greer these days? Her neighbour had seemed subdued earlier, but hadn't opened up to Beth's gentle probing. Very worrying.

At least Greer was back in Bristol; all that nonsense about moving to Birmingham had vanished, it seemed. And not before time. Greer's fixation on Nathan Taylor had been unhealthy, in Beth's opinion. Perhaps now she could grieve for Tom properly.

Beth slung the remaining clippings in her basket and tucked her secateurs into a side pocket. She was just about to make herself a coffee when she spotted a woman walking up the driveway to Greer's house. Tall, a little overweight, her caramel-coloured hair swept up in a messy bun. Beth edged closer to the dividing fence to get a better look.

Oh dear. The woman mustn't have checked in the mirror before going out. An expensive-looking designer jacket, yet buttoned up wrongly. Handbag a dark brown that didn't match her black trousers. No make-up; Beth would have expected a swipe of lipstick, if nothing else. And that scruffy hair...

Poor love. She didn't look well, not at all.

As Greer's visitor reached out to ring the doorbell, Beth spoke up. 'Greer's not home right now. She popped into town earlier and won't be back for a while.'

The woman stared at her. Now that Beth saw her full-face, she looked really ill. Eyes red-rimmed, an unhealthy pallor to her skin.

'I'll stop by later,' the woman said. Her tone was curt.

'Can I give Greer a message?'

'Tell her Isla Taylor called. And that I'll be back.'

Nathan's mother. Greer had mentioned her to Beth with unmistakable dislike.

Not good. Had this woman come to hassle Greer? She definitely sounded angry.

But so unhappy, too. Beth recognised misery when she saw it, and Isla seemed as if her entire world had imploded.

'Would you care for a coffee?' Surely Isla wouldn't say no? 'It's about to pour down, and I'm sure you haven't got an umbrella in that tiny bag.'

Isla stared at Beth, clearly unsure how to respond. 'It's kind of you, but—'

'No buts. It'll be my pleasure.' Beth needed to get Isla inside right away. The woman was so pale she might faint any minute. The rain fell more heavily, and Isla nodded. 'All right. Just a quick coffee.'

She made her way down Greer's drive, and up Beth's, following her inside. Beth led her into the kitchen and pulled out a chair at the table.

'Make yourself comfortable. Tea or coffee? Milk, sugar?'

'Coffee, please. Black, no sugar.'

Beth busied herself with mugs and spoons, as well as sliding two chocolate brownies onto a plate. Isla's haggard face indicated she'd not bothered with food recently.

Minutes later, she placed the coffees and cakes on the table. 'Greer might not be back for a while. I'll tell her you called. Get her to contact you.'

'I doubt she'll do that,' Isla said. 'She murdered my son.'

Beth's mouth fell open with shock. Greer hadn't mentioned that Nathan had died. 'I'm sorry—*what* did you just say?'

'My Nathan is dead. That bitch killed him.' Isla's face crumpled, and her noisy sobs filled the room.

Well, this was weird. Worrying too. Greer might be a cold fish, but *murder*? Isla's grief must mean she wasn't thinking straight. The woman had Beth's sympathy, but...

At last Isla seemed to have sobbed herself dry. 'It was his heart. Organ rejection, according to the hospital.'

Beth set down her coffee mug, pausing before she responded. Isla was so fragile, so wounded, and she needed to proceed carefully. 'I don't understand. If Nathan's body rejected his new heart, why would you say Greer killed him?'

'Because his last check-up, almost a week before his death, showed everything was fine. I kept asking him whether he was taking his medication, and he always assured me he never missed a dose. I can't help thinking Greer tampered with his tablets, or brought on heart failure somehow, or—'

Both options sounded unlikely, in Beth's opinion. 'I realise you're looking for answers. But you can't go slinging wild accusations around. Besides, the diagnosis was organ rejection, not a heart attack.

I'm no doctor, but surely they're different. I'm sorry, but I can't fathom why you'd point the finger at Greer.'

'You don't believe me.' Isla's tone was flat. 'Nobody does.'

'Isla—'

'My daughter said the same thing. I told the hospital I wanted a post-mortem done on Nathan, but the doctors tried to talk me out of it. Insisted their diagnosis was correct. They implied grief was clouding my judgement. I did my best to insist, but Jessica—that's my daughter—told me that Nathan had shown all the classic symptoms of organ rejection. She's a nurse, so she should know.'

'You should listen to her.' Beth needed to choose her words with care. 'You're grieving, and I'm so sorry for your loss, truly I am. A post-mortem, though—would you really want to subject your son's body to that?'

Isla wiped away a tear. 'That's what Jessica said.'

'She's right. How are you holding up?'

Isla blew her nose. 'Like you'd expect. I'm not eating, barely sleeping. Can I ask you something? How well do you know Greer Maddox?'

Beth shrugged. 'We're friends, but she's a closed book. Why?'

'I just have a strong gut feeling that something isn't right with that woman. She was at Nathan's flat the day he died. I called round and there she was, behaving like she owned the place. Nathan had already gone into cardiac arrest and she'd phoned 999, but her manner seemed off. The way she looked at Nathan, as if she hated him. Until then, she'd been obsessed with him, like he was a substitute son. I've no idea what changed, or why. But I can't help wondering if she engineered Nathan's death.'

'But you've no concrete evidence?'

'Only the fact I caught her grinning, just for a second, while we waited for the ambulance. The minute she spotted me staring, she switched to looking all concerned, even though she obviously wasn't. What she shouted at him made me suspicious too.'

'What was that?'

Isla paused, drew in a deep breath. 'When I arrived at his flat, I heard voices before I rang the bell. Nathan said something I didn't catch. Greer yelled back about how Nathan had to admit he'd driven her son to suicide. How she'd only call an ambulance if he did. I was so shocked I froze and didn't hear Nathan's reply. Then the word 'ambulance' sank in, and I realised my son needed urgent help. That's when I pounded on the door, desperate to get inside.'

What a dilemma. Beth had no wish to betray Greer's trust or speak out of turn. 'I'm no psychologist, but I suspect Greer is mentally ill. Like you, she's dealing with the death of her child. I won't go into details, but she's had a tragic life. I think she deflected her grief by becoming obsessed with Nathan.'

'So what changed? One minute she's all over him, the next she loathes him, couldn't care less that he was dying in front of her eyes.'

'Please don't get upset, Isla. But it's a long way from shouting at someone to actually killing them. Are you certain you heard right?'

Isla looked unsure. 'It all happened so fast. And once I realised Nathan was seriously ill, everything became a blur. That's why I haven't gone to the police. They're like the NHS—overstretched and under-funded, and I have no concrete evidence. Just a gut feeling that Greer knows more than she's letting on.'

Beth took the plunge. 'Why did you come here today?'

'Good question. I hoped if I confronted her, I'd get my answer, no matter how she replied. I've always been good at reading people. I just wish I understood why she turned against Nathan so much.'

'Like I said, Greer might be mentally unbalanced. She got it into her head that Nathan dated, and then dumped, her son, leading to Tom committing suicide.'

Isla shook her head. 'No way. Nathan only dated women. Besides, even if he slept with men, what are the odds of him receiving a heart from one of them? Almost zero.'

'That's exactly what I told Greer.' Beth wasn't about to get Jessica in trouble with her mum over her claims about Nathan and Tom. The girl must have got some essential details wrong. The two men had most likely never met, let alone formed a relationship.

Isla was silent for a while. Then: 'You're probably right in thinking she's unbalanced. But I can't get it out of my head that she's responsible for Nathan's death.'

CHAPTER 58

Beth stared at the big guy browsing the beer aisle in Sainsbury's. He looked familiar, but for a second she couldn't place him. Ah, yes; Charlie, that nice young man she'd met when visiting Greer. She tapped him on the shoulder. 'Hi, Charlie. Remember me? I'm Beth. We met at Greer's house.'

He turned, clearly surprised, but then smiled. 'Of course I do. How could I forget those delicious brownies?'

'It's good to see you again.' He appeared hungover. Not that it was any of her business. She barely knew the guy, but from the little she'd seen, she liked him.

He managed a smile, despite the tiredness in his eyes. 'Yeah, you too.'

'Do you fancy a coffee?' He looked lost and unhappy, and she never could resist a lame duck. Take Isla Taylor, for example. Besides, she longed to discuss her worries about Greer.

He'd probably say no. A good-looking young man wouldn't want to chat with a middle-aged mother-hen like her. Time to turn up the pressure. 'I'm concerned about Greer. Can we talk?'

'Sure. I could murder a strong black coffee.'

He did look rough. She mustn't say so, however. 'The cafe's over there.'

Beth and Charlie seated themselves at a table. An espresso for Charlie, a latte for Beth. She took a quick sip. 'Have you seen Greer recently?'

'Mrs M, you mean? Not for a while.' Charlie blew out a breath. 'Which is a shame. She's like a second mother to me, and I'm worried about her. First, she wanted to track down Tom's boyfriend. Said she'd make him pay for what he did. All kinds of crazy stuff.' He took a gulp of coffee. 'Then she became obsessed with the man who got Tom's heart.'

'You know Nathan Taylor's dead, right?'

Charlie looked shocked. 'I had no idea. What happened?'

'His body rejected the transplant. He died before the doctors could save him.'

'Mind you, that guy definitely wasn't on the level,' Charlie continued. 'Mrs M wouldn't listen, though.'

'She should have. Greer said he conned money out of her.'

'So he took advantage of her grief to fleece her of her savings. The bastard. The goddamn prick.' He caught Beth's eye and flushed. 'Sorry. I'm concerned about her, that's all.'

'Me too.'

'I met Nathan when I visited him with Mrs M one evening.' He took another gulp of coffee. 'I saw something weird while I was there.'

'What?'

'He had a photo of that woman who disappeared a while back. Her body was discovered only recently. Murdered, apparently. Lily Hamilton, her name was.'

'Yes, I saw that on the news. Lily Hamilton probably knew lots of people, though.'

'Mrs M said the same thing. How Lily was a cardiac nurse, and Nathan must have met her while having treatment in Bristol.'

'Well, that explains it, then. It's tragic what happened to that young woman. I don't doubt that Greer was upset. She told me she feared Rose might have suffered the same fate.'

Charlie gave her an odd stare. 'Who's Rose?'

What a strange question. Hadn't Charlie said that he was like a second son to Greer? 'Her daughter, of course.'

If she'd thought he looked puzzled before, it was nothing to the shock on his face now. 'I've known Mrs M for over twenty years,' Charlie said. 'She doesn't have a daughter.'

CHAPTER 59

What? Beth must have misheard, surely? 'I don't understand. Greer told me about Rose. She showed me a picture of her. Explained she was afraid for Rose's safety because she went on blind dates with guys she met online. She definitely said Rose was her daughter.'

Charlie looked equally confused. 'I'm telling you—Tom was an only child. He never had a sister.'

Beth didn't know what to think. 'I'm desperately worried about Greer. First her obsession with Nathan Taylor, and now this business with Rose, who apparently doesn't exist. Oh, and did I mention I talked to Nathan's mother? Isla Taylor believes Greer killed her son. She's just not sure how.'

Shock edged into Charlie's face again. 'That sounds like grief talking.'

'That's what I told her.'

'Greer wouldn't kill anybody. Okay, so she's delusional about Nathan causing Tom's suicide, but murder? No way.'

'She needs help, Charlie. Counselling, medication.'

Charlie drained his coffee. 'Perhaps you should talk to her? Me and Mrs M—we don't have that kind of relationship. She's been a surrogate mother to me, sure, but I couldn't talk to her about emotional stuff. That would feel weird.'

'I get that. You're right, Charlie, I should probably chat to her. I just don't know where to start.'

That evening, Beth made a quick coffee, then fired up her laptop. First stop Google. Beth typed in 'Rose Maddox disappearance'.

The results contained lots of individuals with that name, but none of them lost or connected to Bristol. Beth typed 'missing persons UK' into the search bar; the website for the charity 'Vanished People' appeared at the top of the list. Beth plugged in everything she knew about Rose Maddox. Female, white, aged twenty-seven when last seen. Country of residence, United Kingdom.

Nothing came up. From what Beth could tell, Rose Maddox wasn't listed as missing.

Well, that was weird. Her search for information appeared to have reached a dead end. Websites weren't infallible, though. Or perhaps she'd misunderstood what Greer had told her.

Hang on a minute. Maybe she should look further into Lily Hamilton. Didn't Greer believe the same man had preyed on both Rose and Lily?

Beth stretched her arms behind her back, easing the tension from her shoulders. Time to try Google again. She typed in 'murder enquiry Lily Hamilton' into her search engine and scrutinised the results.

The main photo was of the taped-off crime scene, showing a tangle of undergrowth and rock. Beth read about the workers who'd found the corpse, the exact location in Bristol, and that the police had no leads. How Lily Hamilton had disappeared from her home in Bristol on September 6 eighteen months ago. Beth scrolled to the next image.

The gulp of coffee she'd just taken spattered against her laptop screen. What the hell?

The photo was of Lily Hamilton. Beth's eyes traced over the loosely waved blonde hair, the freckles dusting her nose, the tiny mole next to one eye. She'd seen that face before.

Beth knew exactly where, too. That photo she'd seen at Greer's. The one her neighbour claimed portrayed her daughter. Rose Maddox.

The pieces were fitting together, one by one. Beth's memory might be playing tricks on her, but she didn't think so.

Lily Hamilton and Rose Maddox were the same person.

CHAPTER 60

A buzz on Greer's doorbell. Should she ignore it? It was night-time, and she was tired.

A second buzz sounded, longer and shriller. Greer hauled herself off her sofa. Whoever had come calling wasn't going away in a hurry, it seemed.

When she opened the door, Beth and Charlie were on the step, their expressions sombre.

'Can we come in, Greer?' Beth prompted, when Greer didn't speak.

'We thought we should talk to you, 'Charlie chipped in.

Greer stared at him. 'About what?'

'Please let us in,' Beth said. 'We're worried. We only want to help.'

Then they should leave her the hell alone. Hadn't she suffered enough?

Beth and Charlie must believe she was some delusional nutter. Well, she didn't need their interference.

Beth edged past Greer into the hallway. Charlie followed. Stunned at their presumptuous behaviour—why hadn't she resisted?—Greer walked into the kitchen. 'One of you should get the kettle on.' Sarcasm laced her tone. 'Seeing as you're so keen to *help*.'

A flush crept across Beth's cheeks. She busied herself with mugs, spoons, and coffee. Charlie stood, silent and with arms folded, against the worktop, his gaze on Greer.

She really should tell them to leave. Now. Greer opened her mouth to speak, but Beth got in first. 'We know about Rose. Talk to us, Greer.'

An iron fist squeezed Greer's heart. 'Go away. Please.'

Somehow, Beth had discovered the truth. Hadn't Greer always feared this day would come?

'I've done some digging,' Beth said. 'Into Rose, and her alleged disappearance.'

'No.' If she denied everything, Beth and Charlie would leave, and Greer could... *what*, exactly? She had no family, no money, and, after today, probably no friends.

Her lips set themselves in a tight line. 'How can you be so cruel? There isn't a day goes by that I don't think of her. Hope and pray she comes back.'

'I found out when your daughter was born,' Beth said, as though Greer hadn't spoken.

Terror tightened the clamp around Greer's heart. 'Don't say it. Please.'

'She never went missing at all, did she?'

'Yes. Of course she did. I told you, and the police—'

Beth poured hot water into the mugs, set them on a tray with milk and sugar, and turned to face Greer. 'Why don't we all sit down?' She grabbed the tray and walked towards the living room, Charlie behind her. Greer had no choice but to follow.

Beth and Charlie settled into armchairs, with Greer on the sofa, facing them. Almost like they were her interrogators. She should act now, demand they leave. But Beth *knew*, didn't she? She must do, otherwise she wouldn't be saying all this. And if Beth knew, so did Charlie, and...

'I'm sorry, Greer. This must be beyond painful. But the only way we can help you is if everything is out in the open.'

'I told you before. I don't want your help.'

Charlie cleared his throat. 'Please, Mrs M. Just listen to Beth.'

'I also found when she died. How, too. It's easy to check birth and death certificates online.'

Greer stayed silent. Why wouldn't the woman stop talking?

'It wasn't your mother you lost in a house fire, was it?'

Words surged up to haunt Greer. *I tried so hard to save her. The flames... oh, God, Beth, the flames. My hands and arms got burned trying to put out the fire, but it spread too fast. She died, and I couldn't save her.*

Beth was right. Breast cancer had stolen Greer's mum, not a fire.

'I'm so sorry, my love. I can't imagine how awful losing one's baby must be.'

To hell with Beth Randall, and her two healthy, happy, and *living* children. 'No. You can't. Not in a million years.'

The roar and crackle of a fire, devouring everything in its fiery path, crashed over Greer. She scratched at the burn scars on her arms, fighting the awful memories, but to no avail. The stench of smoke, hot and acrid, invaded her nostrils. Flames engulfed the room. The inferno seared her skin, but Greer continued to flail at the thickened air.

A scream ripped from her throat. 'I wish I'd died too. I tried to save her. But I couldn't.'

What seemed like hours later, Greer wiped her eyes with her sleeve. 'Sorry about that.'

Beth smiled. 'No need to apologise. Won't you talk to us, Greer? Get it off your chest?'

Greer nodded. Yes, she would. Time to reveal the secret she'd hidden for so many years.

She dragged in a deep breath. 'I loved Jake, but we married too young. Rose was born six months afterwards. I struggled to cope with a tiny baby, trapped in a poky rented flat hardly big enough for one. Jake's wages barely covered the bills, and we argued constantly. Somehow we muddled through until Rose was nearly ten months old.' Greer saw only compassion on Beth's face. Charlie's, too.

'She hadn't slept the night before, which meant Jake and I didn't either. I couldn't think straight because I was so tired.' Exhaustion had glued Greer's eyes half-shut and jellied her legs. All she'd wanted was to go to bed and sleep for a year.

'I hadn't eaten that evening. We'd scraped together some cash to treat ourselves to fish and chips. Rose started screaming as soon as we sat down to eat. By the time I'd calmed her, the food was cold and congealed, so I chucked it in the bin.'

She was inching ever closer to the hard part. 'Jake had crashed out on the sofa, fast asleep. I'd already tucked Rose into a blanket beside her daddy. She'd finally dozed off. By then, I was ravenous.'

Beans on toast had seemed an easy alternative. 'I wish to God I'd gone to bed hungry. Then Rose wouldn't have died.'

Beth patted her arm. 'Take your time, my love. No rush.'

'Rose woke up, fretting a bit. I threw down the cloth I'd used to hold the hot saucepan and went to calm her. She'd fallen asleep again, though.' Greer wiped her eyes. 'I was so utterly exhausted. Jake and Rose were both dead to the world, and I wanted that so badly for myself. I'd forgotten all about the beans on toast. So I headed into the bedroom to grab a quick hour of sleep.'

The worst was yet to come. How could Greer ever convey the horror of it all?

'It wasn't your fault, Greer.' Beth's voice was warm and soothing. 'You were young, a new mother, trying to cope in difficult circumstances. And that landlord of yours should have installed smoke alarms.'

He hadn't, though. The cloth Greer had thrown down had landed on the lit gas burner, bursting into flames. The cooker had been next to the kitchen window, hung with a flimsy cotton curtain. That had ignited as well, the fire spreading like lightning into the living room where Rose and Jake slept, oblivious. The bedroom, with Greer in it, was at the other end of the flat.

What eventually dragged her back to consciousness was the frantic pounding on the front door. Their neighbour had smelled smoke and heard the crackle of fire. Greer had rushed into the living room, her hands beating at the flames devouring Rose's blanket, only to be overcome by the dense smoke. She awoke in a hospital bed, arms bandaged, the image of Rose's burned flesh scorched into her brain.

'The inquest concluded that Jake and Rose died from smoke inhalation before the fire reached them.' Sobs choked Greer's voice. 'I've lived my whole life dreading that might not be true. That my beautiful daughter's last minutes were filled with terror and agony. And that it was all my fault.'

CHAPTER 61

Greer smiled sadly. 'Rose's death ripped my heart out.'

Maybe that was when it began turning to bone. Greer's doctor would refute that, of course. 'I loved Jake too, but nothing compares to the loss of a child.'

'I wish I'd known all this, Mrs M,' Charlie said.

'It was too raw, too painful. I couldn't talk about it.'

'Oh, my love. You've suffered hell, haven't you?' Beth rummaged in her bag and handed a tissue to Greer.

'The nightmares were awful. I asked my doctor for sleeping tablets. A bottle of pills, and I'd be with Rose again.'

Charlie squeezed Greer's arm. 'I'm so sorry, Mrs M.'

'She must have realised why I wanted the pills and refused to prescribe them. Instead, she booked me in for group counselling. *I'll show her*, I thought. I'd play along, but keep pestering her until she gave me those pills.'

'Did the counselling help?' Beth said.

'Yes. Everyone else had also lost a loved one, and I didn't feel so alone anymore.' Greer dragged in a deep breath. 'I still intended to kill myself, though. I made a second appointment with my doctor, determined to leave with a prescription for sleeping pills. Instead, we discussed the fact I'd not had a period for almost four months.'

'You were pregnant with Tom,' Charlie said.

Greer nodded. 'At first, I panicked. How could I trust myself with another baby when Rose's death was my fault?'

Abortion had been out of the question. Hadn't she already killed one child?

'I decided on adoption. Then Tom arrived, and I fell madly in love.' For a few seconds, she lost herself in bittersweet memories.

'Go on,' Charlie urged.

'Rose dying made me over-protective with Tom. He was my life, my soul, my everything. If I lost him, I had nothing.' Greer smiled sadly. 'Tom resented me for it, though. I realised during his teenage years that my behaviour was driving him away, but I couldn't help myself.'

Beth nodded. 'I understand your need to protect Tom. Why lead him to believe his father was still alive, though?'

Shame stole over Greer. She wasn't proud of the way she'd acted. 'I was furious with Jake for not waking up in time to save himself and Rose. I know that makes no sense, but in my head, my husband abandoned me, so that's what I told Tom.'

Charlie leaned forward. 'Why did you never tell him he once had a sister?'

'I couldn't bear to talk about Rose. Besides, what good would it have done?'

'You don't think he had a right to know?'

'Telling him wouldn't bring her back. And losing her killed me too, in a way. I've never been the same since.'

'Is that why you pretended Lily was your daughter?' Beth asked.

'Yes. She looked the way I'd always pictured Rose would, and I was so vulnerable when I first met her. It was the anniversary of Rose's death, you see.'

Lily had been one of the cardiac nurses investigating Greer's heart problems. 'I needed a series of diagnostic tests. Lily was always so kind and caring.' Greer's eyes filled with tears.

'I spotted the similarities between Lily and Rose straightaway. Her blonde hair, the tiny mole by her eye. How Lily was twenty-seven, the same age as Rose would have been. She was often on duty when I attended the BRI, and we chatted most times. I felt I'd known her forever.'

'You became close,' Charlie said.

'Yes. Tom rarely visited, and I was so lonely. I sensed Lily was, too. She'd split with her boyfriend and had moved back in with her dad. The two of them didn't get along. I wanted to help her.'

'Is that when you offered her a room?' Charlie asked. 'As your lodger?'

'Yes. I'd always thought of my third bedroom as Rose's. It would have been if she'd lived. It all started from there.'

CHAPTER 62 - Before

She'd been so lonely before Lily. After they first met, hope blossomed in Greer; might Lily become a surrogate for Rose? It made perfect sense. The girl had lost her mother to lung cancer the year before. Greer was desperate for a daughter. Was it so very wrong to cast Lily in that role?

Once Lily moved in, the two of them chatted over endless cups of coffee, cooked meals together, visited local cafes. Just like she and Rose would have done.

Tom had met Greer's new lodger on one of the rare Sundays he came for lunch, and the two of them became friends, often going to the pub or cinema together. As a result, he visited more often, although he clearly preferred Lily's company.

Terror often plagued Greer, though. Lily was beautiful; she'd soon replace her ex-boyfriend. Where would that leave *her*? Lily would move out, and she'd be alone again.

She mustn't think like that. Except she couldn't stop. Incredible how much Lily resembled the way Greer pictured an adult Rose would have done. The names were a lucky coincidence. Greer had been a Hamilton before she married, and both Rose and Lily had floral first names. The similarity went further, however.

'My full name is Lily Rose Hamilton,' she'd told Greer, with a laugh. 'My sister's Daisy Violet, can you believe? Good job Mum never had a son.'

'Lily Rose. That's beautiful.' Greer hesitated. Would Lily think she was weird? 'Do you mind if I call you Rose? It's just that it suits you.'

Lily had looked surprised, but nodded. 'Sure.'

From then on, Greer always referred to her lodger as Rose. A particular pleasure to do so around Tom, of course. Brother and sister together at last, as though that hellish fire never happened. Her obsession wasn't healthy, but she didn't care. What harm could it do?

Life with Lily was mostly wonderful, though. At first, anyway. It didn't take long before things turned sour.

In the end, Greer's smother love had driven Rose from her. Just like it had with Tom.

'Here you go. All ironed and ready to put away.' Greer tugged open the door to Rose's wardrobe and draped clothes over hangers.

Rose stood up, grabbed Greer's arm. 'I've asked you before. Can you please knock before barging in? A little privacy's not too much to ask, is it?'

Her daughter could be prickly. This wasn't the first time she'd asked her to knock, but somehow Greer always forgot.

She needed to be patient. Not expect too much, too soon. Rose couldn't have found it easy living with her father. Maybe she preferred closed doors.

'And please don't open my drawers or rummage in my things.' Rose snatched the remaining clothes from Greer's hands. 'I'm a grown woman. I can do my own laundry and put it away afterwards.'

Greer smiled at Rose, determined to ignore her daughter's frosty tone. 'Come downstairs. I'll open a bottle of Malbec.'

'Can't. I'm going out.' Rose took a blue dress covered in sequins off a hanger. 'If I don't get a move on, I'll be late.'

'Where are you off to?' Greer injected false jollity into her voice. She'd hoped for a cosy night in with her daughter. The prospect of wine for one failed to appeal.

'Just out.' Rose was clearly biting back annoyance. 'A date, if you must know.'

Greer plumped herself down on the bed. 'Who is he? How did you meet him? Where are you going?'

Rose pulled clean knickers from a pile on the floor. 'Listen, I really must get ready. I'll say goodbye before I leave, okay?'

'You're not going on a blind date, are you? Internet dating can be dangerous, Rose. How much do you know about this guy?'

Her daughter let out a theatrical sigh. 'Oh, for God's sake. I can look after myself. Now, will you please go?' No mistaking her annoyance now.

Smother mother. Greer needed to avoid repeating history. She stood up and made her way downstairs, reluctance in every step. Her fingers twisted off the screw-top to the Malbec. She slugged a generous measure into a glass.

Before long, Rose's feet sounded on the creaky staircase. Greer glanced at her daughter, framed in the doorway. 'Will you at least text if you need help?'

Rose nodded. 'Sure. I'll be fine, though. Don't wait up, or any nonsense like that.' With that, she was gone, only the slam of the front door betraying she'd been there at all.

Her precious girl didn't realise how vulnerable she was. Well, Greer would ensure she stayed safe that night.

—ele—

'You followed me, didn't you? Were you spying on me?' Rose's voice shot daggers at Greer.

Greer struggled to an upright position on her sofa, her head pounding. Her mouth felt as though someone had poured sand into it. Desperate for a glass of water, she moistened her dry lips.

'Rose. You're home.'

Her daughter's eyes were dark with fury. 'I spotted you peering through the restaurant window. Do you have any idea how weird that is?'

'No. You're wrong. I fancied an Indian takeaway—'

'Bullshit. I don't see any dirty plates, and I don't smell curry, only your boozy breath. Why couldn't you have let me alone for once? Can't I meet a guy without you spoiling my fun?'

The ungrateful minx. 'I was just looking out for you. Do you really think it's smart to meet a stranger off the Internet? Anything might happen.'

'Yeah. Like me having a good time. Or finding a decent guy.' Rose's face had flushed with fury. 'We met in a public place, for God's sake. I told Tom where I was going, arranged that he'd check in with me by text. I was perfectly safe.'

'This guy could have spiked your drink. Lied to you—'

'He didn't, though. Nobody lies about being an accountant, and he definitely didn't slip a roofie in my wine, because here I am, walking, talking and absolutely fine. You just can't stop interfering, can you?'

The next day, while Rose was at work, Greer walked into her daughter's bedroom. She lay on Rose's bed, inhaling the faint scent of her shampoo. Pathetic, but how else could she feel close to her girl?

Her gaze fell on a pile of photos, obviously printed from Rose's laptop. She flicked through them. They were all of Rose, her arms around her birth mother, or so Greer presumed. Sour jealousy flared in her heart. She was losing her daughter all over again, this time to a dead woman.

Greer stumbled back to her room, a photo clutched in one hand. Rose would never miss it among so many.

She took a pair of nail scissors and cropped out Rose's birth mother. Much better that way.

The following morning, Greer called up the stairs. 'Rose? Can I borrow you for a minute?' She made sure her voice was warm, friendly.

To her relief, her daughter appeared on the landing, dressed in her coat and clutching her handbag. Her expression seemed guarded. 'What do you want?'

'I'd like us to have a little chat. Clear the air, so to speak.' Greer smiled, all nice and warm, but Rose didn't respond. Instead, she came downstairs and stood in the hallway, her arms folded.

Greer shoved her disappointment aside. 'I know you think I'm interfering, but I'm just concerned—'

'Yeah, well.' Rose's gaze slid to the carpet. 'About that. You won't need to bother about me anymore. I'm moving out. Next Saturday, in fact.'

No. No, no, no. That wasn't what she'd planned, not at all. 'Please don't do that. I realise things have been tense recently. But—'

'Sorry. This isn't working for me.'

'But you have a lovely home here. Why leave? I always knock now before I enter your room, don't I? Stay. Please.' Greer hated the whine in her voice.

Rose shook her head. 'I can't stand the lack of privacy. All the unsolicited advice. It's only a matter of time before you barge into my room again. Don't get me started on your opinions about dating websites.'

'I'm only trying to keep you safe—'

Rose's lips set themselves in a thin line. 'My safety isn't your business. Dad, with all his faults, wasn't as bad as you. My mind's made up, so don't try to talk me into staying.' She wrenched open the front door, slamming it behind her.

CHAPTER 63 - Now

Greer wiped her eyes. 'Not long afterwards I had to report Rose—I mean Lily—as missing.'

'That must have been awful,' Charlie said.

'It breaks my heart that we ended on a sour note. She'd given notice for her room, you see. By then, we were barely speaking.'

Charlie leaned forward. 'Remember how I told you Lily and I dated a few times? When the police questioned me about her disappearance, I felt like shit.' He caught Greer's eye. 'Sorry, Mrs M. But I get where you're coming from. Me and Lily ended badly, and I'd give anything to change that.'

Greer nodded wearily. If only they'd both leave. Two people now knew about Rose, and the fire, and that was too many. The burns on her arms itched, and she scratched at her flesh, wishing she could claw it off.

'We're here for you, love.' Greer saw Beth shoot a glance at Charlie, who signalled his agreement. 'But you need to help yourself, too. Have you considered counselling? After all, it worked before.'

If it would persuade them to go, she'd agree to anything. 'Okay. After the funeral, though.'

Beth and Charlie exchanged looks. 'Nathan's, you mean?' Beth said. 'Are you sure that's a good idea, love? You need to rest after your recent heart attack. When is the funeral, anyway?'

Greer shrugged. 'I need to find out.' It was now after midnight. She'd have to wait until the morning to call Jessica.

'But didn't you fall out with Nathan? Over him being your son's boyfriend?'

'I hate Nathan Taylor. Tom's heart, though—that's another matter. It's the last remaining link with my boy.'

'I get that. I just don't think you should be around Nathan's mother.'

'You're probably right. I still need to go, though.'

Beth pursed her lips. 'She came looking for you one day you were out shopping.'

Horror hit Greer. 'Oh, my God. What did she want?'

'Nothing good. She was spouting all kinds of nonsense, which is why I didn't mention it. Stuff about how you'd murdered Nathan.'

Greer froze. Impossible to reply.

'Ridiculous, of course. She was out of her mind with grief.'

Greer swallowed. Good job Beth hadn't been inside her head when she'd planned how to kill Nathan. Somehow, she found her voice. 'I'll be careful, so Isla doesn't spot me. But nothing will stop me from attending that funeral. I need to say a final farewell to my boy.'

CHAPTER 64

The morning after Beth and Charlie's visit, Greer located Jessica's mobile number and pressed the 'call' icon. Had she left it too late? Might Nathan's funeral already have taken place?

'Hello?' Jessica sounded wary. Greer remembered twenty-somethings preferred to send messages rather than phone. That didn't seem appropriate, given what she was about to ask. 'Greer, is that you?'

Once they'd exchanged the usual pleasantries, Greer steeled herself. 'I'd like to know when and where Nathan's funeral will be held.' She held her breath. What if it had already happened?

Jessica didn't reply. How could Greer best persuade her?

'It's Tom's heart, you see. Part of my son, my last link to him, died with Nathan. I need to say goodbye.'

'I don't think that's a good idea. Mum wouldn't want you there.'

'She won't see me. I'll slip in late, sit at the back, and leave as soon as the ceremony's over.'

She heard Jessica blow out a breath. 'I'm not sure.'

'Please, Jessica. It would mean so much to me.'

It took a few more tries, but Greer eventually convinced Jessica to give her the address of the crematorium. The funeral was the following morning; had she left phoning Jessica to another day, she'd have missed her chance.

An idea occurred to Greer. 'I'll drive up later today and stay overnight. If you're free, do you want to meet up? We probably won't be able to talk tomorrow.'

'I'd like that.'

That was a relief. She'd been bracing herself for rejection.

They arranged for Greer to text Jessica once she was at her hotel. 'I'm glad you called,' Jessica said, right before the conversation ended. 'There's something I have to tell you. Not over the phone, though.'

―⁂―

That afternoon, once she'd checked into a shabby guest house, its only virtue being its proximity to the crematorium, Greer sent Jessica a message. *In Birmingham. When and where to meet?*

Within ten minutes, she received a reply. *Edgbaston Reservoir, close to where I work. There's a path around it we can follow. 5 pm after I finish my shift. Is that OK?*

Perfect. See you later.

―⁂―

By five o'clock, Greer had parked at Edgbaston Reservoir. She got out of her car and leaned against the bonnet, her eyes searching for Jessica. Above, the sky was overcast, but the greyness held no hint of rain. A breeze ruffled Greer's hair and whipped the water into peaks. She hugged her wool jacket closer around her. Ah, there was Jessica.

The younger woman hurried towards her. 'It's good to see you again, Greer.'

'Likewise. Even if it's in sad circumstances.' They shared a quick hug.

Jessica looked pale and unwell. Besides her own grief, she also had to deal with Isla's pain.

'We can walk around the lake.' Jessica waved a hand towards the water. 'The views of the city are incredible.'

The two women set off in silence. The water glinted in the sparse light that made it through the clouds. Ducks paddled towards a child throwing bread at them. The faint pulse of a Bob Marley song reached Greer's ears from a passing jogger, sparking a gasp of pain. Tom had loved reggae. Why was it the little things that hurt the most?

'Are you all right?' Jessica's concern tore Greer apart. She burst into noisy sobs, fumbling in her pocket for a tissue.

'Let's sit at those picnic tables over there,' Jessica said. Greer blew her nose, unable to reply. Jessica steered her towards the nearest one, sitting opposite her.

Shame stole over Greer. 'I'm sorry. Tomorrow is about you, not me. You've only recently lost your brother, whereas Tom died a while ago.'

'Don't be silly. You're grieving too. I get why you need to attend the funeral. Tom's heart, and all that.'

Now was not the time to impose her own sorrow. 'You mentioned you had something to say to me?'

Jessica didn't reply at first. Greer stole a glance at her. Was it her imagination, or did Jessica look nervous?

'I owe you an apology.' Jessica blurted out at last.

Well, that was a surprise. 'For what?'

'For lying to you. About Nathan, I mean.'

'I don't understand.'

'He didn't have a fling with your son. I made that up. Nathan's straight.'

Beth's words drifted back to Greer. *All so weird... doesn't sound right to me... an incredible coincidence...* She'd been correct, it seemed. 'Why did you lie?'

'I was jealous. You'd formed such a bond with him, and I felt excluded.' Jessica's cheeks turned pink. 'I'm not proud of my behaviour. The main reason, though, was that I was worried about you.'

'Why?'

Jessica's gaze fell away. 'You'd given him money, and I knew he'd bleed you dry. So I lied about Tom, hoping to turn you against Nathan.'

How selfish. Childish, too. 'You took advantage of my grief. Used it for your own ends.'

'No, don't you see? I did it for you, Greer. You'd never have believed me if I'd said Nathan was conning you. So I tried to make you hate him instead. That way, you'd stop lending him money.' She smiled sadly. 'I only wanted to help. Can you forgive me?'

Really, Jessica had done her a favour. Greer had been foolish, too enthralled by Tom's heart to realise Nathan's manipulations. The girl had lied, not killed anyone. 'I forgive you.'

Jessica burst into tears, and Greer pulled her into a clumsy hug across the picnic table. For a second, Jessica became Rose, and Lily, and the daughter-shaped hole in Greer's heart shrank a little.

Jessica dabbed at her cheeks with a tissue. 'You didn't deserve that from me. You were so kind when I felt unappreciated over Nathan.

Mum's never paid me much attention, and there you were, always ready to listen, and I hoped—' Sadness crept into her expression. 'It was stupid, I know. But I thought of you as a mother figure. Is that so very wrong of me?'

'No. Not at all.' Life had damaged this sweet girl, as it had Greer. 'I could tell your mother wasn't giving you the love you needed. I care about you too, Jessica.'

'Do you mean that?'

Greer smiled. 'With all my heart.'

—⁂—

Later, back at the guest house, Greer berated herself. Stupid, stupid. How ridiculous of her. Nathan hadn't been Tom's secret boyfriend. As Beth had pointed out, the chances of him receiving a transplant from someone he'd once dated were almost nil.

That meant she was no closer to uncovering who'd driven her son to suicide.

Charlie was right. She should let the whole thing go.

CHAPTER 65

The wind blew strongly on this chilly morning in Birmingham, a day that found Greer bracing herself against the cold at the Yew Tree Crematorium. Mindful of the need to avoid Isla, she'd concealed herself among the trees that lined the grounds. In less than fifteen minutes, Nathan's funeral would begin. Today she would lose her last connection with Tom.

The mourners filed into the squat red-brick building. There weren't very many of them: Isla, Jessica, and two older guys, presumably from Nathan's employment. When everyone was inside, Greer hurried across the damp grass. Thank God the door was automatic. No heavy hinges or creaks to announce her arrival. She slipped into a seat in the back row behind a pillar; her plan was to leave right before the end. Nobody would ever know she'd been there.

Ahead of Greer were Isla and Jessica, with Nathan's casket on the platform in front. Isla had chosen a nice solid oak, with lilies on top, that must have cost a fortune. Nathan would have approved.

The service didn't take long. Greer wiped away silent tears while the celebrant was speaking. She waited until the coffin sank into the cremation vault, then left quickly as Isla and Jessica were rising from their seats. Once outside, she paused, her breath coming in heavy pants. An iron band encircled her chest, and a dull ache filled her heart. She wiped sweat from her brow.

No wonder she felt unwell. Inside the crematorium, flames would soon engulf the last part of Tom.

'Goodbye, my darling.' The wind whipped away her words, Greer's voice a mere whisper.

The doors of the crematorium opened behind her. Isla came out, followed by Jessica. Greer froze.

Fury flamed into Isla's face when she almost collided with Greer.

'What the hell are *you* doing here?' Spittle flew from her mouth. Her eyes were bloodshot, her skin grey. Her black jacket hung loosely across her scrawny shoulders.

'I'm sorry.' Faced with Isla's rage, it was all Greer could offer.

'For what? Causing my son's death?'

Greer stared at Isla, too stunned to speak.

'I've always thought you had something to do with it. *She—*' Isla jerked her head towards Jessica— 'persuaded me not to press for a post-mortem. Said the hospital was correct, that Nathan died from organ rejection. I wish to God I hadn't listened. The whole thing seemed off somehow. I think you know more than you're saying.'

'Mum, please.' Jessica tugged on her mother's arm. 'This isn't doing anyone any good. Greer didn't kill Nathan.'

Isla shrugged off her daughter. 'I don't agree.' She took a few paces in the direction of the car park, then stopped. 'Are you coming?' she said to Jessica.

Jessica shook her head. 'I'll see you back home. I want to be alone for a bit.' She stepped forward, one hand tucking a strand of hair behind Isla's ear.

Such tenderness in Jessica's eyes. Greer would give her life to have a daughter—or son—who'd look at her that way.

Isla nodded. With a venomous glance at Greer, she strode towards the car park.

'She doesn't mean it,' Jessica said. 'It's just the grief talking.'

Greer huddled into her coat. That chilly wind was getting worse. 'I should go. You said you need to be alone.'

'I don't. Not really.' Jessica's face held a wealth of sorrow. 'I just can't be around Mum right now. You saw how she is. All bitter and twisted. Saying awful things.'

'Do you want to grab a coffee somewhere?'

'No. Too many people in a cafe.' She pointed towards the exit. 'There's a park over that way, only a few minutes' walk. Can we go there instead?'

'Of course. Anywhere you like.'

They walked the short distance to the park in silence. Something Greer had seen earlier wasn't sitting right with her.

Maybe it was nothing.

Or it could be everything.

'There's a path that runs alongside a stream,' Jessica said once they'd passed the park's entrance. 'It's steep in places, so few people use it. There's a bench halfway we can sit on.'

The two of them set off towards the distant trees. Jessica was right; the track was tough-going, and overgrown too. The frigid air wound around Greer as she followed Jessica, the only sounds the crunch of twigs under their feet and birds flying through the branches. The so-called stream was more of a trickle, thick with algae and barely moving; an odour of rotting weeds hit Greer's nostrils.

The path levelled off and widened out, with a bench to their left. It had turned green with lichen in places but looked sturdy enough. Greer sat on it, with Jessica beside her.

Isla's accusation returned to Greer's head. 'Your mother accused me of killing Nathan. I don't get why she'd say that.'

'I'm sorry about her rudeness. Like I said, it's the grief talking. She won't accept Nathan died from organ rejection. I explained it's always a risk after a transplant operation, but she won't listen.'

'I guess she needs someone to blame.'

'She says you had the means, motive and opportunity, as the police say. How you'd turned against Nathan because he conned money out of you. She guessed he'd done that from something I let slip. Claimed you were always hanging around him like a bad smell.' A flush rose to her face. 'Her words, not mine.'

Greer scraped at a piece of lichen on the bench. 'That's motive and opportunity, but what about means? How does she think I sent Nathan into organ rejection?'

'She reckons you tampered with his medication.'

'That's ridiculous. I didn't murder him.'

'That's what I told her. You're far too lovely to kill anyone. I told her I monitored Nathan's medication, put it in his pill boxes every day. He never missed a dose. He knew how risky that would be.'

'That's what's so weird. Like you say, he always took his tablets. Why would his body reject his heart if he was on immunosuppressants?'

'It happens, especially in the first few weeks and months after a transplant. The tragic thing is, Nathan was due for his weekly check-up the day after he died. I was supposed to drive him there.'

'You were a brilliant sister. Helping with his laundry, medication, etc.'

'Yeah, I suppose.' Jessica shifted restlessly on the bench. 'Not that he was ever grateful.'

'What about your mum? I hope she appreciates everything you do.'

A tear slid down Jessica's cheek. 'She's too lost in grief.'

Oh, the poor sweet girl. So taken for granted. 'She'll realise one day. Give her time.'

Jessica's expression hardened. 'How much, though? I've waited my whole life for her to love me, the way she did with Nathan, but she barely notices me. Everything's always been about *him*.' She spat out the words like poison.

Fury sat on Jessica's face. 'All she'd say was stuff like, "Make sure Nathan takes his medication. He'll die if he doesn't." Yeah, I ensured he got his pills, all right.' Her mouth twisted in an ugly grimace. She was almost shouting. 'I'd dole them out each day, and if I was there when he was due a dose, I'd watch while he took them. Cotrimoxazole to fight infection, fluvastatin for lowering cholesterol, apixiban to thin his blood, hypericum—' Jessica stopped, her face red with rage.

When she next spoke, she seemed calmer. 'Listen to me rabbiting on. You don't need to know all that.'

Around them the wind blew fiercer, causing Greer to shiver. Not just with the cold.

That weird thing she'd seen earlier? At the time, she hadn't been sure. Now she was.

Greer eyeballed the other woman. 'Why did you kill your brother, Jessica?'

CHAPTER 66

For a moment, Jessica stared at her, her mouth open. Then she edged away, panic in her face. 'What do you mean?'

'I saw you smile. After the funeral, when your mother accused me of killing Nathan. You thought I didn't see, but I did.'

'You're mistaken. I wouldn't—'

'You grinned. Like you were pleased with yourself. As though you were guarding a precious secret.'

'No.' Jessica looked stricken. Had Greer got this all wrong?

Her gut instinct insisted otherwise. Hadn't Jessica persuaded her mother not to request a post-mortem? Perhaps she'd also suggested cremation rather than burial for her own ends, too. Jessica couldn't risk the woman she worshipped discovering the truth.

'I didn't kill Nathan. Why would you say that?'

Greer smiled sadly. 'After I met your brother, I familiarised myself with his medication regime. Like you said, he was on blood thinners, anti-cholesterol tablets and immunosuppressants. I know about cardiac medication because of my own heart problems.'

Jessica looked defiant. 'So?'

'You talked about the tablets you gave Nathan each day. You never mentioned prednisone, the anti-rejection drug essential for his recovery.'

Jessica shrugged. 'He took so many pills. What does it matter if I didn't tell you every single one?'

'By itself, it probably doesn't. Although I'd have expected a nurse to mention prednisone first, given how vital it was. What you *did* mention, though, was hypericum. That was your mistake. You were so angry, and I guess it just slipped out.'

'No. You must have misheard me.'

'Hypericum perforatum, commonly known as St John's Wort. You're a health professional, so you used its Latin name. It's a herb used for mild depression, but Nathan didn't suffer from depression. His doctors would have alerted him to anything that might interfere with his medication. St John's Wort, for example. I got the same warnings.'

'You're crazy.'

'You omitted to give Nathan his predisone. Without it, his immune system would reject his new heart. Instead, you substituted St John's Wort, known to have a negative effect on anti-cholesterol medication. That's how you killed him, with a double whammy. What I don't understand is why.'

'Bullshit. This is all a load of crap.'

'You were jealous of Nathan. Desperate for your mum's love. That doesn't explain murder, though.' Greer squeezed Jessica's hand. 'Tell me what happened. I'm not judging you.' How could she? Hadn't Greer also considered tampering with Nathan's medication?

Jessica stared at her for a long moment. Then she appeared to arrive at a decision. 'I want to tell you a story.'

'I'm listening.'

'Imagine discovering that a relative had done something unforgivable. You'd always disliked him. Suspected he was a sociopath. How would you feel?'

Greer didn't have to think about that one. 'I'd want to kill him.'

Jessica nodded. 'Underneath the veneer, humans are still wild animals. Society teaches us that murder is wrong, however. So most of us never act on our urges. What about justice, though?'

'I agree it's important. People often do things that aren't illegal but which hurt others.'

'Exactly. So occasionally—hypothetically speaking, of course—angry people decide to exact revenge.' Above them, a crow cawed, the sound harsh and ugly.

'Imagine you're caring for someone who's had major surgery. You're a nurse, so you assume responsibility for ensuring they take the correct medication at the right time. The other person doesn't appreciate your efforts, however. Instead, they're rude and spiteful. Then you discover they did something terrible. That unforgivable thing I mentioned.'

Greer stayed silent. Best to let Jessica release the pent-up hurt inside her.

'The other person doesn't give a toss how much pain he's caused. You cry, and you rage, and the worse of it is, there's nobody you can tell. Your mother is emotionally distant. Your only friends are work colleagues. You've recently met a lovely woman who's kind and caring, but you're reluctant to burden her with your problems.' Jessica gave

Greer a thin smile. 'Your whole life becomes hate and rage. Until all you think about is revenge.'

Greer got it. Of course she did.

'You've noticed something. While the other person always takes their pills, they never actually look at them. They just open their pill box, tip out their tablets, and take them. Thanks to your medical training, you know certain substances interfere with medication. For example, St John's Wort can hinder the uptake of anti-cholesterol drugs. As for immunosuppressants, it's dangerous to miss even one dose. Several? That leads to serious problems. The immune system kicks back in and decides that a transplanted organ, such as a heart, doesn't belong in the body.'

Greer nodded. Simple, really.

'You switch out his medication for the coming week. When he dies, everyone believes it's an obvious case of organ rejection. Which it is. You return to his flat, remove the St John's Wort from the pillbox and replace it with the immunosuppressants, in case anyone checks, which they don't. You flush any remaining St John's Wort down the toilet. All hypothetically speaking, of course.'

She fell silent. The wind whipped through the trees, and the stink of rotting vegetation seemed stronger. Greer wrapped her arms around herself to keep out the cold. The wooden bench felt hard under her buttocks.

Greer still didn't get *why*. 'You said Nathan did something unforgivable. What was it?'

Jessica narrowed her eyes. 'Let me tell you another story.'

CHAPTER 67

She sucked in a deep breath. 'I grew up in Nathan's shadow, painfully aware of Mum's preference for him. Oh, Mum loves me in her own way. She just doesn't express it much or make me a priority.'

How blinkered of Isla. Didn't she realise what a precious gift a daughter was?

'As for my father, he abused her, both mentally and physically, before their divorce. It's why I'm so protective of her now.'

'Did he abuse you too?'

Jessica shook her head. 'He mostly ignored me, thank God, but I still copped his rage on occasions. As a result, I developed low self-esteem, worried I'd always come second best.'

Greer's heart went out to Jessica. Really, the two of them weren't so different.

'In my early twenties, I got involved with a guy who treated me like his own personal punch-bag. He claimed it was my fault he hit me, and why did I always provoke him? He'd buy me flowers and swear it would never happen again. Except it did.'

The age-old story. Greer squeezed Jessica's hand.

'Then I fell pregnant. My boyfriend went crazy. He said he knew I'd been sleeping around. I hadn't, though. My only option was to move back in with Mum once I'd decided to keep my baby. I adored my son—Ollie, his name was—and for a while I was ecstatic.'

Greer well remembered those heady first few months with both Tom and Rose, glorious despite the sleepless nights, the crying, the dirty nappies. Every second of them had been worth the world.

Jessica's face was chalk-pale, her eyes wet with tears. 'I'd found a part-time nursing position, and Mum helped with Ollie's childcare. Until the day she'd arranged a weekend in London with friends. I couldn't afford not to work, and I didn't have anyone to babysit Ollie. So I asked Nathan to step in.' Jessica's tears spilled down her cheeks.

'He made a big fuss, said I shouldn't expect him to sacrifice his Saturday to mind a screaming brat.' Her hands clenched into fists, fury in her eyes. 'Mum intervened for once, though, and eventually he agreed. I dropped my baby off with him and drove to work.' Jessica's sobs were coming thick and fast.

Greer pulled her into a tight embrace. 'Sshhh. I've got you, sweetheart. Let it out. Let it all out.'

Jessica eventually pulled away, her face red and blotchy. 'Sorry,' she muttered.

'You have nothing to apologise for.'

'That weekend was the hottest of the year. I hurried round to Nathan's the second my shift ended so I could collect Ollie. I knew something was wrong the moment I walked in the door. Nathan wouldn't look at me. Just said that Ollie was asleep in the spare bedroom. I ran in, picked up my baby, and he was limp, not breathing.' The expression on Jessica's face almost broke Greer's heart. 'I screamed at Nathan to call an ambulance. Ollie was already dead, though. At the inquest the coroner ruled it a cot death.' She burst into sobs again.

'I'm so sorry, sweetheart.' Greer's mind spiralled back through time, to the stench of smoke, her own screams ringing in her ears, Rose's burned flesh.

'Something inside me died that day. It must have been the same for you, right? With Tom's suicide, I mean.'

'Yes. It was.' For Rose's death, too, although Jessica didn't know about that.

'Then, recently, I was at Nathan's, cleaning his flat. I was tired and cranky after a long shift. Nathan was his usual spiky self. We got into an argument. It turned ugly.' Jessica's face was stony-hard now, all traces of tears gone. 'I yelled how I couldn't forgive him for Ollie dying while with him, even though it was a cot death. He shouted back that Ollie had been fine when he checked before going to the shops.'

'Nathan left your baby alone?'

'Yes. While buying beer. He'd never mentioned that before.' Jessica's words fell like rocks from her lips. 'He said he put another blanket over Ollie, because he'd been, in Nathan's words, bawling his ugly head off. Said he reckoned the extra warmth would send him to sleep. To make matters worse, he closed the window. The temperature outside was over thirty degrees. Nathan said he was mindful of security, given that his flat was on the ground floor. This was back in Bristol, you understand.' Jessica's fists were clenched so tight her knuckles were white. 'When I returned, the window was open and Ollie didn't have a blanket over him. All Nathan was worried about was not getting blamed. So he covered up his negligence.'

'He killed your baby. Not deliberately, but still...'

'I'm to blame too.' Jessica gulped back a sob. 'I left Ollie with Nathan even though I knew he had no experience with babies. I'd credited him with more common sense, though.'

Something clicked in Greer's mind. 'That time I saw you leaving his flat, and you'd been crying. You'd just discovered the truth, hadn't you?'

'Yes. I was so angry. I never thought I could hate anyone as much as I did my brother.'

Greer couldn't blame her. She'd have reacted the same way.

'I'll deny it if you tell anyone,' Jessica said, startling Greer from her thoughts. 'I've destroyed all the evidence. It'll be your word against mine.'

What would be the point of telling the police? Jessica had covered her tracks too well. She was a productive member of the community, a caring girl driven to extremes by grief. Greer could relate to that, and then some. Besides, she needed to consider Isla. Greer might not have much love for the woman, but she'd not inflict *that* kind of horror on her.

Raindrops spattered the ground, the sky dark with cloud. Time to go. Greer got to her feet. 'I've not told you everything about my life. Let's just say I understand why you did what you did. Your secret is safe with me.'

Jessica also stood up. 'Somehow I believe you.' There didn't seem to be anything to say after that. Sometimes secrets brought people together; other times, they split them apart. This was one of the latter.

They climbed the steep bank to the main part of the park in silence. As they reached the entrance, Jessica turned to Greer. 'Maybe Mum will love me more now that Nathan's not around.'

Oh, the poor girl. Somehow, Greer doubted that.

CHAPTER 68

'Greer! Are you all right?' Beth opened her front door as Greer walked up to hers. Greer sighed inwardly. Traffic had been heavy on the M5 from Birmingham to Bristol, and she was exhausted.

She mustn't be rude to Beth, though. 'I'm fine.'

'How did the funeral go?'

'As they always do. Black clothes. People crying.' Greer unlocked her front door. 'I'll catch up with you tomorrow, okay? Right now I need tea, toast and bed. In that order.' She offered Beth a conciliatory smile and stepped inside, closing the door.

Home at last. Thank God.

Greer busied herself in the kitchen, toasting bread, brewing tea. The last twenty-four hours had been intense, and then some. Jessica's revelations had sent Greer into a tailspin. Not over Nathan's death—Greer didn't care about *that*—but her lies about Nathan and Tom dating. That meant someone else had driven Tom to suicide. The question was, who?

Wait. What about Tom's journal? The likelihood was that she'd never uncover the identity of Tom's lover, but the last few pages her son wrote before his death might reveal something. She had to at least try.

She also needed to tell Charlie that he'd been right about Nathan and Tom. Greer tapped out a quick message. *Back in Bristol. Any chance you can come round tomorrow? Say 8 pm?*

She'd just finished her slice of toast when a reply pinged through. *Sure. Be great to catch up. Hope you're well.*

Greer smiled. Good old Charlie.

She grabbed her mobile and made her way upstairs. Tom's journal was still in Greer's bedside cabinet. She took it out, settled herself on the bed, and read the next entry.

December 4. Can't believe it's been over two years since I last used this journal. Thank God Linda's never asked to see it. I've told her I write everything I'm feeling in it, and it's the only time I've lied to her. I feel bad about that, but after Blue ditched me, talking with Linda helped more than a journal ever could. She's been so wonderful to me, but it's not enough anymore. I need to write stuff down again.

Blue's back in my life. I'm seeing him tonight. He's made it very clear we'll end up in bed.

I'm hoping he's changed. Perhaps he'll realise what he's been missing, decide he wants a proper relationship. We'd be good together, Blue and me. Somehow, I'll make him see that.

Greer set the journal aside and rubbed her tired eyes. December 4 wasn't long before Tom's death.

Blue, Blue, Blue. Why couldn't Tom just give the guy's name? Charlie had been right in advising her to let all this go. Tom was dead, and nothing could bring him back, so what was the point?

Yes. Decision made. It was time she stopped searching for Blue.

Tom, though? The words he'd written brought him a little closer to her. Greer picked up his journal and continued to read.

CHAPTER 69

The following evening, Greer's doorbell buzzed at eight o'clock exactly.

When she pulled open the door, Charlie made as though to hug Greer, but she stepped back. Surprise flitted over his face, but he followed her into the kitchen without a word. A distinct smell of beer accompanied him. The atmosphere thickened with tension as she sat opposite Charlie at the table.

'Everything okay, Mrs M? You seem a bit... wound up.'

When Greer didn't respond, he continued, 'Got anything to drink? Beer, wine?'

'Sure. I'll open some Malbec.'

She grabbed a bottle from the rack, along with two glasses. This would go so much easier if lubricated by a decent red. She shoved Charlie's glass, twice as full as her own, across the table. He took a huge mouthful.

'Why did you ask me here tonight?' he said.

Greer eyed him for a second before replying. 'I want you to admit what you did.'

He gulped down more wine. 'No idea what you're referring to.' He wouldn't look at her, though. Oh, yes, he'd obviously realised what she meant. Getting him to confess might be another matter.

Charlie's glass was almost empty. Greer pushed the bottle across the table. He wasted no time in pouring himself a large measure. His fingers were shaking.

'Come on, Charlie. Confession is good for the soul, they say.'

'I haven't a clue what you're talking about.'

'I think you know exactly what I mean.'

'Look, whatever I've done to upset you, I'm sorry. Okay?'

'No. I know what you did. I've read Tom's journal.'

December 12. Charlie got drunk last night. Told me he once killed someone. Wouldn't say who at first, but eventually he spilled the beans.

Charlie's glass fell from his hand. The wine spilled in a blood-red tide across the table into his lap. He didn't appear to care, or even notice. Was it Greer's imagination, or did a glimmer of relief flicker in his face? That was understandable. His guilt must be a millstone around his neck. He was probably glad Greer knew the truth.

A tear trickled down Charlie's cheek into the stubble below. He looked like a man about to be escorted to the gallows. Eyes red and bloodshot, skin flushed with booze and self-pity.

'I'm sorry, Mrs M. I never meant for it to happen.' His words emerged in a slur, as though someone had sanded their edges, rendering them indistinct and muffled.

Greer needed to hear him say it. Admit what he'd done.

'Can I tell you about it?' Without asking, Charlie pulled another bottle from the wine rack and grabbed another glass, into which he poured a generous measure.

'Go right ahead. I want to hear everything you have to say.'

CHAPTER 70

The police interview room grew increasingly warm. Should Greer ask them to open a window? She gulped down some water, her hand sweaty around the paper cup. 'You heard me correctly. Charlie Prescott admitted he murdered my lodger, Lily Hamilton. He was drunk when he told me, and filled with remorse.'

DC Blyth frowned. 'Can you go through again what he said, please?'

Frustration seethed inside Greer. How many times could they ask the same question in different ways?

'He told me things turned sour after the third time they went out. He wanted to keep seeing her, but she wasn't keen. Explained she wanted to date other men. Told him if he didn't like it, tough.'

Blyth nodded. 'Specifically, the part when Charlie admitted he murdered Lily.'

'Sorry. Yes, of course. He said, 'She shouldn't have tried to dump me. That's why I killed her.' After that, he couldn't speak for crying.'

God, this was hard. She'd once loved Charlie like a son.

'He told me he stole something from her dead body. Wouldn't say what, or where he kept it. Just that it was personal to Lily. Said he needed it to remember her by. He begged me not to tell anyone. I had to, though. For that poor girl's sake.'

Blyth was silent for a while. Then: 'Why did you wait four days to report this?'

He was bound to ask that, of course. 'I was so shocked I couldn't think straight. I gave myself the weekend to get my head in order before I told you.'

'You should have come in sooner.'

'You're right. I realise that. It's been hard, though. Part of me is grieving, because he's a sweet boy really. He's always meant the world to me.'

The interview wrapped up soon afterwards. DC Blyth and the other officer present had been tight-lipped about what happened next, but they'd obviously bring Charlie in for questioning, given what she'd told them. Justice needed to be served.

Greer hurried back to her car and headed towards home. Her route took her close to where Charlie lived; on impulse, she steered her Fiat in the direction of his house and parked nearby. And watched.

Waited some more.

Eventually, after about an hour, a police vehicle drew up outside Charlie's home. Two officers got out and walked up the driveway. One of them rang the bell.

When they got no response, the men stepped back to confer with each other, then moved closer to the window. The curtains were open slightly, allowing a glimpse of Charlie's living room. The taller of the two men peered inside. He immediately ran around the side of the house, shouting something at his colleague.

Things happened quickly after that. An ambulance arrived amid a storm of sirens. Paramedics rushed inside, only to leave soon afterwards with a stretcher. Greer watched as they loaded it into the ambulance. She glimpsed Charlie's arm as it flopped, limp and pale, over the side of the gurney. Then the doors banged shut, and the vehicle drove away.

CHAPTER 71

Two days later, Greer was watching the local evening news while forking lasagne into her mouth. Charlie Prescott had made the headlines.

'Police have confirmed that a man they wanted to interview in connection with the murder of cardiac nurse Lily Hamilton has died in hospital from a suspected overdose,' the female reporter said. 'Charlie Prescott appears to have committed suicide before anyone could question him over her death.'

Greer sat up straighter in her seat, her food forgotten. The woman carried on, but Greer was no longer listening. Charlie, the boy she'd first met as a shy and awkward five-year-old, Tom's best friend, was dead.

Greer walked into the kitchen, where she poured herself a large glass of Malbec. Charlie was now the main—the *only*—suspect in Lily's murder. Her sweet girl, her Rose by another name, who'd died too soon, too young. Greer wiped tears from her eyes.

Charlie, though—she wouldn't be crying over that bastard.

December 12. Charlie got drunk last night. Told me he once killed someone. Wouldn't say who at first, but eventually he spilled the beans.

A further bombshell had awaited Greer, though.

I can't call him Blue anymore, not even in my head, now that I know he doesn't want me. That's a boyfriend thing, and we'll never be that. Yesterday he dumped me, just like when he flew off to Australia. Men are a diversion for Charlie, a bit of added spice. Women are his main thing. I think I've always known, deep down, he'd never be mine.

Charlie's insistence that Greer shouldn't read Tom's journal. The lie he told her about talking to Tom's friends. All a smokescreen to hide Blue's true identity.

He'd confessed to being Tom's on-off boyfriend. 'I never meant to hurt Tom.'

'Why did he call you Blue?'

'Because I'm such a huge fan of Birmingham City Football Club. They're known as the Blues.' Simple, really. Nothing to do with eye colour, as Greer had once thought.

Charlie, choked by sobs, had revealed he'd viewed Tom as a safe way of exploring his sexuality. 'The first time it happened, we were both drunk. Somehow, we fell into bed together, and a few times after that, too. We shared some more hook-ups after I returned from Australia. Tom told me he'd been in love with me for years. He got clingy. Demanded more than I could give. That's why I ended it. Not as a friend—I assured him I'd always need him as a mate—but the sex had to stop.' He reddened. 'Sorry, Mrs M. You won't have wanted to hear that.'

Greer hadn't wanted to hear any of it. She'd not mentioned she knew the reason for Charlie's heavy drinking. Who he'd really killed, and it wasn't Lily.

December 14. Last night Charlie told me who he killed. The winter he turned fourteen, he was shovelling snow in the garden with his dad. They argued about something silly, and Charlie shoved his dad, who slipped on a patch of ice and crashed into the greenhouse. A piece of glass sliced through his jugular and he bled out in minutes. His mum had a breakdown afterwards. According to Charlie, she was already mentally fragile. She ended up in a psychiatric institution, with Charlie in foster care. He feels responsible for his dad's death and his mum's suicide attempts, and drinks to numb the pain.

They say confession is good for the soul. In Charlie's case, that's not true. He says he doesn't deserve love, not after what he did.

Greer agreed. For very different reasons, though.

CHAPTER 72

It had been easy to kill Charlie. Greer had simply turned up unannounced at his house, saying she wanted to talk. It was after dark on Saturday evening, and Greer had walked to avoid parking her car outside Charlie's house. Charlie had seemed surprised, but pleased, as he ushered her inside.

Good to see you, Mrs M! I've been worried you must hate me.
I don't hate you, Charlie.
Make yourself comfortable. Want a drink?
I've come prepared. Brought this single malt whisky with me.
Whisky? That's unusual for you, isn't it?
We could both use a stiff drink, don't you think? God, this screw-cap's tight. Open it for me, would you, and I'll fix us the drinks in the kitchen.

Thirty paracetamol tablets, ground to a fine powder. A quarter tipped into a glass of Lagavulin, the other three-quarters in the remains of the whisky. Greer, unseen by Charlie, had wiped off her prints off the bottle and covered her hands with her sleeves to avoid leaving fresh ones. Charlie's were now the only ones on it. She watched him take a swig of his drink.

Tastes weird, Mrs M.

You're right. I opened the bottle a while ago, so I guess the contents must have oxidised. Drink up, Charlie. After a glass or two, we won't care if it tastes odd.

Charlie's words grew increasingly slurred as Greer spurred him on to drink more whisky. By now, he'd imbibed four full glasses and thirty paracetamol tablets. He could hardly speak.

'Don't feel so good,' he muttered, before his head lolled onto his chest. His eyes fell shut.

―eee―

Greer barely managed a few minutes of rest all night. Charlie's snores filled the room until dawn nudged its way through a gap in the curtains.

He opened a bleary eye not long after nine o'clock.

Feel like shit. My head's banging, and I've got pains under my ribs. Could do with a puke too.

You're hungover. That's why I put a packet of paracetamol on the table for you. A glass of water, too.

Charlie downed a couple of the tablets and fell back to sleep.

He woke up again just after midday. *The pain in my side's getting worse. I think I need a doctor.*

Good luck with that on a Sunday. Try another paracetamol.

By now the whites of Charlie's eyes were yellow, as was his skin. His breathing was shallow and rapid. His liver, fragile after years of heavy drinking, was struggling to cope.

'Help me,' Charlie moaned shortly before four that afternoon. He stared around him, clearly confused and disorientated.

He didn't speak again.

Greer took two empty fifteen-pill packets of paracetamol from her bag, careful to cover her fingers. She grabbed Charlie's senseless ones and pressed them over the back of each blister to make it appear he'd popped the tablets out himself. Greer tossed the packets on the coffee table beside the drained bottle of whisky.

Charlie was still alive, but unconscious, when Greer slipped from the house before dawn the following morning. Death from a paracetamol overdose could take a few days, so she wasn't worried. By now, his liver would be so damaged, Charlie's only hope would be a transplant. The odds of finding a suitable donor in time were almost zero.

Damn. She'd forgotten to ask Charlie about the letter he'd sent to Tom.

December 17. That awful letter. I've read it so many times that I know it by heart. I still can't believe what I'm reading. I'm hurting so badly. I don't want to live any longer.

Greer had slammed the journal shut at that point, unable to read any further. All she could think about was Tom lying in his own vomit. Whatever Charlie's letter had said, it had obviously pushed Tom towards suicide.

For that, Charlie deserved to die. Greer refused to mourn his loss, not with a single tear.

Lily Hamilton, though? She'd cried herself to sleep often enough over *her*.

Eighteen months after she killed Lily, Greer had removed her lodger's locket from its hiding place and taken it with her to Charlie's house. All part of her plan to frame him for her death. A nice touch, and why not? Not that the police had ever suspected her where Lily was concerned.

Greer had wrapped Charlie's hand around the locket to transfer his prints. She'd already wiped her own off. Her guilt over murdering Lily had meant she'd never worn it.

She'd concealed it in Charlie's bedside cabinet.

And then lied to DC Blyth. *He told me he stole something from her dead body... wouldn't say what, or where he kept it...*

CHAPTER 73 - Before

Lily was going to leave her. Like all the others. Greer couldn't call her Rose anymore, not after the bombshell her lodger had dropped. The gulf between them had widened too far by then.

After Lily slammed the front door, Greer sat, immobile, on the sofa. She had a mere seven days in which to turn their relationship around. But was that even possible? Lily had been so adamant about moving out.

She'd hoped she'd got her daughter back. The next best thing, anyway. How could she have been so stupid?

Lily was like all the rest. That damn girl hadn't a clue how hurtful she'd been. She'd peeled off Greer's skin, revealing the raw vulnerability beneath. And now she was just going to up and leave?

Hours later, Greer still sat there. The day slid into evening, and the room grew dark. Lily hadn't texted or called. She must have gone out with friends after her shift.

Lily eventually came home at eleven. She went straight upstairs without speaking to Greer.

The next morning, Greer was finishing breakfast when she heard Lily's footsteps descending the stairs. Now might be a good time for them to talk. She got to her feet. 'Good morning. Have you got time for a chat?'

Lily appeared in the doorway. 'Can't it wait? I'll be late for work.'

'This won't take a moment—'

'If you're hoping to persuade me to stay, don't bother.'

She mustn't get angry. 'I'm sorry if I've overstepped the mark.'

'Yes. You have. Several times.' Lily sat down with a sigh. She gave Greer a rueful smile. 'My temper's always on a short fuse, which doesn't help.'

'I realise I'm a bit intense. Tom called me a smother mother.'

Lily drew in a deep breath. Released it slowly. 'Yeah, about Tom. You need to tell him the truth. He doesn't know, does he?'

'About what?'

'His sister, the one that died. How his father's also dead.'

Lily's words ripped the breath from Greer's lungs. 'How did you—'

'I heard weird sounds coming from your room last night. I wanted to check you were okay. You'd passed out on your bed, an empty wine bottle beside you. You were muttering in your sleep, about a fire, how you needed to rescue your baby. On the floor were a couple of photographs and two death certificates.'

Tears trickled down Greer's face. Her beautiful Rose. And Jake, Rose's daddy.

Compassion shone in Lily's eyes. 'She had a similar mole to mine. Born around the same time as me. I became Rose to you, didn't I? That's why you wanted to use my middle name.'

Greer could only nod.

'When I spotted the photos, I cried. I can't imagine losing a baby, but you did. Your husband, too. I read on the death certificates how they died.' Lily pushed up Greer's sleeves to run gentle fingers over the burn scars.

'I'm sorry for your loss,' Lily continued. 'You've suffered so much. Tom deserves the truth, though.'

'I'll tell him, I promise. Just give me some time, okay?'

'Of course. I'm still going to move out. I think that's for the best. But while I'm still here, let's be friends, yeah?'

'What the hell, Greer? Explain why you took this, then chopped Mum out like she never existed.' Lily brandished the photo Greer had stolen from her room. Her face was puce with rage.

Greer edged away from Lily's fury. How careless of her to leave the photo on her bedside cabinet. She'd only taken it out for a moment, forgetting it was there when she'd called out to Lily, hoping for another chat. Maybe the chance to persuade her to stay. Lily had spotted it as soon as she'd walked in.

'On second thoughts, don't bother. You're obsessed with me. I get that. But this is a step too far. You're fucking nuts.'

'I'm sorry—'

'Stay the hell away from me. I'm warning you.' Spittle flew from Lily's mouth. 'The sooner I move out, the better.' She flounced out, the ruined photo in her hand, slamming the door behind her.

Something inside Greer snapped in that instant. A bone breaking like a brittle twig inside her heart.

CHAPTER 74 - Before

The following Saturday dawned salmon-pink, the sky dotted with fluffy clouds. Dry and sunny, too. Perfect for Greer's purposes. Lily surfaced late, having gone out the night before without a word to her. Greer hadn't asked where she was going; she knew better by then. They'd barely spoken since Lily's outburst.

At eleven o'clock Lily came downstairs in her dressing gown, her face pale and drawn. Dark circles had smudged themselves under her eyes. Not surprising. The little minx hadn't come home until two am.

'I thought we could go for a picnic.' Greer poured Lily a coffee and handed it to her across the kitchen table. 'I know somewhere quiet and pretty. As a child, I used to play there.'

Lily looked startled, then annoyed, as she slid into a chair opposite Greer. 'I'm sorry, what? You can't be serious.'

'I'd like us to spend time together today. A picnic would be perfect, don't you think?'

Lily scowled. It made her look ugly. 'I'm still furious about that photo. Bloody weird, if you ask me. I'd prefer not to be around you. '

'And I'd prefer us to part as friends. Much nicer, don't you think?'

Lily shook her head. 'I need to pack my stuff up. I called Dad yesterday. He's away in London, not back until Sunday, but I told him I'd move in later today.'

'There's plenty of time. We don't need long.'

'Couldn't we just go for coffee? I've got a thumping headache.'

'All the more reason for some fresh air. I'll make sandwiches and pack some cold drinks. Please, Lily. A couple of hours together. That's all I ask.' Greer was counting on her being too hungover to argue.

A sigh. 'If you insist. I suppose you're right about ending things nicely.' Lily set down her coffee. 'I've been meaning to ask. Have you told Tom about his dad and his sister?'

'Not yet. I called him last night, though. We've arranged for me to go to his flat tomorrow. I'll tell him then.'

'That's great. It's the right thing to do. You understand that, don't you?'

Greer nodded. 'We'll set off at two. I'll drive.'

Three hours later, Lily descended the stairs, looking summery in shorts and a pink camisole top. 'Are you ready?'

'Of course.' Greer picked up the cool-bag on the table. 'I've packed food and drink for us. Where we're going's not far.'

Fifteen minutes later, Greer drove down a narrow lane and parked up. She steered Lily towards a footpath, difficult to see because it was so overgrown. They walked in silence for a while in the direction of a wooded area. The path veered off to the left, and in the distance, a child's laughter rang out. Followed by a woman's voice.

Lily pointed to a sign, rusty and hanging by a couple of nails tacked to the fence. 'It says Private Property—Keep Out.'

'The man who owned this land is long dead. Nobody will care we're here.' The noises from the woman and child were louder now. Who the hell were they? Few people knew this place existed. They only had seconds, if that, to conceal themselves.

Greer placed her hands on the fence and climbed over it, the way she'd done many times as a girl. Lily followed without further comment. The remnants of a path, thick with overgrown grass and blackberry bushes, snaked away from them. Greer pushed through it with difficulty, Lily trailing behind. The trees and bushes soon hid them from sight.

The track bent round to the right before emerging on the edge of a field. Greer could no longer hear the woman or the child.

Under her feet was a rocky outcrop. She'd stood on it many times as a child, before availing herself of the protection it offered. Her special place, away from the vicious arguments between her parents. Greer would lie under the rock, hidden by the long grass, and dream of a different life.

She sat down, patting the stone beside her. 'Sit here. We'll eat, then set off that way.' She gestured towards her right. 'The path leads through a wooded area to a pond. You'll love it.' There was no wood, or pond, or even a path, but Lily wouldn't know that.

'Are you sure? It looks kind of wild.' Lily appeared uncomfortable, as though she wanted to return to the car. She was hot and sweaty despite her skimpy clothing.

'Trust me. I know this place like the back of my hand.' Greer unzipped the cool-bag and offered Lily a ham sandwich. She thrust a thermos towards her. 'Drink this. Homemade lemonade, and it should be ice cold.'

Lily downed the contents in noisy gulps. She wiped her mouth with a tissue Greer passed to her. 'I needed that.' She bit into her sandwich. 'Mmm. Tastes good.'

Greer took a swig from her own drink. Her stomach was too tense for food. She watched and waited. There didn't seem to be anything to say, not now.

It wasn't long before Lily's eyelids drooped. She yawned, stretched her arms above her head. 'Think I'll lie down for a bit. Not feeling so good.' Her words sounded slurred. She collapsed backward onto the flat stone, her eyes closed.

Greer waited.

And waited. Lily's breathing grew harsh, laboured. Her skin was a weird, waxy shade of pale. Unlike Greer's, her drink had contained a hefty dose of sleeping tablets. Charlie had been correct in saying Lily had known her killer.

It was time; Greer didn't want Lily to vomit, then choke to death on her own puke. She took a carrier bag from her pocket, placed it over Lily's nose and mouth, and pressed down with both hands. Above them, the purr of a light aircraft's engine sounded as the plane chugged through the sky. A bee buzzed nearby.

Lily put up little resistance; her body bucked a bit and strangled gasps came from under the plastic. Her eyelids remained shut, though.

Greer leaned harder on the bag. Before long, Lily became immobile, unresponsive.

Greer removed the plastic bag. She held her fingers under Lily's nose while watching her chest. No sign of life. Tears stabbed Greer's eyes.

She hadn't wanted to do this. But Lily had left her no choice.

'Rest, sweetheart. You're at peace now.' This way, her surrogate daughter would never leave her. Or blab to Tom about things that needed to remain secret. Greer couldn't risk Lily blurting out the truth when drunk, or telling him once she realised Greer hadn't.

Just one thing remained to be done.

Greer undid Lily's locket and slipped it into her pocket. Something to remember her sweet girl by.

She slithered off the ledge, bushes snagging her hair and scratching her arms. Carefully, so as not to hurt Lily, she tugged her body towards the edge of the rock, then pulled it over. She'd not expected it to take so much effort. Lily thudded to the ground, upon which Greer, panting and sweating, rolled her under the ledge.

With any luck, nobody would find her for a long time, if they ever did. Over the coming weeks, the elements would remove any footprints or forensic evidence.

She trailed her fingers over Lily's waxen cheeks. 'Goodbye, my darling. It's better this way.'

Greer called Lily's phone that night, leaving ever more frantic messages. The next morning, too. All calculated to mislead the police.

Cold, cunning. But what choice did she have? Prison wasn't an option. She had to be there for Tom should he ever need her.

The following day, Greer reported Lily as missing.

CHAPTER 75 – Now

The day after Greer learned of Charlie's death dawned dry and sunny. Greer showered, dressed, then fetched her coat and bag. Into the latter she slipped Tom's journal. However painful it might be, she needed to read the last page. She'd do that later.

Greer put a flask of coffee into her bag, along with two other items. Time to go.

As she closed her front door behind her, she saw Beth in her garden, pruning shears in hand. Her neighbour hurried over to the fence that divided their gardens.

'I was going to call round this afternoon,' she said. 'Greer, did you see the news last night?'

'About Charlie dying? Yes.'

'They say he murdered that poor girl. Lily Hamilton.'

'So it seems.'

'I can hardly believe it. He came across as such a nice young man.'

'Appearances can be deceptive. A while ago, he tried to convince me Nathan might have killed Lily.'

'Wow.' Beth shook her head. 'Cunning as well, then.'

Greer nodded. 'Indeed.'

'I know how much he meant to you. How are you holding up, my love?'

A shrug. 'I'm dealing with it. What else can I do?'

'Come round anytime if you need to talk. I'm here for you.' An awkward silence fell.

'Off out, then?' Beth said at last. 'Lovely day for it.'

'Thought I'd take a walk. Revisit old haunts.'

Beth peered at her. 'You're looking well. Surprisingly so.'

Greer smiled. 'I feel much better. In fact, I've decided on the way forward.'

'You're going to try counselling, then?'

'It's a great idea. Thanks for suggesting it.' She leaned over the fence and hugged her. 'You've been a fantastic friend, Beth.'

Greer got out of her car, eyeing the overgrown footpath that led away from the road. Her legs felt heavy, and the heaviness in her chest rendered her breathing laboured. It didn't matter; she hadn't far to walk. She pushed through the bushes, thorns snagging her clothes.

It wasn't long before Greer reached the rocky outcrop where she'd killed Lily. It seemed a fitting place to end her life. She swung her legs over the edge and sat down, placing her bag beside her. A soft breeze ruffled her hair, the sky blue and cloudless. A sliver of crime scene tape, all that remained of it, fluttered from a branch.

Greer gazed at the landscape before her. So much had changed.

Green fields had become a building site, the farmhouse that once stood on them demolished. A sign announced in bold purple: *Coming Soon! An Exciting New Development of Spacious Family Homes!*

Greer was totally alone. Easy to imagine she was the only person on earth.

She'd lost everyone she'd ever loved. Her parents. Jake. Rose. Lily. Tom. Nathan. Charlie. They'd all left her, one way or another.

Greer reached into her handbag and extracted the urn containing Rose's ashes. It was heavy, given its small size; brass, coated in silver, and engraved with two dates that were far too close. *Rose Marie Maddox. Forever in my heart.*

She kissed it, running her fingers over the cool metal. 'We'll be together again soon, my darling.' She took Tom's journal from her bag and placed it beside her on the rocky outcrop. Next came the flask of coffee. Followed by a packet of sleeping pills.

First, though, Greer would finish Tom's journal. Closure, of a kind, before she died. She picked up the journal, located the last page, and read the final entry.

December 18. I'm not scheduled to see Linda until the New Year. Actually, I won't see her, or Charlie, anyone else, ever again. The depression is back, but a thousand times worse. It's time to end my miserable existence.

It's not just that Charlie dumped me, although that hurts like hell. He's partly why I want to kill myself. The final straw, though, has been Mum.

I hate my mother. She's lied to me my entire life. I can't ask her the reason. She'd only tell me more lies.

I've burned the letter I received from the tracing agency. Every word is seared into my brain anyway. My father, the man who Mum claimed walked out when she was pregnant with me, is dead. He didn't abandon us, though. He died in a house fire before I was born.

I'd so wanted to find Dad. Tell him how much I missed not having him around when I was a kid. Shout and scream at him, ask him why he left. Except he didn't, of course. Was anything Mum told me about him true?

Now that I know she's a liar, I'll never trust her again.

That's not all she's lied about, though. The tracing company told me I once had a sister. Rose, her name was. She died in the fire too.

I can't forgive my mother. Not ever. She should have revealed the truth years ago.

I've lost everything. Charlie, my father, the sister I didn't know about. Except I never had any of them, did I?

I can't go on another day. Dad, oh Dad—I wanted so badly for us to be together again. The lies have been the final straw.

Tom's journal fell from Greer's hand onto the rocky outcrop. *I hate my mother.* Oh, dear God.

Not as much as Greer loathed herself.

Despite her precautions, Tom had uncovered the truth. Impossible to stick her head in the sand any longer. She'd driven Tom to suicide, not Charlie. If she'd been honest with her boy earlier, he'd still be alive.

She wouldn't have had to kill Lily and Charlie, either.

Awareness, sour and loathsome, slapped Greer in the face. She could hardly breathe, suffocated by self-hatred.

She'd been blind to the truth. Now she needed to put things right.

———

The following afternoon, Greer walked into Bridewell police station and headed towards the front desk. 'I'm here to see DC Blyth.'

She'd left a message for him the previous evening. 'Call me back, please. I have further information about Lily Hamilton's death.'

After what seemed an eternity, Blyth had obliged. 'I need to speak with you in person,' Greer had said. 'I can't go into it over the phone.' He'd eventually agreed.

In the meantime, she'd returned Rose's ashes to their hiding place in her wardrobe. Placed Tom's journal in her bedside cabinet. She'd contemplated burning it, but decided it would be disrespectful. She'd already failed her son enough.

An officer showed her into a room furnished only with a table and chairs. Greer pulled one out and sat on it.

How calm she felt. The storm was about to break, and she was ready.

———

Greer signed her name to the statement she'd just given. The day had proved long and tiring. None of it had been easy, but like she'd told Charlie, confession was good for the soul.

Charlie Prescott didn't commit suicide. I killed him because I mistakenly believed he drove my son to take his own life. It was me who was responsible for Tom's death, though.

And: *He didn't murder Lily Hamilton. I did.*

Blyth and the other police officer present had been harsh. Greer had expected nothing less. The contempt in Blyth's eyes was nothing compared to her own self-loathing. She didn't deserve forgiveness. Certainly not for Lily or Charlie. As for Tom and Rose, she'd failed both her children. Such negligence didn't warrant mercy.

Still, she'd got through the worst part. Sentencing, and prison, held no fear for her. She needed to be punished. Three people had died because of her. Five, if she included Jake and Rose.

Besides, she wouldn't be in jail long. Nobody could force her to take her medication. Her heart would soon harden into bone, the physical matching the metaphorical. She'd die, and be reunited with Tom, and Rose, and everyone she'd ever loved. There was a certain comfort in believing that.

'We're done here,' Blyth said. 'Stand up.'

Greer tried, but an explosion of pain ripped the breath from her lungs. Sweat beaded her brow. Her hands clawed at her chest, then her throat. Where had all the air gone?

Blyth's frantic yell for help faded away as Greer slumped from her seat. The floor rushed up to meet her in an unforgiving punch.

So this was how her life ended. A massive, and final, heart attack.

Well, death was a welcome relief. Soon she'd be with Tom and Rose.

Wait. What was that sound? Ah, yes, Tom's heartbeat, strong and regular. How she'd missed the comfort it offered. As Greer listened, the sweet scent of baby Rose caressed her nostrils.

Darkness closed in. Her eyes fluttered shut. The terrible pain ended. All was well again.

Postscript

I hope that you enjoyed *Heart of Bone*! If so, would you consider leaving a review on Amazon and/or Goodreads? It would be much appreciated.

Heart of Bone is a book set in the UK with British characters, written by a British author, so it adheres to UK spelling, punctuation and grammar. You'll see 'tyre' instead of 'tire', 'realised' instead of 'realized', 'windscreen' instead of 'windshield', etc. None of these are wrong, just different from what readers in other countries may be accustomed to.

Thanks to my wonderful beta readers, Colin Garrow, Heather Larson, Kath Middleton, Lynda Checkley and Mary Moss. Your help has been invaluable.

To find out more about my other novels, please visit my website at www.maggiejamesfiction.com.

Follow me on Facebook (Maggie James Fiction) or via Twitter (@mjamesfiction). You can also follow me on Amazon.

About the Author

Maggie James is a British author who lives near Newcastle-upon-Tyne. She writes psychological suspense/domestic noir novels.

Before turning her hand to writing, Maggie worked mainly as an accountant, with a diversion into practising as a nutritional therapist. Diet and health remain high on her list of interests, along with travel. Accountancy does not, but then it never did. The urge to pack a bag and go off travelling is always lurking in the background! When not writing, going to the gym, practising yoga or travelling, Maggie can be found seeking new four-legged friends to pet; animals are a lifelong love!

Find out more via www.maggiejamesfiction.com or https://author.to/MJF